SIN

Miguel brought [...] that made me shudder as it cracked across Violette's big white buttocks. She cried out, clenched her cheeks and writhed but the thrashing continued.

It was potent stuff to watch and my thighs ground together as I squirmed in my seat. Then Lysette, the little French maid, stood in front of me, blocking my view. Her naked bottom, so sweet and pert, was just inches from my face. I had fancied her earlier, of course. Now, to be presented with those smooth rounded cheeks within kissing distance was too much. I pressed my lips to each sphere, not caring what Manny might think. He was making free with my breasts anyway. This was some cocktail party, it was just as well my husband hadn't brought me . . .

Also by Lesley Asquith

Sex And Mrs Saxon
In The Mood
Reluctant Lust
The Wife-Watcher Letters (editor)

Sin and Mrs Saxon

Lesley Asquith

HEADLINE DELTA

Copyright © 1993 Lesley Asquith

The right of Lesley Asquith to be identified as the Author of
the Work has been asserted by her in accordance with the
Copyright, Designs and Patents Act 1988.

First published in 1993
by HEADLINE BOOK PUBLISHING

A HEADLINE DELTA paperback

10 9 8 7 6 5 4 3 2 1

All rights reserved. No part of this publication may be
reproduced, stored in a retrieval system, or transmitted,
in any form or by any means without the prior written
permission of the publisher, nor be otherwise circulated
in any form of binding or cover other than that in which
it is published and without a similar condition being
imposed on the subsequent purchaser.

All characters in this publication are fictitious
and any resemblance to real persons, living or dead,
is purely coincidental.

ISBN 0 7472 4228 3

Typeset by
Letterpart Limited, Reigate, Surrey

Printed and bound in Great Britain by
HarperCollins Manufacturing, Glasgow

HEADLINE BOOK PUBLISHING
A division of Hodder Headline PLC
338 Euston Road
London NW1 3BH

Sin and Mrs Saxon

Chapter One
AMERICA

Of course, I should really have got to my feet and left the apartment. As the wife of a senior appointee to a specialised agency of the United Nations, I was risking being involved in a sexual scandal during his first few days in office. Not more than a yard away from me, our hostess for the so-called cocktail hour was tipsily leaning her back against one of her guests while he fondled and cupped her breasts from behind.

The man was a tall and handsome South American diplomat in an immaculate evening suit. His full sensuous lips smirked under the pencil-thin moustache as he squeezed and jiggled the pair of tits he had uncovered from her low-cut evening gown. She giggled and pressed her full bottom back into his groin and rotated it against what I presumed was a rampant erection. Her husband, Monsieur Marcel Lefarge, watched his exhibitionist wife with a glow of pride.

The cocktail hour, I decided, was an excuse for attractive people to get together for an orgy. I hardly knew any of them, as my husband Harry and I had only taken up residence in the exclusive Vanderbilt apartment building the previous day. I'd met Violette Lefarge

Sin and Mrs Saxon

in the lift that morning and she'd introduced herself. Later, her French maid came to our door with the invitation to take cocktails with her. I wondered if, eyeing me up as searchingly as she had, Madame Lefarge had decided I was a likely candidate to add a new face, or more properly a fresh pair of tits and a cunt, to her organised romps. Not that I've anything against good sexual fun and games when conducted discreetly. However, considering Harry's exalted new position I couldn't afford to be involved in anything that might become the talk of the town.

'Go, Diana,' Harry had urged as we perused the invitation. I had just emerged from the shower cubicle and dried myself, standing beside him naked in the ballroom-sized lounge as he read out the words on the gold-edged card, his other hand idly fondling my bottom. 'I'll be at the office all evening getting the hang of my new post, but you go, dear. Get to know some people – they'll all be diplomats and such, so no doubt you'll be meeting them at receptions and balls. They'll take to you, you're such a beautiful creature. There's little doubt, my love, you'll have the best pair of tits in the room—'

His hand had sidled up from my bum and around my back to fondle those same tits. Frankly I thought sometimes, like when playing tennis or trying to contain them in a bikini top, that they were too big, but Harry loved them; and the adoring stares I had received from other men all my adult life proved they were breasts to be admired. 'Don't be so crude,' I chided him, laughing and holding up my tits for him to give them the attention they deserved – kisses and nipple-sucking. I tried to draw him back over me onto the bed but he pulled away, promising to see to me later and saying that his staff were waiting to meet their new chief. So I dolled myself up in the new House of Fellowes evening dress I'd bought myself before leaving London and crossed the carpeted corridor to ring the bell of the Lefarge apartment. The maid, in black silk dress with lacy cap and frilly apron, was a pretty young thing not more than twenty. She bobbed from the knee as she ushered me in.

The Lefarges, I decided on my first look around, were no paupers. Apart from bringing her personal maid from Paris to New York, Violette Lefarge's lounge was carpeted so deep that my feet sank into the pink pile. The room was furnished with genuine Louis XIV antiques, the drapes over the wide picture window overlooking Central Park matched the decor, and the walls were hung with a Renoir, two Gaugins and a Van Gogh, among others. I was quickly introduced to an assembly numbering about a dozen, all beautifully turned out in evening dress and tuxedos. I accepted a drink and sat beside a youngish American man who I found to be half-drunk and morbid.

'What do you do?' I asked him, trying to be sociable. I wanted to add, 'Apart from drowning your sorrows,' for he knocked back two large Scotch on the rocks and accepted a third even as I was joining him on the *chaise longue* (like the rest of the goodies in that lounge no doubt shipped over from France).

'Wall Street,' he slurred and, as if I didn't know what he meant, he added, 'stocks and bonds, you know? Investments, gilt-edged securities. Unlike the rest of the parasites in this room I work for my living. I add to their goddam wealth. What are you, some kind of Limey broad come to join in the fun—?'

Sin and Mrs Saxon

'I'm not sure what you mean,' I said demurely. As our hostess was getting her tits fondled across the room, it was a leading question. 'They seem very – friendly – don't they?'

The man laughed bitterly. I could only guess he had a thing, a lech, for Violette Lefarge and resented the handsome South American making free with her. 'Christ, where did you appear from?' he said. 'This is going to be a free-for-all. Violette and that big slob Martinez are just starting the ball rolling. Soon there'll be fucking in every corner of this room. If you don't know that, you shouldn't be here—' He steadied his eyes to peer at me. 'You're a looker, lady, I'll say that. Do you perform?'

'Not in a roomful of people I don't know,' I said. 'Who knows what gets around later? As far as I was concerned this was a simple invitation to a cocktail party.' Although reluctant, I added, 'I think I should excuse myself and leave—'

'Do you indulge?' he asked me. 'I mean, do drugs? There's good pot going around, the best. And other stuff, if you want, all on the house. Some prefer nose candy. I can tell it's been going the rounds. There's a few here on a high already.' He lifted his glass. 'I don't touch the stuff myself now. I prefer this.'

'I don't even smoke cigarettes,' I said.

'You got a husband?' he asked offhandedly. 'I bet you have. You been a model or an actress?'

I told him I had a husband who was working in his office that evening and I'd never been a model or actress, though I was pleased to think he'd thought so. Around the room several couples were kissing deeply and fondling each other. Several women had their breasts out and were surrounded by admiring males. As ever, seeing lewd goings-on had its effect on me. The urge manifested itself in a fluttering in my stomach which transmitted itself to a pulsing and moistening in my cunt. I was no doubt looking around with fascinated eyes. Tipsy as he was, my companion guessed my strong interest.

'Stay and watch,' he advised. 'Hell, you might learn something. I'm not getting in on this, so keep me company if you like. They might ask you to join in, but they won't make a big deal if you decline. Anyway, they welcome spectators. Someone watching adds to their kicks. That's why they like a crowd. I'll bet Violette asked you along to see if you'd be shocked – or go along—' He eyed her moodily as she turned her face to kiss the man cupping her breasts. 'She doesn't care. Anything goes with her. If you stood up now and screamed at her she was a filthy bitch for inviting you to such a degenerate party, she'd laugh in your face.'

'I've no intention of doing that,' I said. 'What she gets up to is strictly her business.' I could have added that in my lifetime I had been involved in sexual adventures that made what was going on around me pretty tame stuff. No doubt things would liven up and the party would swing. 'I take it you know Madame Lefarge well?'

'I was here for dinner the other night,' he said. 'Good old Manny Levinson invited over supposedly to discuss some investments. She began to feel me up under the table and had my dick out. She was doodling it with her nutty old man sitting opposite and their goddam French maid serving us. Then she drops a serving spoon and bends to pick the thing up, but Lefarge tells her he'll do it. They're both looking under the table while she's pulling on my prick and jerking me off. She didn't even bother to stop. Christ, I had to cover myself with a napkin quick to save flooding the place—'

He saw my amused grin. 'Whatever turns them on,' I said. 'Were you complaining?'

'You think that was all?' Manny Levinson asked. 'I tell you they're both plain sex crazy. Later she invited me to stay the night and he just smiled—'

'Very hospitable of them,' I suggested, finding the conversation getting funnier. 'Did you take them up on it?'

'Well, hell, I thought, what kind of a fuck would that be with her old man watching and getting his rocks off? But I did. Violette can be very persuasive. Just look at her now.' I did and saw she had clasped her man friend's prick in her hand – a huge upright thick stalk. 'I can't compete with Martinez,' he complained. 'I'm not revealing myself with that big dago bastard showing off his superdong—'

It was, I had to admit, a monster of a weapon, thick and rigid and rearing long inches above Violette's grasp. My cunt palpitated at the thought of accepting all that tubular flesh with its uncapped purple helmet as big as a hen's egg. 'I can see what you mean,' I commiserated. 'They surely can't *come* any bigger, if you'll excuse the pun. You were hoping to have Violette again tonight, I gather?'

'So I'm getting drunk instead,' Manny admitted. 'That French dame can screw like nobody's business and I thought I was back here for a repeat performance. *You* don't fancy a fuck, I suppose?' he ventured, the hand not holding his glass sliding over my thigh. I lifted it and put it on his own leg.

'Thank you for the offer, but no,' I said nicely. At that moment Violette Lefarge came across to us, leading Martinez by his prick. For all that, I saw his dark eyes take me in with interest, the classic undressing-you-with-his-eyes look. He nodded at me arrogantly, as if marking down future prey.

'We've been neglecting our new guest,' Violette Lefarge said of me, her bared tits thrusting out of her dress, her hand still gripping the big dick. 'Has Manny been entertaining you? And your glass is empty, *chérie*. There is everything you may desire here, just ask. Everything—'

I knew she meant a variety of drugs if I cared to indulge and to prove it she turned and snapped her fingers. Her maid appeared bearing a tray on which there were drinks, cigarettes of marijuana and tiny bowls of a white powder. I took a champagne cocktail, noting that her pretty maid was now completely naked except for the tray which was supported by broad silk ribbons around her neck. The girl's pert little tits were uptilted with rouged nipples that stuck out quite amazingly, at least three-quarters of an inch long on the upsweep of her perfect breasts. From my seated position I could see below the tray and saw youthful rounded thighs that parted at the crotch, revealing a wispy-haired sweet little pouch of a cunt with rolled-in lips. My tummy did flips again, aroused immediately by the lovely creature. I barely restrained myself from reaching out to finger her tempting slit. I could have left there and then and taken her to bed.

'*Merci*, Lysette,' said her mistress and I observed that Martinez gave her rounded bottom cheeks a fondle as she turned to pass on to the other guests. 'You will note that we have nothing to hide at our little *soirées*,' Violette said to me, her eyes gleaming wickedly. 'I hope you are not shocked?'

'Not yet,' I said calmly, 'but Manny and I thought we'd sit this one out, take in the scene, if you don't object.'

'Of course not,' she enthused. 'All we ask is that what we do here never goes beyond this room. I'm sure that with your husband in such an important and responsible post he would not want any scandal attached to his wife or her friends while in New York.' Violette had evidently done her homework well before inviting us to her party. 'I'm sure you'll make nice friends here,' she added.

'I'm sure I shall,' I said, 'but I'm not sure my husband would approve of your idea of a party.' I'd decided that Harry would be better off not getting in with this wild crowd, but reserved the right to know them on my own terms at times that suited me. 'Let's just say that I'm enjoying myself and will sit this one out—' Across the room the maid's tits attracted me.

'Which is a great pity,' her companion Martinez joined in. 'Such a beautiful woman, so ripe, so rounded.' His words oiled off his tongue sensuously, meaning as plainly as if he had said it: I would love to fuck you. 'I was hoping we would see more of you, in every sense of the word,' he added lecherously. 'Please introduce me, Violette, to this charming creature—'

'Senor Miguel Franco y Martinez,' said Violette, as the suave Latin took my hand and kissed it lingeringly. 'Mrs Diana Saxon. Her husband is—'

'Husbands I do not care to know,' Martinez grinned to me. 'You must call me Mig and call me soon. Or I shall

Sin and Mrs Saxon

call you,' he threatened boldly.

'Violette,' said Manny wearily from beside me. 'Why don't you take this big prick with you and do whatever you intend to do with him? Mrs Saxon and I will sit and drink your excellent champagne and watch him fuck you, for no doubt that's what you want him to do while your husband enjoys the sight.'

'Don't let us stop you, please,' I added, looking at the monster cock in her hand which had not lost its upstanding rigidity during the conversation. I knew if I were holding on to all that I'd want it badly. 'It would be a shame to waste it, wouldn't it?'

'I feel so naughty today,' Violette giggled. 'I've been bad, so bad. I deserve to be punished. I should be punished. Miguel, you know what to do—'

She held up her dress, turning around and showing what women are made of – a pouting cunt at the front with a mass of black hair foresting her prominent bulge and her crinkled outer lips pushing through the bush. Hairy and pink, an enticing stink – as my husband would say of mine. She smirked down at her fig as if to say have a good look, then she waggled her arse imperiously, well aware that the full fleshy moons presented a tempting target.

Miguel pulled her dress over her head and she threw out her arms to display all. Underneath she was bare-arsed and bare-cunted, her big pointed tits doing the shimmy-shake. Now others had gathered around, clapping and urging her on. She performed a little dance, letting her tits swing out, bending to show off her bum and the hair between the cheeks, passing her hands over her cunt and up her stomach to clasp her tits, holding them out as if on offer.

'I've been so *bad*!' she repeated. 'So wicked. I should be punished—' There were cries of 'Thrash her, Miggy. Give it to the bitch. Fuck her till she begs,' and Martinez picked her up bodily and carted her off to a vacated settee. There Lysette handed him a short leather belt divided at the end into several thongs. He dumped her unceremoniously on the length of the settee and she fell face down, covering her face among the cushions. Her thighs were wide-spread and her arse cheeks separated, showing her cunt hanging like a pouch with the mass of hair curling up to her arsehole. Then she raised herself on an elbow to look around to make certain all were enjoying the show.

Miguel brought down the tailed strap with a swish that made me shudder as I watched it crack across her raised buttocks. She cried out, clenched her cheeks and writhed, but the thrashing continued until she was crying out for mercy. Miguel then threw the strap aside and covered her, his bare arse and flanks thrusting away as he entered and fucked her mightily. She howled at the treatment and he paused to give her two hearty smacks across her arse before continuing. It was potent stuff to watch and I felt my thighs grind together as I squirmed in my seat. Beside me, Manny's hand came across to squeeze both of my breasts in turn down the neck of my dress. I sighed and let him continue.

On the settee Miguel was pumping his load into Violette, raising his head and gasping throatily as he jerked in his last spasms. His place was immediately taken by the first man in line behind him and Violette's cunt was filled by a new prick. From her continuous bucking and the hoisting of her arse it was evident she relished the perpetuation of the fuck. Manny meanwhile was pinching my nipples in turn, making my whole breast swell and stiffen with arousal. I crossed my legs tightly and rubbed my thighs together to induce a climax. I watched the relay screwing of Violette through the crowd gathered around the settee. Then the little French maid stood in front of me, blocking my view. Her bottom, so sweet and pert, was just inches from my face and I reached out with both hands to draw it nearer to me. In my excitement I couldn't help myself.

I had fancied her earlier, of course. Now, to be presented with those smoothly rounded cheeks within kissing distance was too much. I pressed my lips to each sphere, not caring what Manny might think. He was making free with my breasts anyway. Lysette turned her head as I lovingly kissed her bottom and smiled down at me. Then the wicked nymphet parted her legs in invitation. My hand slipped in beneath her bum, an outstretched finger curling up to enter her fat little lipless cunt. I heard her sigh as she thrust her neat bottom out to me. I swirled my finger in the moist warm folds, found the erect button of her clitty and flicked it. 'Yes, oh yes, madame,' I heard her whisper softly as her bottom rotated against my wrist. Then I was coming and she was coming, and across the room Violette was crying out that it was killing her, *killing her*, as her arse rose and fell in her umpteenth climax.

It was, I felt, time to take my leave. I disengaged Manny's hand from the neck of my gown and made my way to the door. Lysette followed me, ostensibly to see me out as a good servant should, but at the door her eyes were alight as she regarded me. Here we go again, I thought. I've never been able to resist temptation, only give in to it. 'That was so sweet, what you did for me,

Sin and Mrs Saxon

Madame Saxon,' she smiled. 'I should so like to do the same for you.' And before I could stop her, her arms were around my neck and her soft mouth pressed to mine. Her pliant little tits pressed into the silk of my evening gown, the nipples like sharp points against my breasts. We kissed long and lingeringly, our tongues touching before we parted. Her hands came up to my tits, cupping them gently as if testing their fullness. 'They are so big, so beautiful, madame,' she whispered almost shyly. 'I would love to see them, to kiss them and suck them and make love to them. Would you mind?'

I returned to our apartment a shaken woman. Surely I wasn't falling in love with a slip of a girl? I undressed, enjoying the feel of the cool air on my naked body. I sipped a drink while looking out from the tall height of the apartment over the brightly lit Manhattan skyline with its skyscrapers. Harry came in soon after and stood behind me, arms around me and holding my tits, his thumbs flicking my nipples. 'How big they are,' he observed. 'Were you thinking of me, Di?'

'Of course,' I told him, pressing my bottom back into his crotch. 'I've been standing here naked just for you, thinking we should christen this apartment with a really good fuck.'

'It is rather splendid, isn't it?' he laughed. 'Remember the one-roomed attic we moved into when we married? Things have got a little better since then.' I felt his prick rising against me as he held me. 'The offer of a knighthood and this vastly important job with the Food and Agricultural Organisation of the U.N.' Harry never could take anything seriously and that's why I loved him so much. 'Do you think they'll find us out, a couple of peasants like we are among the powerful of this world?

Sin and Mrs Saxon

How did you get on tonight? Old Lefarge is a multi-millionaire banker who could swing funds for aid projects I have in mind for developing nations. He's an adviser to the World Bank. There must have been an ambassador or two and many statesmen at his party tonight. I'm sorry I had to miss it but I'm sure you represented me well. How did it go?'

'Promising,' I said, leaving at it that, taking his hand down to between my thighs. 'I'm sure I shall enjoy New York.'

Chapter Two
ENGLAND

Palatial apartments such as those in the Vanderbilt Towers had not always been the style to which I was accustomed. My early years of girlhood in Scotland had been spent as the youngest daughter of a labourer eking out a scant living for his brood. All of us were ensconced in a cottage with wooden sides and a corrugated iron roof, which was owned by the quarry master for whom he worked. However, my mother picked potatoes and turnips to add to the family income, kept our home snug and fed us on the cheapest cuts of meat and vegetables grown in our garden plot.

This good wholesome food, I'm sure, is what filled me out at an early age. My womanly curves attracted grown men. My liaisons with Geddes the local coalman and Mr Saxon the quarry owner are well detailed in a previous story*, as are my sexual adventures in London when forced to flee from home to avoid a scandal. There I met Mr Saxon's handsome son Harry and we later married when he came home from service in the Royal Engineers at the end of the Second World War. A foray into Africa

* *Sex and Mrs Saxon* (Headline, 1993)

Sin and Mrs Saxon

followed, his work there leading to his appointment with the U.N., his speciality being irrigation of arid areas of Third World countries, then just emerging as independent nations. Hence our arrival in New York, but much had happened before which has not been told.

After we met again in London at the beginning of the war, Harry Saxon slipped an engagement ring on my finger and took me to a small hotel with a friendly night porter. He turned a blind eye as we slipped up to a bedroom and there we duly celebrated our betrothal with a non-stop night of fucking and sucking. We were two healthy young sexual animals enjoying each other's nakedness in a loving and lustful session that continued until dawn. Harry then went off to report to his depot and we were not to meet again for five long years after he had seen action in North Africa, Sicily, Italy and Germany.

Left alone that morning, seventeen years old and still warm and romantic from a night of love, I decided that I should do my bit for the war effort too. I took a number seven bus to Victoria and the Combined Recruiting Centre situated there. I was resolved to join the navy and presented myself to a female officer in a smart uniform who was enlisting recruits for the Women's Royal Naval Service.

'Any skills?' she asked, pen poised over a printed form as I stood before her desk. 'Shorthand and typing? Mechanical knowledge of cars and engines?' My heart sank, for most of the girls in the line before me at least had secretarial experience. As for a skill, I had been a successful and popular young whore with an upper-class clientele, what is known as a callgirl these days. I'd never worked the streets but a prostitute is one by any name.

Sin and Mrs Saxon

'I can cook,' I volunteered. I was good at it too, my mother having seen to that. The woman officer nodded, rubber-stamped the completed form and I was sent through to the room where a physical inspection was taking place. The long room had benches with hooks on the walls for hanging up clothes, and a good dozen or so girls and women were in several stages of undress as I joined them. At the far end were desks with women doctors in white coats looking into ears and throats, sounding chests and hearts, taking pulses and blood pressures, even examining pubic hair, vaginal entrances and anuses. Some of the girls awaiting their turn held up their dresses shyly to cover their nakedness.

I had no such inhibitions, being nude before others having been a big part of my life. Also, I was aware, I had nothing to be ashamed of. I was proud of my full breasts and violin-shaped hips, as I'd once heard them described by a male admirer. Undressing and looking around me I saw every type of female shape: big tits, pear-shaped ones, the droopy pendulous kind, and some so underdeveloped they were what my Harry called 'bee stings'. There were as many kinds of fannies too: great thatches of hair and prominent outer lips, some thinly covered with a few wispy hairs and tight little quims. There were bottoms that curved and bulged with large fleshy moons plus neat little bums of adolescent girls. I felt I could more than hold my own with any of them.

My turn came to face the doctor, a large and well-developed female of around forty with a handsome if severe face. I handed her my completed entry paper and she stood up. 'Drop that dress and lay it on my desk, girl,' she said, coming to me with her stethoscope raised. 'No false modesty here, we've too much to do.' I could

Sin and Mrs Saxon

have told her I had none, but had simply covered my nakedness by holding my dress up before my body like all the other recruits. I laid the dress over her desk and she nodded as if pleased with me. 'You look very fit,' she said, as she regarded my figure. Sounding my heart, her hands brushed over my breasts, lightly passing across both nipples as if testing them for stiffness. 'Any major ailments? Any serious illnesses?' she asked.

'None at all, doctor,' I said, taking a sharp intake of breath and giving a little shudder as she squeezed both my tits, to test for lumps or a growth I supposed, but her so-called professional touch seemed very like someone enjoying a fondle to me. She gave me a sharp look as I sighed quite involuntarily. My traitorous nipples, already somewhat reddened and tender-looking from Harry Saxon's ardent sucking on them during our previous night of sex, stretched out and tilted rigidly.

'In the Wrens you will properly address me as First Officer Calthrop or alternatively as ma'am,' she said severely. 'Not as doctor.' I stood still, not daring to move or breathe as her hands inspected my lower regions. My pouting cunt still felt moist from Harry's big prick and I blushed to think she might know. 'You're quite a fine specimen of a young female. Diana Mackenzie, is it?' she said, glancing at my entry form. 'In the navy you'll meet up with all types of men. Don't let them take advantage of you.'

'Yes, ma'am,' I said humbly as another woman in a white coat came across to us.

'Finished with this one, Mona?' she asked. 'I'll take her off to be weighed and measured.' So the doctor's name was Mona. She gave me a last long searching look that I'd seen other women give me before, making me

Sin and Mrs Saxon

well aware of her sexual preference. It didn't matter, I never guessed that I would see her again.

That afternoon I was on a privately chartered bus on my way to the Portsmouth naval base in the company of other girls who had passed the tests to be accepted as Wrens. We were taken to a large building on Southsea front called Pendragon House that had once been, I supposed, an hotel. There we were shouted at, bullied into squads, examined once again for bad teeth, hair lice and pubic crabs, and finally kitted out in our uniforms and laughable stiff cotton underwear, before being allotted to our rooms.

I was in one with seven other girls, the furniture consisting of double-decker bunks and bedside lockers. For me, used to being away from home and enjoying new experiences, it was fun and I busied myself making up the bottom bunk I had grabbed while others stood dithering. I packed my locker with my kit too, then looked about me. The girl who had been left with the bunk above me stood sobbing quietly, with her head in her arms, resting on the unmade mattress. She was about my age and a slender blonde girl I'd heard addressed at roll call on arrival as Wren Daphne Seymour. Her shoulders lifted as she sobbed and she looked the picture of misery in her dejection.

I had been told a Petty Officer Wren would inspect our quarters and all had to be shipshape for her. She was a plump girl of about thirty who had gained her crossed anchors of rank on her upper left sleeve by being the kind of strict disciplinarian well suited to whip trainee Wrens into shape. How apt that was I would learn the hard way. Petty Officer Bella Watson's reputation was imparted to us gleefully by staff at the base on our arrival. Poor Daphne Seymour was crying her eyes out and doing nothing to make up her bed with the sheets and blankets provided or tidy away her kit.

'We've got a right cry-baby here,' said one of the Wrens, a tarty-looking girl called Lil Canty, who had proudly informed us all that she had been a barmaid in a Liverpool pub not known for its gentility. 'Kick her up the backside so we can get ready for room inspection. The Petty Officer will do her nut if dopey Daphne doesn't sort out her bed and locker. Then we'll all be up shit creek, as they say—'

'You may say it, you foul-mouthed bitch,' I had to reply. 'Daphne here is just homesick, I expect. Let's either help her get her bed made or pipe down if you won't help.' I liked the 'pipe down' bit, it sounded very nautical in my new situation as a Wren. I'd already heard our room was to be called nothing else but a cabin and the floor a deck, just as the dining hall was the mess and the officers' quarters the wardroom. It did not impress Wren Canty.

'And who's going to make me pipe down, you Scotch cow?' she threatened. Daphne turned her head from the bed and let out a howl and a flood of tears, muttering she did not want to cause trouble between us. I took hold of her sheets and blankets and began to make the bed. It was no chore for me. 'I said who's going to make me pipe down?' repeated Wren Canty. 'Not you, you big-titted slut.'

I noted the other girls in our room, sorry, cabin, looked on and listened with dismay, being well-brought up young things unused to such rough language and threats from the ex-barmaid. 'Big titted-slut,' I laughed. 'Flattery will get you nowhere, Canty. Any time you think you can scratch my eyes out and pull my hair, you're welcome. Now if you wish. Want to try?'

'I've nothing against you, Scotty,' Lil Canty said sullenly, backing down. I saw the other girls regarding me in admiration and realised I had gained their respect. I had Daphne's bed made and was fitting her gear in her locker while she wiped her eyes on the handkerchief I'd handed her. Then Petty Officer Bella Watson entered, sauntering up and down between the beds and inspecting our efforts closely. As she passed me she paused to inspect my uniform, eyeing me contemplatively.

'Name?' she demanded.

'Wren Mackenzie, ma'am,' I said.

'Officers are ma'ams. You will address me as Petty Officer, Mackenzie. Your uniform jacket is too tight, you're all front, girl, with your big bosom. Tell them at stores to change it in the morning. Say I said so.'

'Yes, Petty Officer,' I answered dutifully but had no intention of doing so. The jacket revealed my top contours admirably. We were then told to go down to supper, after which we returned to our so-called cabin and the other girls got into their nightdresses. It was the one item of clothing that the navy had not issued but all seemed to have brought them from home. I didn't own one, having slept naked since my time in London. I slipped into bed enjoying as ever the cool sheet against my body, then Daphne came back from brushing her teeth, her eyes still red from her crying.

'Thank you for making my bed and putting my kit away so nicely, Diana,' she said quietly, sitting on the edge of my bed. 'Being away from home for the first time made me so homesick and sad. You must think me a real baby blubbering my eyes out like that. Even now I

Sin and Mrs Saxon

want to cry. I'm trying not to. You seem so brave, I do admire you—' Her tears flowed again and in a moment of compassion I sat up to put my arms around her, my bared breasts over the bedcover. Somewhere in the building a bugle sounded and suddenly all the lights in the cabin went out leaving us in darkness. Daphne sobbed into my neck and clutched me. The next moment she had slipped into my narrow bed and was cuddling up as if seeking comfort from another human being in her misery.

I was glad of the friendly darkness, for with blackout curtains at the window our cabin was in utter blackness. I was pretty certain that two recruits sharing a bed was not what the navy would look upon kindly. Therefore no one else present was aware of Daphne joining me, innocent as she may have considered such an action to be. She was, undoubtedly, a naive girl from a close-knit family and quite unaware of such a thing as sex between two females. She cuddled into my warm naked softness with a quiet sob and a sigh, feeling comfortably secure, no doubt, after a first day away from mummy and daddy and thrown into an entirely alien way of life.

Thus it may have been for her but I was a sexual creature, easily aroused, and Daphne's slim boyish body pressed into mine with only her thin nightie separating our flesh had its usual effect on me – sexual desire. My arm was around her and with her nightdress raised by her action of slipping in beside me, my hand made contact with her smooth bottom cheeks. For a moment I caressed them as she nestled into the curve of my neck, then I decided that seducing the sweet innocent would be rather underhand in her vulnerable state. Her skin was so soft however, the temptation was great. I withdrew my hand before my fingers could seek between the cleft of her curved buttocks and reach to infiltrate the virgin slit. Then, with a shock to my being, Daphne muttered something about my being so sweet to her, so kind in her misery, and pressed a succession of grateful kisses on my cheek.

I felt I was being used as a mother substitute, though we were of the same age. It had been a hectic day for all of us and from the bunk beds around us came the sound of regular breathing of girls in a deep sleep. 'There, there,' I consoled Daphne in a whisper. 'You'll soon settle down here—' But, in turning my face to say so, our lips met and clung for a long moment. Such sweet lips and sweet breath! Again came the temptation – this time to slide my tongue into her mouth and roll over on top of her. 'You'd better go to your own bed,' I told her, as much for her sake as my own. My tummy was on fire with a lust that burned in my cunt. I pushed her away.

'Don't send me away,' Daphne whined, cuddling back to me. 'Let me stay, it's so comforting and cosy here with you, Diana.' Her hand sidled over my stomach, going up tentatively to cup my right breast which was already swollen with excitement, the nipple stiff and erect. 'Please, please,' she added, kissing my chin and neck before her mouth sought and suckled on my nipple. Little moans of contentment escaped from her as she fed on both breasts in turn like a contented baby. 'They're so nice, so big and beautiful – do let me—'

My nursing her was such an erotic experience for me that it had gone far beyond stopping her. I could only draw her closer, in the classic mother feeding her child posture, lifting and holding up my breasts for her as my free hand went down between my legs to finger myself.

Sin and Mrs Saxon

I found an opened-mouthed slit dripping with my lubrication and palpitating for release, the inner folds juicy and hot to the touch, my clitoris standing out taut and erect from its hood like a stiff fingertip. With Daphne's sobs fading into the swell of my soft tits as she sucked contentedly on my nipples, I reached a continuous orgasm as I stroked my clitty. I tried to contain myself, gritting my teeth, trying not to jerk my pelvis as I was swept into the throes of a blessed release. After a previous sleepless night of sex with Harry and a tiring day following with my entry into the Wrens, I fell into sound sleep almost at once as Daphne's mouth sucked gently on a nipple.

I was awakened with a start, a shaded beam of flashlight in my eyes. Holding the torch, in the dimness beyond it, I saw the gloating face of Petty Officer Bella Watson looking down upon us. 'What have we here – two love-birds?' she smirked in a stage whisper. 'Don't you know you can be dishonourably discharged for such conduct?' She clapped a hand over Daphne's mouth as she awakened and was about to let out an anguished howl.

'Come with me, both of you, and don't awaken the others,' the Petty Officer hissed. 'You pair of horny sluts are in trouble!'

Chapter Three
AMERICA

Cocktails at Madame Violette Lefarge's plush apartment had seemingly introduced me to a pretty gang of lechers. I was wary of getting too involved with them and intended to remain on the fringes, as it were, suiting myself if and when I thought their company would enliven my stay in New York. Though I did not approve of drugs I considered the sexual freedom of their gatherings as interesting to say the least, never having been able to resist attractive partners. The pretty little maid Lysette, for instance, and the outsized cock of the handsome and suave South American Martinez had more than intrigued me. I wouldn't refuse the chance at either given the right time and place.

This by no means meant I found my husband unsatisfactory in bed or wherever else he took me. We were both adventurous and imaginative when it came to out-of-the-ordinary situations and places to enjoy fucking. It was what had kept our marriage so strong and exciting over the years. Having a bit on the side, to put it crudely, had never been considered by me as being unfaithful to Harry – it was a purely physical happening to be savoured with someone new. Fucking is too good a gift of nature not to be enjoyed at every chance, I considered. Anyway, a fuck is a fuck was my philosophy, and the same applied whenever I learned that Harry had been tempted by other women. A change may be hard to resist but it doesn't mean that one's wife or husband is no longer desired.

Others may fiercely disagree with this outlook but, looking around, I knew of no other couple as happily suited and married as Harry and I. The following morning after the cocktail party – well named, I considered, as there were many cocks on display and the women were certainly 'tails' – I awoke after a good night of loving sex to celebrate our new home. We had employed no maid as yet, so I cooked Harry a breakfast and saw him off to his office, then soaked in a deep sudsy bath.

Our bathroom, like all the other rooms in the apartment, was a splendid affair – adjoining the bedroom yet with a separate door into it from the hall. It was thickly carpeted and had tiles and mirrors, washbasin and shower cubicle, bidet and toilet and glass-fronted cabinets were set around the walls. The circular bath with its golden taps was big enough for three people to splash in, and Harry and I had already shared it. Lying back, with my breasts floating like twin horned sea-mines, I considered that the bathroom area was as big as the whole cottage I'd been brought up in. I'd come a long way from the Saturday nights when my mother had filled the long tin bath with kettles of hot water and my father had smoked his pipe in the outhouse while I and my sisters, Isobel and Jennifer, had shared the water in front of a roaring fire.

I dried myself, threw on some sweet-smelling talcum powder and was surprised to hear the telephone ring. I answered the receiver in the kitchen. It was one of the receptionists permanently stationed at a desk in the ornate foyer of the building. No one entered without a security check, it seemed. 'Mrs Saxon,' said the male voice. 'You have two visitors here wishing to come up to your apartment. One is a Senor Martinez and the other gentleman is a Mr Levinson. Do you wish to see them, or shall I say that you're not available right now?'

I'm sure he heard my little chuckle. It had not taken long for me to receive visitors. 'Send them up, please,' I answered, and before he replaced his telephone I heard his deep American voice direct them to the elevator. As I was naked, I put on a long silken housecoat with a belt of the same material. It was naughty of me perhaps as the garment clung tightly to what was underneath – nothing but me. Two horny admirers in one go, I pondered. Such happenings always made my day.

I answered the door to find Manny Levinson bearing a couple of dozen long-stemmed red roses encased in cellophane. The tall figure of Miguel Franco y Martinez towering over him, resplendent in polo-playing gear: white tee-shirt, flared sharkskin jodhpurs with highly polished brown kneeboots and a knotted cravat at his neck. Hairs sprouted from his shirt, curling over its neck – he was the very picture of the macho male. As I stood aside to let them enter, he elbowed little Manny aside and, much as I fancied him with his huge prick and heavy hung balls, I decided he should be shown I wasn't about to fall into his arms. If that ever came about it would be on my terms with him doing the grovelling. It was an ambitious thought considering I did not know him well.

'How flattering to have two such handsome callers at this time of morning.' I smiled sweetly, noting that both were eyeing up my breasts and thighs clearly revealed by the thin silk housecoat which clung to my contours like the last of the seven veils.

'The pleasure is all mine,' Martinez said suavely, giving me the old lingering hand-kissing treatment again. 'I thought I'd pop in on my way to practise at the polo ground—'

'Don't let me keep you then,' I suggested.

'It can wait,' he smiled, not in the least put off. I realised he was a persistent fellow, not easily diverted from what he wanted. 'Manny here is a busy little investments adviser and I'm sure he has lots to do right now. Like leaving us, for instance. I came here to say how lovely I thought you were last night—'

'Thank you,' I smiled, 'but actually it was I who asked Manny to call to discuss my investments. Wasn't it sweet of him to bring flowers? Go into the lounge and take a seat, Manny,' I added. 'Senor Martinez is about to leave.'

I heard Manny give a delighted chuckle and walk into my lounge, leaving me at the door with Martinez, who regarded me with eyes alight with villainous humour. 'There will be other times, you delectable Mrs Saxon,' he assured me. 'Did you like what you saw at Violette's little party last night?'

'What I saw wasn't so little,' I replied cheekily.

'Quite so,' he said proudly. 'It has pleased many ladies in its day. Do let me know if you are curious—'

'Off to your polo practice, you Latin lecher,' I laughed, pushing him out of the doorway. 'The only mount you'll have this morning will be your horse. On your way—' As I closed the door he pouted his sensuous lips at me, pecking a kiss in my direction, approving of my light-hearted manner. I returned to the lounge where Manny sat looking at me with adoration.

'Coffee?' I asked. 'Is it too early for a drink? I don't want to start you off, young man.'

'No,' he said. 'I don't hit the sauce until later on a good day, and this one has started well, with you seeing off that big lug Martinez like you did. He thinks he's God's gift to all women. When you said you wanted to discuss investments, was that just a ploy to get rid of him, or have you business you'd like to discuss with me? I'm a hot-shot financial adviser, believe it or not, and would be delighted to help—'

'I leave all that to my husband, Harry,' I said, 'but he might be happy to have you advise him.' He followed me into the kitchen where I put on the coffee and found a vase for his roses. 'It was sweet of you to bring flowers,' I thanked him. 'I did mean that—'

'It's by way of apology,' Manny said. 'I must have been drunk as a skunk last evening when you were with me. I didn't do anything I shouldn't have, did I?' I handed him a cup of coffee and studied his face, wondering how much he remembered and deciding to tease him. 'It's pretty much a blank,' he added.

'Such as fondling my breasts?' I challenged him impishly.

'How could I forget that? I'd have had to be dead not drunk,' he admitted self-consciously. 'God, they are big and beautiful. I just thought this morning you might think the worse of me—'

Manny was looking at the high swelling mounds under the silk robe as he spoke, eyeing the cleavage where the garment opened at my neck. I had no doubt he wished he had my tits in his hands right then, and I would not have stopped him if he had reached out to uncover them.

'Things got a bit wild in there,' I said. 'Forget it.' I was tempted to add, 'Any time, Manny,' but held my tongue. Instead, I asked him, 'What do you think of the apartment? Rather grand, isn't it?'

'Violette Lefarge had it before she moved across the passage to get the view of Central Park when the last occupants left,' he said. 'You know about the mirror, do you?'

'It's news to me,' I had to say. The apartment was full of ornate mirrors on every wall. 'What about a mirror?'

'Come with me,' he said, leading me off into the bathroom. On the walls between the glass-fronted cabinets were several framed pictures of mermaids and leaping dolphins. He tilted one aside and I saw right into the bedroom where Harry and I slept. 'Two-way mirror,' he explained. 'Violette had it put in as she used that bedroom as the guest room. She liked to peek on her overnight visitors, that's if she and her nutty husband weren't in with them. Or more likely he stood here taking in the scene of his wife getting screwed, if you'll excuse the language. I thought you should know about it.'

'I'm glad you did,' I said, amused by the trick mirror. We were looking right through the wall facing the bed, giving an excellent view. The door bell chimed at that moment and I went to answer it with Manny remaining behind, no doubt staying to keep his presence unobserved.

I opened the door and was faced with Lysette, the pretty little French maid. She lowered her eyes as if shy, the little devil, well aware I knew why she had called on me. I recalled the feel of her bared bottom, the pliant freshness of her young breasts with the uptilted elongated nipples, and her sweet tongue in my mouth, making me hot immediately. She came straight into my arms, pressing her lithe figure against my silk-clad one and I was lost, forgetting that Manny Levinson was in the apartment.

'I could not wait, Madame Saxon,' she said breathlessly as our mouths parted. 'After last evening, oh, I did not sleep and played with myself thinking of you. Tell me you do not mind me calling? The Lefarges have gone to the polo ground and will be lunching at Del Monaco's, so I am free the whole day. Do not send me away—'

With her sharp-nippled tits and crotch hard against mine, her mouth poised to repeat her kisses, how could I refuse? I was trembling with emotion or lust, whatever, wanting her so badly that I couldn't have resisted the sexy little minx had Harry appeared. The thought of him joining us further aroused me and I filed the idea in my mind for some future occasion. Our lips still entwined, hands fumbling at each other's breasts and crotches, we made a beeline for the bedroom. There Lysette pushed my robe from my shoulders, standing back as the silky garment slithered to my feet, taking in my nakedness with wide eager eyes. Her hands came to my breasts, little palms that could only cup my heavy curves over the circles of my aureoles, flicking the stiffened nipples with both thumbs. Then her wet red lips fastened on to one, drawing it and some breast flesh with it into her mouth, such was the suction she applied.

Weak at the knees, I sat back on the bed and she gently lowered my shoulders to the covers. Between my splayed tits, over my stomach, I saw my parted thighs, with the forested cunt mound between, raised as if on offering. 'I have wanted to see you like this so very much, dear madame,' Lysette said hoarsely. 'I shall make love to you as only two women can. We shall reach heaven—'

I was sure we would, but I wanted to see all of Lysette too. 'Undress, dear,' I begged her. 'Then come to me. Let me see you and touch you—' I am not usually so helplessly aroused before actual bodily contact, but this little witch was so desirable that I was clay in her hands. I realised that she was already the dominant one and I her passive slave. Lysette crawled forward over me, squatting on my face, opening the lipless slit of her pouchy little quim directly above my mouth.

'Lick, Madame Saxon!' she ordered harshly, her tone very different from before. 'Use your tongue well to please me, or I shall beat you severely. Do it now, clean me out!'

Sitting up and facing forward, she reached back and used a hand to slap hard at one of my hips as a jockey might urge on a mount. Her salty-tasting cunt fast to my lips, I protruded my tongue and lapped and licked. Though somewhat abashed and resentful at my treatment, I was still aroused, perhaps made even more so by the bitter-sweet sense of being humiliated, which I on occasion find irresistible. 'Yes, yes, Lysette,' I managed to mumble, drawing breath before resuming reeming out her tight little fissure. My tongue tip found her clitty and I swirled around it, making her body give little leaps. Pleased, I supposed, she reached back with a hand, curling two fingers into my cunt, probing deeply and roughly. My thighs jerked and above me she was squirming, her crisis coming with mine as we bucked and floundered together in a long drawn-out orgasm.

She rolled over beside me, regarding me arrogantly as I huffed and puffed to regain my breath. My breasts rose and fell with the exertion and she sat up and grasped them both tightly as if to still them. 'Such teats,' she laughed. 'You are a cow and I will milk them.' I murmured that she was hurting them, gripping them too tightly, and she gave them both a harder squeeze. Right, I thought, just now I am too aroused by you to want to stop the proceedings, though you are a slip of a girl younger than my own daughter. So have your way, little one, next time I shall be the one to threaten punishment.

She nipped both my nipples with her sharp teeth and I gave a little yelp.

'You don't need to be so cruel,' I protested. 'I want you here with me but I'm willing to do what you want without hurting me— '

'But I enjoy being cruel,' Lysette smirked. 'When I set out to seduce an older woman, they often expect it, love it. If you want me, you must do as I say, Madame Saxon. Do you know where I learned that is what many women enjoy?'

Always fascinated by the sexual secrets of others, I shook my head obediently, just as the little bitch expected. 'No, I don't know,' I said. 'But I expect you're going to tell me—'

'My dear step-mother in Paris,' she gloated. 'Papa's dear wife. She beat me as a child. As a young woman I went to her bed and seduced her. Then I would beat her, hard across her buttocks with a strap. When papa found out, he sent me away, but she cried to see me leave. Then I found employment with Madame Lefarge—'

'Do you beat her?' I was dying to know.

'No, she is too strong-willed. I beat her husband, we

Sin and Mrs Saxon

both do. When she is tired, I take over—'

What a great little set-up, I thought, there's no end to what people get up to, is there? Then, looking across the room, I saw the mirror opposite and remembered that Manny Levinson was no doubt closeted behind it getting entertained. The thought made me chuckle and Lysette frowned angrily.

'What do you find so amusing?' she demanded. 'Do you wish to be beaten?'

'Not just now, dear,' I replied lightly. 'I'd rather we pleasured ourselves again. I'd enjoy another come, wouldn't you? I'll sit on your face for a change—'

'Don't tell me what I must do,' she said angrily.

'But I am,' I said calmly, having had enough of letting this kid order me about. That was a temporary lech which I'd enjoyed at the time. 'If it comes to dealing out a beating, taking you across my knee to smack your pretty bum, little girl, I'm bigger and stronger than you. This time I'll be queen, won't I? Use your tongue well, darling, or I'll be angry.'

She studied me like a sulky schoolgirl, then lay flat on the bed waiting for my arse on her face. 'Get on with it,' I ordered, as much to show my authority now as to receive pleasure. I was delighted to hear her mutter a grumpy 'Oui, madame,' and I squatted with my feet flat on the bed on either side of her slim shoulders. I felt her draw my quite ample buttock cheeks apart and commence a tentative lapping with her sharp-pointed little tongue. I slapped at her hip as she'd done to me and she began to delve into my cunt beautifully, making me groan out my pleasure as I felt her warm to the task. Her tongue flicked at my clitoris; her lips pushed hard into me and sucked the stiff nub, making me rotate my

Sin and Mrs Saxon

bottom in acute pleasure. I leaned over to reach for her tight quim and she parted her legs widely, bucking her hips. It was at that moment, as I began titillating Lysette's cunt, that I caught a glimpse of Manny Levinson approaching, his prick stiff and erect in his hand.

'This is too much,' he protested, 'I can't stand any more of seeing you two at it without doing something about it. I'm only bloody human.' The cock in his hand had an appealing bulbous circumcised head. No monster, it was at least a good thick-looking cock and my pulsating cunt, being tongued so thoroughly now by an excited Lysette, craved the bigger object. My bottom was near the edge of the bed so I brazenly tilted it in Manny's direction, to the consternation of the girl below me as my cunt was withdrawn from her mouth.

'Do it, I want it,' I moaned my willingness to Manny, and the next moment he had closed to me, curling over my back, his length gratefully accepted up my greedy burning fanny.

'She's licking my balls,' Manny grated as his shafting began, his circumcised knob nudging the nub of my clitoris, driving me crazy with the feeling. I gulped out wild words, urging him on to fuck me, *fuck me*. What a sight we presented: Manny shafting me vigorously, his hands grasping my tits for leverage as he curled over me and, below, the nymphet using her pointed tongue on his balls and stem as it withdrew from me before ramming in again.

This magnificent, lewd tableau was proceeding apace, with accompanying noises of squelches and slurps and the slap of Manny's belly against my raised bottom. Several stomach-heaving climaxes had already been achieved by me when a brilliant flash momentarily

Sin and Mrs Saxon

dazzled us, followed by another instant bright light. I turned in alarm to see Madame Lefarge in the bedroom with her husband beside her raising his camera.

'How dare you intrude,' I screamed, even as Lefarge came closer and continued taking his pictures. 'What are you doing in my apartment?'

'I think it is obvious, *chérie*,' Violette Lefarge said amiably. 'Taking some very interesting pictures.' Her maid wriggled out from below me and sat up, smiling triumphantly, while Manny stood back, trousers to his ankles and Marcel Lefarge continued taking photographic evidence of our debauch. 'Good girl, Lysette,' Violette Lefarge praised her maid. 'She obviously believed we would be away all day like we told you to say, and the result is even better than we could have wished. And Manny, too, involved in your adulterous behaviour, Mrs Saxon. Tut, tut, what would your husband say? What if we sent some copies of our pictures to him, or even the head of the F.A.O. that employs him? Think of the scandal that would result—'

'The bitch has set you up,' Manny growled, making a grab for Lefarge's camera but stumbling as his trousers caught around his feet. 'Christ, Mrs Saxon, I didn't mean for this to happen—'

'I know you didn't, Manny,' I said calmly. 'They sent Lysette over here to trap me. Your being here was just a bonus for these two bastards. I'd be interested to know now what they intend to use the pictures for—' I looked defiantly at Violette Lefarge. 'It can't be to obtain money. They've plenty of that, it seems. I would think it's a more subtle blackmail, to rope me into their sex *soirées*, doing as they bid or else—'

'How clever of you, Mrs Saxon,' Violette positively

cooed. 'Or now I'm sure we can call you Diana, as we are on such intimate terms. Yes, we would like you to add to our little orgies when required. I don't think you'll refuse to help entertain our guests. They are all nice people, of course – bankers and heads of governments whom my husband will wish to entertain in his business dealings. Watching you just now, seeing what a highly sexual creature you are, you should enjoy it.'

'I'm for calling the police,' Manny threatened. 'Blackmail is a serious crime in this country—'

'Do so,' Violette offered, 'but the sandal for Mrs Saxon would ruin her husband. End their marriage too, I suspect.' She smiled sweetly at me. 'What do you say, Diana?'

What could I say? Once again my unruly sexual nature had landed me in a difficult situation. However, there had been others and I'd wriggled my way out of them safely, as I was sure I would this latest.

'No police, Manny, thank you,' I said. 'I'll have to sort this out for myself.' Whatever I'd be called upon to do, I decided, one way or the other the Lefarges would use me and I'd have to go along until I saw my way clear of their hold on me. 'It's for the best,' I added. 'I can't risk my husband's reputation.' And, of course, there was the knighthood he'd been promised. I had too much to lose by being defiant at that moment.

Lysette was eyeing me, her sharp cat's eyes bright green with malice. 'She threatened to beat me, madame,' she informed her mistress. 'I should like to beat her for her insolence. Tell her to lie across the bed with her bottom out so that I may make her eat her words—'

'Bitch,' I snapped at her but, warned I'd better do as

ordered by Violette, I stretched out on the bed with my bared bottom over the edge. I heard Manny protest and saw they had taken the belt from his trousers. Lysette, the vindictive little bitch, doubled it in her hand and whacked it down across my cheeks. It landed with a painful crack that brought tears to my eyes and made me bite my lips to prevent myself crying out. After several good thwacks I howled in pain and humiliation. My buttocks went red hot and stung agonisingly while the camera clicked. Then my thrashing was over, the belt flung aside, and I was left alone with Manny standing beside me full of concern.

'Don't worry,' I told him. 'My turn will come somehow and I'll get more than my own back. Meantime I'm bound to do some of their bidding. Not a word of any of this mess to anyone, mind you. They can't kill me, can they?'

'I don't trust that crazy lot, they'll try anything,' Manny said unhappily. 'I'm in this with you too, Mrs Saxon. Any help I can give, count me in. I shall wrack my brains to do those bastards—'

'You can start by calling me Diana,' I smiled to cheer him. 'We know each other well enough for that, I feel.'

'That's another thing I have to apologise to you for,' he said.

'Because you fucked me?' I said kindly. 'I was there begging for it, wasn't I? Seeing that girl and I doing what we did must have been too much for any man. I didn't refuse it, did I? I seem to remember enjoying it. Pity it ended like it did but that's not your fault.'

'Diana,' Manny said. 'I've never met a woman like you. All I can say is that your husband is one lucky guy. I hated it when that little bitch strapped your lovely ass but you took it like a lady.'

'I'm just about to take a bath and apply soothing cream to that lovely ass,' I grinned, 'so you'd better leave, Manny. Don't worry about me, I can take care of myself.'

Later that afternoon Harry came home pleased with the start he had made in his new position with the F.A.O. 'There's no end of schemes I've in mind for developing countries,' he said. 'What kind of day did you have, my love?'

'I was in the house all day,' I said, which was true.

'You can't get into any trouble staying at home,' Harry laughed, 'so I'll take you out to wine and dine on the town tonight to make up for a dull day. When you get to know people, your life will be quite hectic here in New York, I'll bet. You wait and see, my dear.'

I could hardly have put it better myself. Then the chimes went at the door again and Harry returned with a huge bouquet of flowers, masses of them in a large gold-painted basket. 'Who in the world gave you these?' I said. 'Who was it at the door?'

'A real high-class chauffeur in uniform,' Harry laughed. 'I don't suppose it was from him, so you must have a rich admirer already. Look at the card.'

'It's from a Senor Miguel Franco y Martinez, or Mig as he's signed it,' I read out to Harry. 'He was at last night's cocktail party at the Lefarges and I saw him give me the eye.'

'He has good taste,' Harry teased. 'Are you sure you didn't encourage him? He was impressed enough to spend a fortune on these flowers. Do you know he's a member of the richest family in Rosaria and a special envoy to the United Nations?'

'I've never even heard of Rosaria,' I said, adding most

innocently, 'Why, I hardly spoke to him, I was just introduced.'

'Rosaria, my love,' Harry said, 'is a South American country of no great size with great wealth in timber and emeralds. This Martinez is as rich as Midas while his countrymen scratch for a living. I'd like to meet him, see if I can't interest him in doing more for the people. That's the kind of job I've got—'

'He's probably more interested in playing polo,' I said without realising my slip. 'I mean, he's the kind that would play polo, don't you think?'

'That and sending flowers to beautiful women he has a fancy for,' Harry teased again. 'You'd better watch out for him, my love. If he does contact you, before you spurn his advances and throw him out, tell him your husband would like an appointment to meet him. The object, to improve the living conditions of peasant farmers in Rosaria.'

I knew why the flowers had arrived, because he had seen Manny with his bouquet and wanted to go one better. 'If I am ever in his company again,' I said, 'I'll tell him that. But I don't suppose we'll move in the same circles. Now let's go out for the night, Harry. Show me the town.'

'Poor lamb,' Harry sympathised. 'You must have had a long boring day here all by yourself—'

Chapter Four
ENGLAND

Not for one moment did I suppose that innocent little Daphne Seymour had ever been branded a horny slut. Terrified of our severe Petty Officer, she followed me silently into the corridor and into Bella Watson's private cabin. Our tormentor closed the door for privacy and immediately Daphne burst into a flood of tears, sobbing uncontrollably. I stood beside her naked, my big thrusting breasts and nipples still showing signs of the fondling and sucking they'd received. Never shy of being naked before others, vulnerable was how I felt as the stoutish Petty Officer regarded me, hands on her flaring hips.

'Your first night in the service and you two couldn't keep your paws off each other,' Bella berated us. 'If I report this little affair, you two will be out on your pretty arses. Just what were you doing snuggled up together? I want the truth now!'

'Please, miss,' Daphne began through her sobs, as if addressing a headmistress.

'Don't *miss* me, Seymour,' snapped the awesome woman. 'I'm addressed as Petty Officer and don't you forget it if you are around after this. Did Mackenzie invite you into her bed? Did she seduce you? She looks

Sin and Mrs Saxon

like she would, the naked hussy standing there so brazenly.'

Looking forward to enjoying life in the Wrens, for once discretion was the better part of valour and I held my tongue. Bella glared at me as if expecting a riposte but, getting no reply, continued cross-examining Daphne as the one she rightly gauged would crack. 'Did she lure you into her bunk for sex?' she demanded again. 'The truth might just save your skin.'

'I don't know what you mean, Petty Officer,' the frightened girl blubbered. 'It was just that I felt so terribly homesick and unhappy. Diana had been kind to me and when it was lights out I got into her bed for company—'

Petty Officer Bella Watson laughed grimly. 'I can guess the sort of comfort you mean, Seymour. Did the pair of you touch each other up—?'

The sadistic bitch, I thought, but kept silent. Daphne looked amazed through her tears. 'I was lonely,' she said miserably. 'It just happened. I cuddled into Diana and it was nice. I'm sorry if I shouldn't have—'

'You'll be sorrier if you don't answer my questions,' threatened Bella. 'I want to know what went on between you two. Coming clean might just save your skins, or would you like me to report this breach of discipline? If I do, you two will be ex-Wrens by the morning. What would your parents think of that?' Having threatened the ultimate, she put her round face close to Daphne's. 'Give with the gory details,' she ordered sharply. 'Did Mackenzie suck your breasts or go down on you—?'

'I'm not sure what you mean, Petty Officer,' Daphne whined, wringing her hands.

'A spot of muff-diving, hunting the beaver,' Bella said

Sin and Mrs Saxon

callously. It was then I knew, seeing her eyes light as she tormented the innocent girl, that our Petty Officer was a fully paid-up dyke and a butch lesbian if ever there was. 'You may play the homesick little mummy's girl on her first night away from home, but you don't fool me. What went on?'

Daphne looked at me appealingly, as if begging my forgiveness. I had been in similar situations in my time and had survived, so I gave her an encouraging smile. 'Tell her, Daphne,' I said. 'She won't believe you if you say nothing happened, so tell her it was all because you were so unhappy—'

'I sucked Diana's breasts,' Daphne whispered shamefully. 'That was all. I cuddled into her and it just happened. It felt nice and comforting—'

'I'll bet it did,' Bella said sarcastically. She transferred her gaze to my breasts, nodding in approval. 'Plenty to feed on there and no doubt Mackenzie enjoyed it too. I can see she's still aroused. Now what do you think I should do with the pair of you? Shall I report you, or will you take whatever punishment I think fit in the circumstances and then forget the matter?'

'Oh yes, Petty Officer,' Daphne murmured gratefully. 'Don't report us, please! My father is a naval officer and I daren't think what he'd say if I was discharged. Any punishment you think fit would be better. I mean extra work, cleaning the cabins, whatever you say—'

From the way Bella Watson was regarding us, as if completely at her mercy, I rightly knew that extra chores in our off-duty time was not what she had in mind. Her next words affirmed my suspicions. 'Physical punishment was what I meant,' she said sweetly. 'You've been naughty girls and naughty girls need to be taught a

Sin and Mrs Saxon

lesson. Off with that nightdress, Wren Seymour—'

'You mean—' Daphne gasped. A moment later, cowed by a glare from Bella, she pulled her nightdress off, standing dejected in her nakedness, a shapely slim girl with small pointy breasts and wisps of hair surrounding a tight little virgin's cunt lips. She tried to cover both her top and bottom bits with her hands, only to have them knocked away by our Petty Officer.

'Such a girlie-girl,' said Bella Watson, walking around her, a hand smoothing Daphne's little curved bottom sensuously. 'I don't suppose that sweet arse of yours has ever felt the belt, has it?'

I saw Daphne standing silent, eyes rimmed with salty tears. 'No, Petty Officer,' she whined.

'Do you think a good strapping of your bottom is fair punishment for what you did tonight?'

'Yes,' Daphne said hesitantly. 'If you think so—'

'Go to my bed and bend over it.'

Daphne swallowed hard, braced herself, and walked to the bed, resting on her elbows as she dipped her back and revealed her naked rear, a sight that no doubt excited our superior. It was indeed a pretty bottom, white as marble and boyishly small. Petty Officer Watson regarded it lovingly from beside me, then went to her bedside cabinet and drew out a length of webbing belt, wrapping the end of it around her hand. Daphne, waiting apprehensively, glanced around and drew in her breath in a loud gasp. I saw the cheeks of her buttocks flinch.

'This will hurt me more than it does you, Seymour,' Bella said sadistically. 'I'm sure your naval officer father would approve of what his naughty daughter is about to receive. Don't you think so?'

Sin and Mrs Saxon

'Ye-yes,' came from Daphne. She buried her head in the bedcover.

'What about me?' I dared ask. 'If I lie there beside her, you'd have two bums to whack at the same time. That would get it over with—'

'Nobody asked you, Mackenzie,' said the plump woman. 'Tempting as the thought is, you'll stand there and wait your turn. As it was your bed she was in and you were the one I found naked, I'll deal with you later.' I shrugged my shoulders, accepting the inevitable and she turned her attention to Daphne's raised rear. 'Not a sound from you,' she warned. 'Can't wake up the whole building, can we? So grit your teeth and bear it. You don't want to be thrown out of the service, do you, girl?'

The webbing strap came down immediately, cracking across Daphne's bottom and producing a stifled yelp. As I watched helplessly, the girl's cheeks were reddened by a dozen or more hard strokes that criss-crossed both mounds. Daphne sobbed out a plea for mercy, clenched and unclenched her buttocks, but did not try to crawl away from the blows and took the punishment well. Bella Watson thought so too, throwing the strap on to the bed at last, regarding Daphne's ruddy posterior with satisfaction.

'That wasn't too bad, was it, Seymour?' she said. 'You could even get to enjoy it.' *She* did, for sure, I knew, looking at her eyes bright with lustful pleasure. 'Girls of your type do learn to like a beating, especially when they know they've been wicked. It warms them up. Do you feel warmed up? Does the heat from your thrashed bottom go on down to your pussy? Has it made it hot and itchy for something?'

'I don't know, Petty Officer,' Daphne begged. 'Can I

Sin and Mrs Saxon

get up and put on my nightdress now, please?'

'You don't know,' Bella Watson said mockingly. 'At your age you ought to. Stay where you are and we'll find out, won't we?' Standing over Daphne, she used a foot to push apart the girl's legs, revealing her parted buttock cheeks and the hanging bulge of her cunt with the tiny lips. 'In that bedside drawer, Mackenzie,' I was ordered, 'you'll find a jar of cold cream. Bring it to me—'

She had left the drawer open when she'd taken out the webbing belt. I looked in to find the cold cream jar and saw a double-dildo in the shape of a vee with straps attached, some short lengths of silken cord, and a massager with dozens of little raised rubber bumps on its surface and a loop on the other side made for a hand to hold it while in use. It was a complete kit for lesbian loving and handily placed at her bedside. I found the cold cream and passed it over. Poor Daphne was turning her head when she dared, not daring to guess her fate.

'Such a well-thrashed bottom,' Bella Watson said quite sympathetically, as if she had not been the cause of it. 'A little soothing cream will cool it, Seymour. You would like it soothed, would you not?'

'Yes,' Daphne said timidly. 'If you think so—'

'Oh, I do.' A good scoop was taken from the jar and Bella put a generous dab of cream on both Daphne's cheeks, using both hands to rub it in gently, sensuously, over the bottom presented. 'Nice, eh?' said Bella. 'Lie still, girl, and enjoy the feeling. Such nice smoothly rounded cheeks you have. Reach back with your hands and part them for me—'

'Please, please,' began Daphne, but a warning smack on her bottom made her obey. I saw Bella take more cream and, with an upsweeping movement of her hand,

Sin and Mrs Saxon

trail it over Daphne's cunt and tight little anus, smoothing in the oily substance as far as the girl's outer lips and beyond. 'Oh, ooh,' gasped Daphne, 'what are you doing—?' Her groan that followed was of sheer humiliation, as the expert fingering of her tight little quim produced loud slurping sounds. 'Please—' she begged.

'Please what, Seymour?' taunted Bella Watson. 'Please stop or please continue? I'm sure this must feel rather nice. I want to hear you say that it's nice—'

From where I was standing, seeing the greased moving finger curled into Daphne's cunt, well beyond the knuckles, the hand doing the manipulating twisting in circular motions, I wondered how long it would take to make Daphne submit. It was the kind of punishment I'd enjoy, and being forced to endure it by a blackmailing bitch of a woman only added a certain piquancy to the act. Daphne's whimpers and sobbing moans continued; Bella's insistent titillation of her cunt was having an effect.

'You haven't answered my question,' our Petty Officer dyke snapped, ceasing her fingering momentarily. Daphne turned her face as if questioning why. I noted her buttocks gave little involuntary jerks, desiring the frigging to continue of their own accord. 'Say you like this,' ordered Bella. 'Tell me!'

'It's not right, it's not nice,' Daphne whined in protest. 'You're a beast, doing this to me—' The touching-up restarted and she shivered, her bottom lifting and making little circular movements against the hand working on her. She gave a shuddering groan as if giving up the struggle, now thrusting back to get full measure of the fingers in her, for I'd observed Bella had added two more. 'Oh, I do like it,' she helplessly admitted. 'Don't stop now, please. Oh, oh, it feels so funny—'

Sin and Mrs Saxon

Daphne, it was obvious, was about to come and no doubt by some other hand besides her own for the first time. 'Yes, yes,' she uttered loudly. 'There, just there! Oh, my goodness, I'm dying, dying! Oh, oh, ah! Aaaarrrgh—'

This last was an exhalation of breath turned into a groan of relief as Daphne's buttocks jerked rapidly, thrusting higher as each helpless spasm shook her to the core. I could only think she was badly in need of a good come and she'd certainly got one. Even then the inhibited girl felt remorse. 'I didn't mean to,' she whispered as if in apology for her lewd behaviour. 'I couldn't help myself. It just happened—'

'Of course it did, Daphne,' said Bella, sounding quite friendly and using the girl's first name as if to reassure her. 'Off to your own bed with you now and you'll sleep well. You simply needed release. I won't be reporting you; all this will remain our secret.'

'Thank you, Petty Officer,' Daphne said gratefully, putting on her nightdress. 'I do feel better now.' She brushed her cheeks with the back of her hand to remove the residue of her tears. She was apprehensive still but I noted she regarded Bella with the kind of adoring look dogs give to their masters. As if on a sudden impulse, she pecked a quick kiss to the woman's cheek, a gesture of more than a simple thank-you. Then Daphne hurried from the room, her thoughts no doubt full of the wonder of another woman giving her such a strong orgasm, mixed with her sense of relief for escaping being reported and discharged the service.

Alone with the Petty Officer, I awaited my fate, aware I would not fool her with such an exhibition as put on by Daphne. 'What did you think of that, Mackenzie?' Bella said, her tone of voice aggressive again. 'Under that repressed little virgin's hide lurks a horny bitch. You no doubt saw that and got her into your bed for your own lecherous purpose.'

'She came to my bed, like we said,' I answered calmly. 'I in no way expected it—'

'You didn't throw her out,' Bella said nastily.

'How could I? She held me like a limpet, crying her eyes out. Really, she's not my type.'

'What is your type? Am I?' she asked, testing me.

'Not really,' I smiled my reply. 'And I'm not your type either, am I? You like 'em innocent and easily moulded into willing subjects, like Daphne, no doubt. You've got a convert there. Now if it's all the same to you, I'm off to bed—'

'Not until I allow you to, Mackenzie,' Bella said, taken aback by my insolence. 'There's a little matter of suitable punishment to be administered—' Regaining her composure, she leered at me maliciously. 'We'll dispense with the pleasure your sort would get having a climax and stick to meting out a good thrashing. Bend over the bed—'

'Not this or any other time, Bella,' I said boldly and cheerfully, remembering I had a hold over her. 'You wouldn't dare report me, not when I'd give a full and lurid description of your little dalliance with Daphne if you did. That makes us quits, I think, so I'm off to bed.'

'You bitch,' Bella said, but there was humour in her voice. 'We know where we stand then, don't we?' She regarded my nakedness, her eyes going down from my breasts to my mound with its bush of chestnut-red hair. 'If you are off to bed, come into mine for a while. Touching up Daphne has made me tremendously

Sin and Mrs Saxon

randy—' Her hands reached out to cup both my breasts, thumbs and fingers pinching my nipples. 'You've made it with another woman before, I'm certain. Let me—'

Her offer was tempting, made more so as one hand went down to stroke gently over the outer lips of my cunt. 'Just for a while,' I conceded. 'Seeing you doing that to Daphne got me aroused too. If you want to make me come, I wouldn't mind—'

'Lie across the bed,' Bella instructed me, her voice quite hoarse with her excitement. I watched as she pulled off her uniform jacket and skirt, threw off her slip and bra and stepped out of her knickers, leaving just her black stockings held up by elastic garters that cut into fleshy white thighs of ample girth. Her tits hung fat and pendulously with big rubbery brown nipples. At her crotch was a black growth of thick hair on a prominent mound. I judged her a well-built woman in her middle thirties, a girl-hungry spinster.

She advanced upon my prone figure, trailed a hand over my stomach and down to curl a probing finger into my cunt. 'Drenched,' she exulted. 'Mackenzie, you horny thing, I've rarely felt such a moist fanny. Such a stiff clitty too, poking up like an erect nipple.' Her mouth slid across my breasts, fastening to each nipple in turn, then rose to kiss my mouth, her tongue seeking mine. 'Did you like Daphne sucking your tits, those big jugs you've got on you?' she asked as our lips parted.

'Who wouldn't?' I had to say. 'You suck them now. I like it. Hold them tight as you like—'

'What about your cunt, do you like that sucked?'

'Do it,' I urged her. 'Lick me out, that's what I want—'

'I shall eat you, eat you, Mackenzie,' she threatened,

her voice thick with emotion. 'Get your damned knees up, girl, I want in there—'

Her face went between my thighs and I grasped her hair, holding the pinned-up bun at the back of her head and pulling me to her. Her warm tongue snaked into me, flicking its tip, reeming around the nub of my clitty, making me gasp my pleasure and tilt my cunt into her face. It was now my turn to mutter yes, oh yes, and writhe my hips. I felt the surge of unstoppable arousal palpitate my cunt, thrusting it against her mouth as my orgasm came to the boil. In my throes she crawled forward over me, face to face, breast to breast, nipple to nipple, belly to belly and cunt to cunt. My knees rose and I locked my ankles behind her back, heaving into her as she thrust into me like a man, our pubic mounds grinding together. I heard her stifled cry as we came strongly, two naked beings thrashing together until subsiding into less frantic spasms that led to us lying still, sucking in air to regain our breath.

'Go now, Mackenzie,' Bella ordered, regaining her composure in time. 'Not a word of this to Daphne when she asks what went on after she left. Tell her I punished you. I don't want you saying we had sex.'

'You don't want her thinking you do this to all the girls,' I laughed. 'Sly thing. You want her to feel she's special.'

As I arose from the bed, Bella gave my bottom a friendly smack. 'Just remember what I said. I could do a lot to help your career in the Wrens. When your training is finished, my report on your fitness for a specialised job or even for promotion will carry some weight. A bright girl like you shouldn't end up a skivvy, no more than a kitchen hand or a barracks cleaner. There'll be appointments to signal school, driving and motor-mechanic training—'

'I'd like that,' I said.

'Then keep your nose clean while you are here. No more getting Daphne into your bed—'

'You want her for yourself,' I taunted laughingly. 'Shame on you, Petty Officer, setting out to corrupt that innocent girl.'

'Not so innocent,' Bella excused herself. 'You saw the way her bottom wriggled when I was tickling her fanny. Daphne is a natural and I'm never wrong when I spot one. I'm not the only one indulging around here. Put a crowd of females together like we are and sex is bound to rear its head—'

'So I've noticed,' I had to say. 'What did you do before you joined up?'

'I taught French in a famous public school for young ladies—'

'I'll just bet you did,' I had to laugh. 'This can't be very different for you then, is it?'

'On your way, Mackenzie,' Bella said authoritatively. 'Don't think because we had this little session tonight that I won't bear down on you hard if you slack off in your training.'

'Bearing down on me hard was what you were doing during our little session, as you called it,' I said cheekily, leaving her lying on the bed.

That was my first day spent as a Wren and I had already taken to the life, promising as it did very few dull moments.

Chapter Five
AMERICA

There always has to be a common denominator and as I seemed forever to get myself into tricky situations, that common denominator was me. My sexual nature had got me into unimaginable spots of bother since puberty, so if I did not suffer the pangs of guilt or fear my life was ruined by this latest threat, it was because I'd been there before. I had no doubt I'd extricate myself with a clean sheet, albeit none the wiser until I was next in some similar self-inflicted crisis, wondering why it should happen to me! The truth is that I was a sex bomb waiting to explode.

Kissing Harry goodbye in the doorway of our apartment as he left for his office the next morning, I saw the Lefarges' maid posted across the carpeted hallway, ostensibly watering the potted plants but no doubt keeping an eye out for my husband's departure. From the smirk on her pretty face it was obvious her employers had something in mind for me. Expecting something of the sort, having decided I was not going to make it easy for them, I was fully dressed and ready to bolt. Lysette hurried back into the Lefarges' apartment and I made a beeline for the lift, or elevator as the Americans call it.

Sin and Mrs Saxon

Passing the reception desk in the foyer, I was wished a good morning by the man on duty, who had previously introduced himself as Peter Gulay, and I was aware he was fascinated by my breasts and bottom as I went past him. 'Madam Lefarge has just called down to know if you're in the foyer, Mrs Saxon,' he said, as ever his eyes on the swell of my tits. He placed a hand on one of the array of telephones on his desk. 'Shall I phone back to say you are with me?'

'I have appointments, Peter,' I lied. 'Tell them I've already left. Better still, say you never saw me—'

'It's always a pleasure to see you, Mrs Saxon,' the young man said flirtatiously. 'In this case your whereabouts shall remain a mystery. Wild horses wouldn't drag it from me—'

I had to laugh with him, at his light-hearted approach. Such a handsome well set-up fellow too. 'You smoothie,' I told him. 'You're wasting your time being a receptionist. You should be in films or on the stage with your looks—'

'You've noticed,' Peter said with mock gravity. 'It just so happens I am an actor, earning a crust in this temple to wealth while attending numerous auditions and waiting to be discovered as the new Clark Gable.' He grinned at me in a good imitation of the famous star. 'I take it from now on I never reveal to the Lefarges anything about you—?'

'Something like that,' I said, going out under the canopied entrance and on to the pavement where the top-hatted and uniformed door attendant saluted me. If I thought I was free, I wasn't. Parked directly before me was a stretch Cadillac limousine with the liveried black chauffeur holding the rear door open for my entry. 'I

Sin and Mrs Saxon

think you've got the wrong person,' I said.

'Not at all, Diana,' said an accented voice within the car. 'I may call you that, may I not, seeing that we are now on such intimate terms with our little arrangement?' I looked inside to see Marcel Lefarge reclining on the deep leather upholstery. 'Please get in. We thought you might decide to abscond, and we couldn't have that, could we?'

'Not at all,' I said, determined to retain my cool. 'What have you got in mind for me, may I ask?' I sat beside him as the limo purred away.

'A favour for an old and valuable friend,' Lefarge stated, as if arranging a business meeting. I supposed it was, if the person I was to perform for was important to the rich banker. 'Be nice to him, do whatever he wants, and we will all gain. Madame Lefarge and I have provided certain pleasures for him on occasion before. We thought this time that you would make the perfect companion to satisfy his unusual demands—'

'You make it sound so charming,' I said derisively. 'And no doubt you'll be taking in the whole scene, getting your kicks seeing someone more able at it as usual—'

'Not this time,' Lefarge smiled, not in the least minding my insult. 'Milo Circassion is a very private gentleman. I wouldn't dare expect to be present. I deliver you, that's all. When he's through with you, his driver will return you to your home. Don't disappoint him or I, *chérie*. He telephones to return his thanks after an arranged visit, or informs us icily if he's displeased with our choice.'

'I just hope he's not fat or ugly then, like you,' I said easily, intending to offend. 'Just how many such calls upon my body do you intend before I'm in the clear with you? When do I get the photos and negatives you hold—?'

'When we tire of our little game,' he smiled. 'It could be a month, two months, two years. You are a beautiful woman, Diana Saxon. Men should enjoy you—'

It has always worked both ways with me, but I let that go. More on my mind was how I'd get my own back on the Lefarges. Something would allow me to and I'd relish it. The car pulled up in the driveway of an imposing house. 'Ring the bell and say nothing, they'll know whom you have come to visit,' Lefarge said as his chauffeur held open the car door. 'I shall expect a good report about you, Diana.'

A trim little Puerto Rican housemaid in cap and apron ushered me into a magnificent hallway with a curved stairway and balcony. Without expression, she handed me over to a similar-sized Japanese butler in a morning suit, who led me upstairs and tapped gently on a wide door. I went in, finding an airy bedroom with a huge four-poster bed, the walls lined with old masters I recognised from my love of studying art books. In an armchair, sitting up in a splendid silk kimono, was an elderly man with dark glasses perched on a hawk-like nose, his mouth a thin hard line and his body slim and wiry. Beside his chair was a small table with a champagne bottle in an ice bucket, cigarettes in a silver box and a tray with two tall crystal glasses. I noted too a white ivory walking stick beside the chair. He was blind.

'What are you looking at, girl?' he demanded in a voice tempered by a lifetime of being authoritive. His hand sought a cigarette from the box and he put it neatly into a long ebony holder. Crossing to him, I picked up the ornate silver lighter from the table and flicked it alight under his nose. Aware of the heat, I suppose, he steadied my hand and drew on his cigarette.

'I was admiring the Matisse on your bedroom wall,' I said.

'My favourite,' he said, 'even if I can no longer see it. So I've been sent an art lover, have I? Scottish too, from your voice. What are you doing in New York? No, don't tell me. Earning your living pleasing rich old men like me. How did you come to know the Lefarges?'

'I met them at one of their cocktail parties.'

'So they considered you worthy of coming to my home? They have their uses, and expect business favours in return, but I don't like them. Don't get too involved with them, young woman.'

'I intend not to,' I said, warming to this character. No doubt as rich as Midas, like all his ilk in the billionaire bracket he was shrewd. 'What is it you want?'

'Undress,' he said matter-of-factly. 'My hands have to do the seeing for me these days. Put your clothes over a chair and then come to me—'

I stripped, seeing myself naked in the long mirror of the wardrobe: breasts, thighs and hair-covered cunt mound. At my age I was in my prime, I considered, shapely but with not an ounce of fat on rounded limbs. It was rather a pity, I felt, that he couldn't see what he had before him, wondering if he was expecting a younger woman. I went to stand before him, my bared toes sinking into deep carpet pile.

'A drink first,' he decided. 'Pour champagne and help yourself. Have you a name?'

'Diana,' I said, pouring. The bubbles tickled my nose. It was excellent champagne. 'You are Milo Circassion—'

Sin and Mrs Saxon

'You've heard of me?'

'No. Marcel Lefarge told me. Should I have heard of you?'

'No reason,' he said as if pleased. 'Now I play a little game. I do not think you are in the first flush of youth and I'm glad of that. Young girls bore me. I like a well-fleshed woman. I'd say you were in your early thirties, is that so?'

'Dead on,' I said, not minding him being wrong by ten years.

'I think you are well-fleshed too. Approach closer.'

He held out his cigarette for me to stub out, then both hands came forward to rest on my hips. His hands were small and soft, cool and well-manicured. 'I wasn't wrong, was I?' he said, feeling down the sides of my upper legs. 'Big breasts, I think,' he added and reached out to cup both in his palms, juggling them as if to test their mass and weight. 'Beautifully firm and rounded,' he praised them. 'Such raised nipples too, quite taut and erect. You enjoy me fondling your breasts?'

'Ye-yes,' I muttered, for his sensitive hands, the unusual situation of a blind man making so free with my body, had made me aroused, turned me on tremendously. 'Squeeze my breasts harder, pinch my nipples,' I told him. 'I want that, I like it. Suck on my nipples too. I'll hold out my tits for you—' I pushed a breast to his face, holding it out as his mouth closed over the nipple and he sucked avidly. Wanting more, as eager as he, I held his right hand and took it down to the fork of my legs, rubbing the palm over my now swollen outer cunt lips. I pushed my crotch to the hand, jerking against it. 'Feel it,' I ordered. 'Use your fingers. Make me come, you are getting me worked up like this—'

Sin and Mrs Saxon

'My pleasure,' said Circassion, inserting two hooked fingers into my quim. 'You are so moist up there, Diana, I have no doubt you are not putting on an act for me as so many of the girls who visit me try to do. You love this, don't you?'

My hips were bucking as he masturbated my cunt expertly. 'Aaagh, keep going,' I urged him. 'Cut the discussion, just finger-fuck my cunt for me—'

He gave a soft laugh. 'Yes, use those words. Tits, finger-fuck, cunt. They are the right ones in such a situation. You are a highly sexed female, my dear, a pleasure to know.'

I climaxed with a series of shakes and shudders that proved how strong the orgasm was that he'd given me. Then I stood before him breathless, my shoulders heaving. 'Lie on the bed,' he ordered. I did so gratefully and he rose from the chair, coming across to feel all over my hot body, touching my face, lips, neck and down to my breasts and beyond to my cunt. His finger probed among the warm wet folds which still palpitated. 'You did have a good orgasm,' he stated. 'Would you mind turning over, young woman? I wish to feel your buttocks.'

'Of course,' I said, still aroused, rolling over and hoisting up my bottom for him, as an afterthought reaching back to part the cheeks. His hand went between my bum cleavage, fingers like a gently tickling touch seeking out my hanging – the downward bulge of a cunt when in such a position. He circled my anus, stroked the serrated ring and pushed in a fingertip. I groaned with the pleasure and dipped my back to present my rear the better for him.

'Ah, if I could only gaze upon this lovely sight,' he said, his hand wandering over both arsehole and cunt.

Sin and Mrs Saxon

'You can fuck me if you want to,' I said, hoping he would. 'I'd like that. I do want it—'

'There I must disappoint you,' he said but not sadly. 'I'm old, blind and worst of all completely impotent. Even with such a lovely creature as you, there's no life in it.'

I turned to regard him, my cunt itching for fulfilment. 'Shall I suck your prick? Would that help?'

'How kind,' he said genuinely. 'How sweet. But I'm afraid the best doctors in the world have given up hope of my ever regaining an erection.' His hands left me and he stood back. 'Also time has flown in this pleasant interlude. I have an appointment, a business associate due to call. You must leave now. I insist that you visit me again.'

'That might depend on the Lefarges,' I suggested.

'They do as I say,' he said, once again his tone authoritive. 'When you leave, Tako my butler will give you my private telephone number. Call me whenever you like, even just to take tea with me in my garden, my dear.'

I felt I had gained an influential friend and one that might well fix the Lefarges and their hold on me. On an impulse I got off the bed and kissed his cheek. The bleak features broke into a momentary smile and he touched the place I had kissed. 'Thank you,' he said. 'You've delighted an old man. Get dressed and my butler will show you to a bathroom, as you no doubt wish to refresh yourself. Would you like him to run a bath for you?'

'I'm able to do that myself,' I said lightly.

'I thought so, you seem an independent person. You may have lunch here too, if you wish.'

'Thank you, but I shall go home,' I said. The butler

appeared as if by magic and wordlessly showed me into a splendid marble-sided bathroom along the corridor. Large fluffy towels were draped over hot pipes and the bath had gold taps in the shape of open-mouthed dolphins. Behind a glass screen was a spacious shower cubicle and I welcomed a shower in the humidity of a New York summer. More, I was still aroused, left so by the sensuous fondling Circassion had given me while laid across his bed. Casting off my clothes, I let tepid water stream down on me, the spray sharp as needles striking my tits as I held them up and squeezed the orbs.

I must have stood so for twenty minutes, enjoying the sensual thrill of the force of the water on my nakedness. As I dried myself, towelling strenuously and quite frankly desiring a fucking, the bathroom door opened. I was confronted by the surprised face of Miguel Martinez – surprised but still regarding my undressed state with leering approval.

'Well, well,' he said amiably. 'It's you. I've just had a short meeting with Milo Circassion and the old boy told me he'd just had a bit of fun with a remarkably randy and beautiful woman. So I popped along to see who this creature was—'

I held the towel up to cover myself. 'Don't you know people knock before entering a bathroom?' I said angrily. Angry, of course, that I'd been discovered visiting Milo Circassion for purposes of which he was well aware.

He held up a hand as if to make peace. 'Your secret is safe with me, dear Mrs Saxon. I realise full well this is the doing of the abominable Lefarges. Do not bother to hide your charms behind that towel, for they took great delight in showing me the pictures taken of you in rather compromising circumstances. They are no doubt using them to have their wicked way with you. I must admit that you make an excellent subject. Such a ripe and beautiful body.'

'No doubt you would gloat over the photographs with them,' I retorted. 'It's not funny. They threaten to expose me if I don't do as they want. Like coming here this morning. How could I refuse?'

'Don't regard me as your enemy,' he said. 'If I can help you out of this difficulty, I will. Of course,' he grinned wickedly, 'I should expect some small favour in return. I have an insatiable desire to fuck you, madam. Quite insistent. Even now I have the biggest of erections eager to fill your cunt. The very cunt old Milo found so moist and receptive. He's a very hard man to please. Frightens all the call girls to shivering wrecks. After his pawing you, I'm sure you are ready for the real thing—'

'Then you'd better see your friends the Lefarges about making an appointment, hadn't you?' I said. 'You're so in with them.'

'I can't stand them,' Martinez said. 'They do throw good parties though. You want my help, Diana? Release me from this urge I have to fuck you and I'll be on your side—'

'If I could believe that,' I began.

'Why not? I can be a man of my word, especially for such as you. I assure you the pleasure wouldn't be all mine – I fuck to give a woman full measure. After all, respectable wife of a United Nations official or not, you let that little creep Manny Levinson fuck you—'

'That happened in the heat of the moment,' I protested. 'The Lefarges had sent their maid in to seduce me—'

Sin and Mrs Saxon

'I saw the pictures,' Martinez laughed, enjoying my embarrassment. 'What a good job she made of it too. And lucky old Manny lurking in the vicinity. But has he such a weapon as this—?' Before my gaze he unzipped and delved a hand into his trousers, pulling out the monster penis I had admired at the cocktail party. His hand was big, but the engorged stalk rose thick and menacing inches above his grasp. 'Try it for size,' he offered.

I was tempted, reckoning it was as big if not bigger than any I had encountered. 'What if I let you—' I said.

'Apart from greatly satisfying you, I shall try to recover the photographs, or at least use my influence to stop the Lefarges from intimidating you for sexual purposes. You made a friend of old Circassion today, I could get him to help. He could break the odious French couple as he wished.'

'He's so powerful?'

'One of the two richest men in the world, if not the richest,' Martinez said impressively. 'Still with his finger on the pulse of any commercial activity that interests him. He tells people like Onassis what to do, even governments. Ruining the like of the Lefarges would simply mean making a telephone call—' He glanced down meaningfully at his upright prick. 'Go through that door, you'll find a bedroom beyond.'

I did as bid, obeying with the happy thought that salvation awaited with friends to help me. I sat on a bed not bothering to cover myself as Martinez stripped off his jacket and pulled at his tie. After all, he was intent on fucking me, so why be modest? Stripped down, his figure was athletic and proportioned like a weight-lifting champion, his broad chest a mass of black hair. Between

Sin and Mrs Saxon

thighs like tree trunks reared the cock of which he was so proud, ten inches of thick muscle set over massive balls. It bobbed about as he came towards me, standing legs apart before my sitting position.

'Are you into vocal sex, Diana Saxon?' he asked. 'I find it quite a turn-on. Be as descriptive as you wish, as crude and lewd as you will feel when I'm penetrating you; fucking you, as the proper term is. First, what would your husband think to see us here together naked? You with those magnificent big tits and me with this big urgent prick—'

'I wouldn't want him to see us, would I?' I said. 'This is purely between us because of your offer to help—'

'There's always an added piquancy, a zest, about fucking a married woman,' he stated. 'I love it, love to think of the husband cuckolded; love the thought of shafting his supposedly faithful wife's dear cunt while he's at his office. Doesn't it give you the same feeling?'

'Are you going to fuck me, or talk me into a come?' I taunted him.

'I like that,' he laughed. 'Indeed I like you. You're a man's woman, splendidly proportioned in all the important places, built to tempt—' His hand came over to lift the underside of my left breast, weighing its fullness. 'Who could resist you?'

'Mr Circassion,' I said. 'For all that I allowed him to do, he never managed an erection—'

'Don't blame yourself for that, Diana,' he said, twirling my nipple between a finger and thumb. 'Old Circassion has a computer for a brain, but he's dead from the neck down. You impressed him greatly, he was full of praise for the way you pleased him. He's a good man to have on your side. But then you were made to please men. Do you know what I thought the first time I saw you—?'

He took my hand and coiled my fingers around his stalk. I felt the heat of it, the throb, moving my wrist slowly to massage its thickness, excited to know I would be receiving it. Yet, apart from his toying with my nipple and my hand grasping his rigid flesh, we had stayed apart. I was getting the treatment from a master in the art of arousing women, subtly and unhurriedly working his will on me with light, almost careless touches while intriguing with his smooth talk. 'What did you think the first time you saw me?' I asked, squeezing his length and finding it unbending.

'You had your rear turned to me,' he said, as if savouring the memory. 'The curve of your back, the swell of your buttocks, so round and firm under the silk of your gown, obsessed me. What a fine ass on that woman, I thought, the perfect receptacle for the ten-inch beast stirring in my trousers. My well-lubricated penis buried to the hilt in that woman's perfect bottom. It was a disturbing thought—'

'It is to me,' I said, laughing at his suave manner even while suggesting such a thing, 'and that's not on. You're far too big and, anyway, I hardly know you—'

'Then I shall get to know you better,' he said seriously. 'In time you will beg me to fuck you, front and back.'

I was terribly aroused. Who wouldn't be, posed naked beside an Adonis with such an upstanding monster, wooing me with lewd words? But I wasn't giving in, deciding he would do the begging eventually. I released my hold of his shaft. 'You'll wait a long time for me to beg,' I said.

'This is getting better,' he grinned. 'You don't take me

Sin and Mrs Saxon

seriously. Lean forward, woman, let those magnificent tits hang out for me.' I did as he asked, interested in his next move. He moved forward, nestling his upright prick between my cleavage as my breasts parted. I felt the warmth, the damp hardness pressed to my skin, then both hands clutched the sides of my breasts, pushing them together, trapping his great length in the soft folds. He began an immediate rocking on his heels, sliding his penis up and down the channel that was formed. Such was his size that the big plum-like head popped out beneath my chin as he gently tit-fucked me.

'Suck!' he ordered imperiously and I dipped my chin and covered the dark helmet with my lips. The heat of it on my tongue, the salt taste, the thought of what I was allowing this man to do, combined with the movement of the hard stem between my tits, brought out the lewdness so easily gained in such situations. I sucked in more of the length, my cheeks working and my chin lowered to my neck. 'Play with yourself, Diana,' he said matter-of-factly. 'I want to watch you masturbating. Do it—'

I did, glad to, my fingers reaching inside me to pluck at my clitoris. While being tit-fucked and sucking him and playing with myself, he leaned back as if detached, relishing my wantonness. 'Come, you bastard,' I shouted wildly. 'I'll make you come!' He laughed loudly and remained standing before me, in complete control of both of us. My lower belly and cunt were convulsing, churning and burning. I fell back across the bed with my thighs spreadeagled. 'Fuck me then!' I called out. 'Fuck me. That's what you wanted to hear, right? Use that big prick where I want it—'

Being him, he did not leap on me, but bent over my prone form almost gloatingly. I was still masturbating

Sin and Mrs Saxon

myself and he removed my hand. 'I knew this would happen,' he said with satisfaction, covering me and guiding my hand to his length. 'I can always tell if a woman fucks. Gently does it now,' he warned as I tried to direct him into me with some urgency. 'We won't be disturbed. Enjoy.' With a loud and grateful moan of pleasure I felt the big head enter between my cunt lips, its girth stretching me. The full length took my breath away as it pushed deep into my vaginal passage to nudge my cervix. I was filled to capacity, made wildly wanton and shameless by the mass plumbing my innards.

'Fuck it all up!' I screamed, wanting more if possible, my legs clasped around the small of his back, my hands pulling his taut buttocks into me and heaving up to encourage his thrusts. I got two hard slaps across my hip and was told to calm down; we were not two animals fucking. He then began a slow and deliberate movement, sliding in me to the hilt and pulling back until the knob was poised at my outer lips, making me wait agonisingly for re-entry, not daring to thrust up to him as I longed to. Stopping and starting, he expertly kept me on the point of orgasm until I was mouthing pleas to be finished off, to be given climax after climax. 'I have to have it,' I begged. 'Please, Miguel, fuck me harder and I promise you can have me any time you want. Only fuck me.' His implacable cock teased, changed the angle of entry, making me rear under him on the bed, my begging cunt greedy for its release.

By now my knees were at my ears, cunt tilted for his every inch, my thighs a cradle for his pelvis. Even in my loss of senses I decided this was a fuck such as I'd never experienced, quivering halfway between pain and pleasure as the huge prick shunted within me tormentingly,

Sin and Mrs Saxon

delightfully. Martinez looked down upon my twisted features the whole time, smiling goatishly at my helpless state of arousal. 'Does your husband fuck you like this?' he asked meanly. 'Rouse you to such abandonment? You really must answer me.' He ceased all movement as if to threaten me, that I'd be left frustrated. 'Tell me—'

'No, he doesn't fuck me like this,' I grunted traitorously, willing to concede anything. 'You fuck me better than anyone. Keep fucking me now—'

Satisfied, he thrust deeply, penetrating me to the hilt. His flanks now increased pace, getting the rhythm he wanted. Pierced, impaled on his staggering length, I whinnied and brayed, muttering endearments and pleas until my first explosive come. I thrust upwards until my shoulders alone kept contact with the bed. 'Let me see, see!' I cried out, and he raised his body, allowing me to look down over my breasts to watch his thickness entering me below the bush on my raised mound. Then I came and came and he began his ride to climax, his prick leaping inside me, spouting its glut, his body clashing with mine, belly to belly.

How long we lay sated I could not tell. Exhausted by many orgasms I fell asleep and woke to find him dressing. He smiled at me. 'Succulent. You have a most succulent cunt, Mrs Saxon. I look forward to a rematch. We make a good team, don't you think?'

'Remember your promise,' I told him.

'Of course. You look lovely lying there nude. A woman looks her best after a good fucking. Rely on me to help you in your present difficulty. Now I shall leave you to get dressed and return to your husband—'

'You couldn't lace his boots,' I said, using an old Scottish expression.

Sin and Mrs Saxon

'Perhaps not,' his handsome Latin features creased in a smile, 'but I have screwed his wife—'

I lay moments after he had gone, considering my situation, as ever convinced it could only happen to me. Fucking had got me into the present trouble and I had fucked with Martinez in the hope of getting out of it. It had been a marvellous session, I had to admit. The man had drained me. I returned to the shower and refreshed myself, dressed and proceeded down the long stairway. As if on cue the Japanese butler was there with the Puerto Rican maid to hold open the door. Tako, quite expressionless as ever, handed me an envelope. I *felt* what they were thinking and hurried out to the gravelled driveway. There a uniformed chauffeur awaited, holding open the door of a Rolls. 'Say where you wish to be taken, madam,' he said unctiously.

I did not care to let him know I stayed at the Vanderbilt Towers building, so I told him to drop me in Times Square. In the back of the Rolls I lifted the flap of the envelope and looked inside. There were five one-hundred-dollar bills, payment for my visit to Milo Circassion. I took a taxi home, going past Peter Gulay who gave me a conspirital wink, then up to my apartment to hear the telephone ring. Thinking it was Harry, I picked it up to hear the smirking tones of Violette Lefarge. 'We have had such a good report of your visit to Milo,' she cooed. 'He phoned earlier to say he wanted to see more of you. And did he pay you well? He can be quite generous—'

'His butler gave me an envelope when I left,' I said. 'Do you want your share?'

'Of course, no, *chérie*,' her bubbling laugh came over the line. 'You earned that like any whore would. Did you enjoy being a prostitute for me? Milo said you were most obliging.'

'I'm glad to hear it,' I told her calmly. 'And speaking of whores, I'm talking to the biggest one right now.' I plonked down the telephone, going to the drinks cabinet to mix a large gin and tonic. Sitting with my feet up, drink in hand, I was surprised by Harry coming home from his office.

'Not another boring day in the apartment by yourself, I hope, my love?' he asked worriedly. 'I'm sure we'll soon get a circle of friends once we're settled here. You should go out shopping, buy yourself something nice. I've been so tied up with my new post I haven't thought that you might need money. Are you short?'

'I have enough,' I told him. 'And I will go shopping tomorrow. I feel I deserve to treat myself. What kind of day did you have yourself?'

'They want me to attend a conference at the F.A.O. headquarters in Rome,' he said almost apologetically. 'I shall have to go, of course. It will mean you being here by yourself for a week at least, Di. I met our neighbour Madame Lefarge in the foyer as I came in, dressed to the nines and off to a reception. Taking a chance, I approached her and said I was leaving for a conference in Europe. I asked if she would kindly see that you had some company while I was away. She said she'd remembered meeting you – that very beautiful woman who is your wife, she said and would be delighted to make sure you'd meet plenty of other people while I'm abroad. So you'll be kept busy—'

That, I decided, would be true enough.

Chapter Six
ENGLAND

Training to graduate as a fully fledged Wren consisted of leaving a warm bed at an unearthly hour and for the rest of the day being drilled and shouted at, made to endure physical training, being lectured at in classrooms and spending ours in menial chores like cleaning toilets and peeling mounds of potatoes in the galley – which was never to be mentioned as a kitchen. I thrived on it, especially enjoying the swimming and surprised at the number of classmates who feared entering the pool. The days flew by into weeks and passing-out day loomed, when we'd receive our 'drafts' or postings to naval bases around the country.

Not all the girls would make it. Some were dismissed as unsuitable, one or two, including Lil Canty the ex-barmaid, took off of their own choice, and a couple of trainees managed to get themselves pregnant in that period (or lack of period, should I say!). Most girls mucked in and became friends with others of the same mind – such as the boy-mad ones, those who loved frequenting the local dance halls, and the others who haunted the nearby pubs on 'shore leave' as our liberty time in town was named. Not a few took to being on more than friendly terms, kissing and cuddling openly in the cabins, the straight girls accepting this as harmless play if not too blatant. Some mornings I noticed, having to rise before the others for early breakfast duty in the officers' wardroom, that one or two pairs of girls were sharing a bed, no doubt drawn together after lights out.

Daphne Seymour was often absent, supposedly on fire-watch duty, but I knew she was with Petty Officer Bella Watson, locked in sexual pleasures. The shy girl had taken to being the older woman's lover as if born to it, as perhaps she was, remembering how she had sucked on my nipples. She confessed to me that sleeping with Bella was unbelievably 'nice' and she was given such wonderful orgasms by the woman's fingers, tongue and even by the rubber double-dildo I had spotted in the bedside cabinet. Sadly for Daphne, Bella Watson was sent off to be trained as a Wren officer in another depot. In her anguish at being torn apart from her lover, the night after Bella had left a tearful Daphne joined me in my bed and sought solace suckling upon my nipples and then going down under the blanket to give me a most expert tonguing, licking me out until I stifled the groans of my strong climax. Daphne, it seemed, had been taught well by an expert in the art.

Portsmouth was a sailors' town, offering plenty of opportunities to fulfil the tastes of all. This period was known as the 'phoney war' and, apart from the blackout and the number of service personnel, as the bombing of towns had not yet begun, things were fairly normal. The blackout gave more cover than ever before for fucking in shop doorways or on Southsea Green. As an engaged girl, receiving regular letters from Harry at his army depot, I did try to remain faithful. I did not count the few

Sin and Mrs Saxon

episodes of female loving I'd enjoyed as letting my fiancé down. I threw myself into the training schedule and masturbated in my lone bed at nights when the urge was too strong to resist. Then I met George 'Turk' Semple.

One evening, several of us Wrens were having a drink at a corner table in the Anchor public house in Southsea. Aware I was being stared at, I looked up to see a naval officer regarding me intently from the bar. His cap looked old and was jammed down over his forehead almost concealing his piercing eyes. A huge and wild red beard covered the lower half of his lean face, sprouting over his collar and tie. His uniform looked lived-in, but the sleeves bore the gold rings of a Lieutenant-Commander of the regular navy. Unusually, for that early stage of the war, above his breast pocket were two medal ribbons. He nodded his head to me as I caught his gaze, as if saying in effect 'I'll have you, my beauty.'

When it was my turn to go to the bar for drinks, I seemed drawn to his side. 'I'll get these,' he said, no dithering or nonsense about it as he put a pound note on the counter. Our pay being small and his manner so assertive, I was about to say, 'Thank you, sir,' when he added, 'Get rid of your friends and join me.'

I must say I was taken by his style, amused by his arrogance and attracted by his piratical appearance. I was well aware he wanted me for the one thing, so I was not overawed by his rank.

'Is that an order?' I replied cheekily. Gathering up the ordered drinks on a tray, I was about to turn when he caught my sleeve. 'What could you possibly want with me, sir?' I said, playing the innocent.

'Those magnificent tits of yours for a start,' he answered bluntly. 'I happen to be a tit-man, and yours thrust out like torpedo nose-cones. The rest of you is too bloody enticing for your own good too—'

'Should an officer be addressing a Wren rating in this way, sir?' I asked, keeping a straight face.

'No but I haven't the time for niceties. What name do you go by?'

'Mackenzie. Wren Diana Mackenzie, sir,' I said, pulling away and returning to my table. I knew he had not given up on me and the girls I was with were giggling.

'You've clicked there, Di,' laughed one. 'He was undressing you with his eyes. I've seen him in here before and heard the talk. He notches up Wrens on his bedpost. Do you know who he is?'

'The wild man from Borneo?' I guessed.

'He's a hero. Turk Semple, captain of the submarine *Grouper*, and he's already bagged a German cruiser and destroyer. "Groper" would be more appropriate. He hangs about in here between patrols to torpedo naive Wrens. Why do you think they call him Turk?'

That, I knew, was the naval term for a fuck and to 'turk' a girl was to give her one. 'Well, he's not going to turk me,' I said, not minding if he did but in no way letting the girls think I was impressed.

A little later I excused myself to visit the toilet which was situated at the end of a long narrow corridor made narrower by stacks of wooden crates filled with empty bottles awaiting return. Emerging from the toilet, I found Turk Semple leaning on a wall.

'Alone at last,' he said, converging on me, his wild beard almost tickling my chin. 'Ever been kissed – halfway down?'

'I don't know what you mean,' I giggled. His hand sidled under my uniform skirt, going on up slowly between my thighs as we stood face to face. 'You're taking a lot for granted—'

'And you have sex staring out of you, Wren Mackenzie,' he said. 'If ever anyone was born to fuck, you were.' The hand touched my crotch and slipped under the leg of the lacy French knickers I wore. 'I could report you,' he said. 'They're not regulation navy issue—'

'I think I should have worn them,' I said and he gave a wicked smile. My legs came apart as if on their own accord as fingers stroked my mound, pulled at my outer labia. It had been so long since a male hand had ventured between my legs, I sighed and leaned against the wall, enjoying the feeling. 'You'd better make me come,' I warned him as a finger slipped inside my cunt. 'Don't just arouse me—'

'Good girl,' he said, 'saying what you want with no shame to it. We're two of a kind.' His finger was joined by a thumb and he rolled my clitoris between them, pulled on the stiff projection, flicked it until I gave a low moan and pulled his hand harder to my crotch. Then my hips were bucking and I gave a little cry, there in that dim passageway, brought off by the hand of a stranger.

As I straightened my uniform, Turk raised the fingers that had pleasured me and kissed them. 'The Essence,' he said. 'The absolute essence, juice of quim. I would crawl over broken bottles on my knees, kissing your sweet arse as you walked away. The night is but young, Diana. Dump your mates and I'll wait outside for you. This was just a practice run. I shall fuck you before this evening is out.'

I returned to my friends at the table, enjoying the thought that I'd had a good strong come since leaving them. 'Your face is all flushed, Di,' one of the girls

Sin and Mrs Saxon

remarked. 'Are you feeling all right? You do look shaky.' It was, I decided, the excuse I needed.

'It's the drink,' I said. 'We Scots' girls brought up by strict parents aren't used to it. I'll walk back to Pendragon House, the fresh air will make me feel better.'

Before anyone could decide to join me, I left the pub. Outside was a small sporty car with Turk leaning against it. In the dark of the night he pulled me to him, kissing me with wet lips and tongue, his beard tickling my neck, a strong hand cupping one of my breasts through my jacket.

'I keep a flat in Southsea,' he announced as we drove off. That went without saying, I thought. He parked and held my hand, leading me up stone steps. We entered an untidy room bare but for an armchair and a sideboard laden with bottles of spirits and glasses. He poured out a whisky and glanced at me. 'You're a bit young for the strong stuff, aren't you?'

'Not too young for you to fuck,' I laughed. 'I'm doing this because I want it as much as you. No need to ply me with drink to get your wicked way with me.' A glance at my watch told me that I only had an hour or so left before my return to barracks, so I walked through to what I guessed was the bedroom. Turk joined me as I stood beside the double bed. As usual, enjoying the thrill of exhibiting my body to men, I began to undress, slipping off my jacket and skirt.

'By God, this is what we're fighting this war for,' he said, stripping himself while he ogled me. His chest was a mass of reddish hair that continued on down to his balls, over which stood a thick erect penis. I had an instant desire to suck it. I pulled him to me and covered it with my lips. His hands gently clasped each cheek of my face and he rocked on his heels, the motion shunting his cock in and out of my mouth, fucking my face.

Then he pushed me flat on the bed to nuzzle my tits, clasping them and sucking hard on each nipple. His mouth trailed down, to my navel and to the fork of my legs, his tongue assaulting me. 'Turn over now,' he ordered. 'On your hands and knees, girl, let those big tits dangle while I slip you a length.' The palm of his hand cupped my hanging cunt. Drawing it back, he fingered my anus.

The suppressed little 'mmm' I gave made him chuckle. 'You liked that,' he said, probing with a fingertip and making me squirm and rotate my bottom. 'The tradesman's entrance, where it's safe to fire one's salvo. Tilt your bottom up, this can't wait—'

'Fuck me then,' I told him. 'Put it in, I want it. Never mind playing about.' With a sigh of relief I felt his rigid length slide into me, into the moist receptive folds that made entry so easy. My buttock cheeks thrust back to receive his all, feeling his heavy balls bouncing against my flesh. 'Don't you come yet,' I called out anxiously, feeling the first surges rippling through my stomach, palpitating my cunt as it gripped the shaft prodding into me. His hands gripped my tits, holding them like reins as he rode. I gasped out that I was there, there! COMING, you've made me come!

Then he took his cock out of me even as I protested I wanted it to stay. He eased himself up slightly and pressed his crest to my bottom with an insistent pressure that made my ring give and suddenly he was in my back passage.

'Keep still,' he ordered. 'You'll get used to it.' Another inch penetrated, then more, until I felt filled

Sin and Mrs Saxon

with mass and heat, groaning in a curious pain/pleasure, moving my rear carefully as more was eased into me. 'Good girl,' he praised me. 'You take it well. Now reach back and part your cheeks. There, it's in to the hilt. Do you like that?'

'Ye-yes,' I admitted. 'It feels huge, filling me up—'

'You've had this before,' he said, moving his flanks. 'What a lovely arse to bum-fuck.' I couldn't deny his claim, rotating my bottom like a ball into his lap. One of his hands now went to my cunt, cupping it, the middle finger busy inside me. I bucked like a demented creature, came once and then again in the same series of spasms. Then he was groaning gutterally, jerking his hips, flooding me with jets of thick emission deep within my bottom.

'That's better,' said Turk, relaxing on the bed beside me after the bout, using as ever colourful terms. 'Better there than leaving you with a bellyful of liquid arms and legs, Wren Mackenzie. I don't dole out babies on a whim—'

His sticky come was seeping from me and I rose from the bed to wash myself. 'You fired enough up me to make a dozen babies,' I laughed. 'Now will you drive me to my barracks? Good little girls have to report in by ten o'clock while in training—'

'I think you're neither a good little girl, nor in need of training,' Turk commented. 'My word, you are a beauty! Can't you wait awhile and let me fuck you again? Let me play with your big tits – that will do the trick.' I let him do so, massaging his limp dick into life until he mounted me again. I made it to Pendragon House with seconds to spare, the duty officer sitting grimly at her desk as I reported.

Sin and Mrs Saxon

'Another moment or two and you would have been in trouble, Mackenzie,' she said. 'Which would have been a pity, as you've been one of our best recruits. I can tell you, now that passing-out day is so near, that you've been selected for the mechanics' course at HMS Collingwood. Only the top girls have been chosen. You were recommended by Petty Officer Watson before she left.'

Good old Bella, I thought. She had rewarded me for keeping secret her love-ins with Daphne. What I knew about motor mechanics' skills wouldn't fill your eye, but I would learn. I was delighted I had not been selected for the more mundane ratings such as cook or steward. On passing-out day I marched proudly in the parade as a fully trained Wren, going on leave before proceeding to the mechanics' course. That night I went to the Anchor inn and found a glum crowd of customers. In my buoyant mood, I asked Gerry the landlord the reason for the sombre scene.

'Lost one of our best customers today,' he said sadly. 'Commander Semple. The Admiralty has announced the loss of his submarine with all hands. Raise a glass on the house to his memory, lass. You didn't know him but he was quite a man.'

'I'll drink to that,' I said, my eyes blinking with tears. The war I decided, was not all fun and games as I was to discover for myself. As for Turk Semple, at least I had sent him off with the best farewell a woman can give.

Chapter Seven
AMERICA

I was awaiting a further call to do the Lefarge's bidding, which I knew would soon come. In the meantime I decided on safety in numbers until Martinez kept his promise to free me from their clutches. They would not want my husband to be aware of their hold over me, but he had now left for Rome and had since phoned to say he was going on to Somalia after the conference to survey an irrigation scheme. It would be three weeks to a month before I saw him again, during which time I would be vulnerable to be used and abused as the Lefarges ordered. With someone to keep me company, I'd not be so available. So I telephoned my sister to join me for a holiday and was delighted when she said she'd fly to New York within a few days.

I had barely replaced the phone before Madame Lefarge was at my door, inviting herself in. I was about to leave to spend Milo Circassion's money on a shopping expedition to Fifth Avenue. I was looking chic and also looking forward to be free of her clutches for the day. My appearance brought an admiring smile of approval.

'How lovely you look, Diana,' she said maliciously. 'The lucky man you are to entertain this morning will be delighted with you. The car is waiting below to take you to him.'

'I had planned a shopping trip,' I said hopefully, wasting my breath.

'That can wait. Do this little thing and you'll have much more money to buy nice things with, my dear. I'm sure your client this morning will pay well to amuse himself with you. We mustn't keep him waiting—'

'You bitch,' I told her. 'You're using me as a common prostitute to impress businessmen who could be of use to you—'

'Hardly common,' she smiled. 'Very high class. You have been a *find*, *chérie*. Is your sister as lovely as you?'

'What do you know about my sister?' I said, surprised and shaken. 'How could you possibly—'

For a moment Violette Lefarge hesitated, as if she had said too much. 'Your husband told me before he left for Rome. He said you'd invited Jennifer – that's right, isn't it? – as he was having to go on a field trip for some weeks,' she said, regaining her composure. 'Her visit mustn't stop you doing what we've agreed, you know.'

'It will, as much as I can make it,' I said, puzzled as to how she could possibly know that I'd invited my sister to join me, or that Harry would be away for several weeks. The only person I had mentioned it to was the friendly receptionist, the aspiring actor Peter Gulay. He was no doubt in the pay of the Lefarges, befriending me to pass on any information I might impart in general conversation. No doubt, too, from his desk with its switchboard and battery of telephones, he could listen in to my phone calls.

I took the elevator to the foyer and marched up to the reception desk in cold fury. 'Thanks a bunch, Peter,' I

Sin and Mrs Saxon

told him hastily. 'Just keep your big nose out of my business in future,' and strode out, leaving him bewildered at his desk.

The waiting car dropped me at one of New York's finest hotels and, as instructed, I went to the receptionist and announced I was the manicurist sent for by Mr J.D. Coolidge. It didn't fool the smart woman behind the desk for one moment. Raising her eyebrows just the slightest, she called a uniformed bell-boy who escorted me up in the elevator and knocked on the door of a suite of rooms on the ninth floor.

The man who answered the door was gross, a fat middle-aged slob in shirt-sleeves who made my heart sink. He was about as attractive as a toad, nodding at me with a lecherous look as he slipped the bell-boy a five-dollar bill. 'Come in, dear,' he said, leading me through to a plush lounge with a laden drinks trolley. A youth stood there with a glass in his hand, dressed solely in a silk dressing-gown which hung open at the front. He had a boy's penis which was fully erect.

At the sight of me he gave a lewd wink. There was no doubt he was a beautiful boy, his head tight with blond curls and such a cherubic look upon his face that I was conscious of my powder and lip-gloss. His body was slim and I took him to be under age for most adult enjoyment, including the drink he held in his hand. I could only guess that he was being paid to be present, as I was, and cringed at the thought of what would be expected of us in some perverted threesome with our host.

'I don't know what you have in mind,' I said firmly, 'but count me out. That young man doesn't look a day over fifteen.'

'Melvin here is nineteen going on twenty,' said J.D.

Coolidge. 'Don't let that baby face fool you, he's a little devil.'

'You don't have to explain me to a whore, J.D.,' Melvin said arrogantly. 'Tell the bitch to shut the fuck up and get through to the bedroom. I like the look of her, this one has got the shape.'

'Don't mind the little cunt,' J.D. told me, laughing at Melvin's assertiveness. 'He gives me the run-around too when I'm in town. I find him amusing, he likes my money—'

'You like my ass, you big queer,' Melvin retorted. 'You want me to fuck this broad? That will be a pleasure—' He pushed the drinks trolley through to an adjoining bedroom, gesturing me to follow. Curiosity made me join him, helping myself to a good stiff vodka on the rocks to give me courage. In the lounge a telephone rang and our host paused to answer it.

'That'll be J.D. fixing some deal,' said Melvin. 'Talking big bucks. Put on a good show for the old bastard and you and I will be riding the gravy-train. He's loaded.'

'Just who is he?' I said.

'President of some goddam airline among other things. He calls me when he gets to N.Y. and likes an exhibish—'

'Can't *he* get it up?' I giggled as Melvin replenished my vodka to the brim. 'My last one wasn't able to perform. It must go with being rich, the tired businessman—'

'He'll get it up,' promised Melvin. 'Seeing me going at you will work the magic. You willing to let me do as I like? Do as he likes—' He studied my face closely. 'I'll bet you're one of those dames with a home and husband, doing a bit of moonlighting as a hooker for the extra moolah. New at the game, are you?'

Sin and Mrs Saxon

'Something like that,' I said.

'Well, you've struck pay-dirt with J.D.' he said. 'It beats the hell out of being in the factory, I say. Go along with me, doll, and we leave here stacked—'

If I smiled it was a combination of the vodka I'd downed plus his New York vernacular. He slipped off the silk robe to stand naked, slim but well proportioned, looking more than ever like a schoolboy. 'Are you sure you are nineteen?' I asked dubiously.

'Hell, I've served in the U.S. Navy. Would still be in if I hadn't got a D.D.'

'What's that?' I said. 'Not a dirty dick, I hope?'

'Dishonorable Discharge,' Melvin grinned. 'I'll leave your to guess why. I'm a bi. Bi-sexual, if you hadn't guessed. I like my vice versa too. I do a drag act now in Queens—'

'You had an erection when I arrived,' I said, guessing there had been some fun and games going on. At that moment our host came into the bedroom, smoking a long cigar and with a drink in his hand.

'How are you two doing?' he asked. 'Waiting for me?'

'It's the dame,' Melvin said. 'She's gabby. If she can fuck like she can talk, she'll do fine. Get undressed, lady, I want to see if those tits are real—'

I laughed aloud, finding the whole situation ridiculous, but as ever tempted to reveal myself. I undressed, folding my clothes over a chair carefully, my back to the men, hearing their remarks, getting aroused as I always did in company. I enjoyed being the female ogled and commented upon. 'Would you look at that fine ass,' Melvin said admiringly. 'Round and firm as marble. They sent you a looker this time, J.D., no kidding.' I turned around from the chair, presenting my full frontal

Sin and Mrs Saxon

as they say now. My breasts seemed heavier and fuller than ever, nipples peaking with my growing arousal. At my crotch my bulge pouted, with dark reddish hair surrounding my outer lips. 'Tit and cunt,' Melvin added, 'and plenty to go around. Get you on that bed, lover, and lay yourself out.'

As I climbed on to the bed, Melvin's hand went under my rear, touching me up, fingering inside. I remained in that position, on hands and knees, waggling my bottom against his wrist. 'She's all for it, wet as the Hudson up there,' I heard him tell J.D. 'I like big dames—'

'Here, I'm not that big,' I protested.

'Big in tit and ass, I mean,' Melvin said, 'and, sister, you are one built woman.' His fingering was rough, making me draw in my breath and cringe as he forced his hand into me. I yelped out a cry and protested at his treatment, receiving a hard sharp slap across my raised cheeks in reply. 'Stay, bitch!' he ordered roughly. 'You hold still for Melvin now, if you know what's good for you—'

I was about to register a further protest to say I wasn't allowing anything that hurt when J.D. spoke up. 'What was that about? What's going on between you two—?'

'I was aiming to fist-fuck her,' Melvin complained, 'but the cow closed her thighs on me, trapping my hand—'

' "Bitch", "cow",' I said, turning my head to glare at Melvin, 'you really know how to treat a lady, don't you?'

'You ain't no lady, lady,' Melvin sneered. 'You're a goddam whore, here for the money, so I'll call you bitch and cow and do what I like with you, see? Open those thighs and let me in or I'll paddle your ass good.' He gave me another stinging slap and I was pushed back

Sin and Mrs Saxon

down ignominiously, as his whole hand pushed into me stretching wide the outer lips of my vagina.

I felt I would split apart, the fist inside me twisting and tormenting me. It was my first experience of a practice I'd only heard about before. I shrieked, sitting up with knees wide and baying to the ceiling. Turning my head I saw J.D. taking it all in with a look of licentious rapture, and nodding his approval at Melvin's depraved skills. The agitation within my cunt brought gasps and grunts from my mouth as my lower body and hips began to work in concert with the closed fist churning within me. 'God, you're killing me, killing me,' I pleaded, helpless as the mounting surge of an unstoppable orgasm drove me wild.

'Yelp and squeal all you want, bitch,' Melvin said, callously crude. 'She loves it, J.D.,' he observed to our host. 'See those big tits fly on her chest and look at her ass go crazy. You like it?'

'I like it,' J.D. responded happily. 'You have a way with women, Melvin, you little shit, I have to give you that. Dammit, you treat them like crap and they all seem to love it. You've got this one going bananas for it—'

'Fuck me, one of you, fuck me,' I pleaded, shaken by the spasms of a climax. I had fallen forward on the bed with my buttocks still raised, my cunt stuffed and pulsing on Melvin's fist. I desired a prick and its deeper penetration to give me the ultimate sensation. 'Fuck me now,' I murmured.

'What do you make of this bitch?' Melvin laughed. 'She's just been fist-fucked and now she wants a dick up her. Hold it, baby, not so fast, you don't get away that easy. We're gonna have a little fun with that lush bod of yours first. Turn over and sit up, so we can get a feel of

Sin and Mrs Saxon

those big boobs. You want to tit-fuck her, J.D.? Screw her in the ass?'

'Carry on, Melvin, you're doing all right,' J.D. said approvingly. 'I like to see an expert at work. What next?'

'She got a nice mouth,' Melvin said, 'I fancy fucking her face before I have her below. What do you say to that, bitch? A horny cocksucker like you would like that, eh?'

'I'll bite it off, you perverted shrimp,' I threatened.

'And I'll piss down your throat,' Melvin replied, amused. He thrust his pelvis out towards me, hands on his hips and penis dangling limply. 'Suck!' he ordered. 'Do something about that, stiffen it up for me—'

It was that kind of afternoon, I suppose, when it seemed easier to go along with what was expected of me than to protest too much. Privately, too, I was enjoying myself and was especially intrigued by the low-life Melvin who did act the part splendidly, having a flair for being the cocky juvenile. His employer, *our* employer J.D., obviously liked his style. It had no doubt entertained him on previous occasions. Apparently content to watch Melvin operate on me, I wondered what part, if any, he would take in the proceedings later. He drew on his long cigar and emptied his tall glass of whisky sour, refilling it from the trolley as I sucked on the prick held out for me and finding it smoothly rigid as it grew in my mouth.

'The bitch sucks well, she's eaten cock before and likes it,' Melvin observed, obviously deciding the derogatory term 'bitch' was right for the occasion and proving his mastery. As ever, I enjoyed having a prick in my mouth and there was an added almost-illicit thrill in sucking off someone who looked so much like a choirboy. No doubt we gave the impression of an innocent lad being seduced into adult sex by an older woman and our spectator gloated over the scene. When the door chimes sounded, he mumbled a curse and hurried off, returning moments later with a tall man in thick spectacles and a velvet jacket set off by a tied cravat and jeans – an 'arty' type. I saw him as I glanced sideways past Melvin's flat white stomach, by this time having his whole length over my tongue and applying full suction to the throbbing stem. It was an anti-climax in more ways than one when Melvin pushed me flat back onto the bed, withdrawing his cock to greet the new arrival.

'You owe me five centuries for the last shoot, Ziggy, you bastard,' Melvin complained. 'You can hit me now—'

'Sure, sure,' agreed the newcomer. 'I been out of town doing TV commercials. You'll get your dough—'

'Five hundred bucks is five hundred bucks,' Melvin said, 'and an artiste like me don't come cheap. Make with the moolah.'

'So sue me,' Ziggy laughed. 'Don't worry, you'll get your fee. You take a cheque?'

'Nix to that,' Melvin retorted. 'Give it to me in readies. What you here for anyway?'

During this word-play, I was laid back naked as a fish, my breasts lolling on my chest, thighs apart and my cunt terribly aroused, the object of curiosity to Ziggy, who made his fore-fingers and thumbs into a sort of square before his eyes and looked through it at me, moving to picture my reclining pose from several angles.

'Who's the dame?' Ziggy asked. 'I could sure use her for my next pic. Are you available, honey?' he questioned me. 'You want to be in the movies—?'

Sin and Mrs Saxon

I didn't know. I wanted something in my mouth – a tongue or a prick – or, better still, in my cunt. I resisted the urge to put a hand down to finger myself and relieve the tension. There was a definite itch and throb in my warm wet quim which cried out to be satisfied. Instead, I was handed a drink, a long straight vodka and ice. In front of me, Ziggy took a video cassette from his briefcase and handed it to J.D. Melvin was given his five hundred dollars and, being naked, he took it through to stash it in his discarded trousers. When he returned, he had lost his erection again and was more interested in talking to Ziggy.

'What's this about your new pic?' he enquired. 'Is there a part in it for me?'

'It was written for you,' Ziggy stated. 'I got the script with me right here, so you can take it and bone up on your lines. It's a goodie, all my own work, and this lady here is made for the part of the housewife.' As the three men stood debating, ignoring me for the moment, my fingers moved to the fork of my legs. I began to stroke my hairy mound, titillating myself. I was tipsy with drink and playfully wanton.

'If they are so damned interested in discussing business, with me laid out naked as a fish, then stuff them,' I thought. My other hand cupped a breast and pulled at the nipple. The hand below glided over my outer lips, strumming them, opening them, a finger entering to stroke the inner vaginal walls, massaging back to the cervix, plucking at the engorged clitoris. I gave a low moan of pleasure and the three men turned to me.

'The horny bitch can't wait,' Melvin announced. 'She's playing with herself—'

'Let her continue,' J.D. ordered. 'I want to see this!'

Sin and Mrs Saxon

As if in a haze of arousal, I looked up to see all three of them standing over me, adding greatly to my lewdness and increasing the intensity of my fingering. 'If none of you will fuck me, I'll make myself come,' I gritted out through my teeth, my hips rolling on the bed and my pelvis lifting. Melvin, I noted, was massaging his tool. He regained a stiffy and moved as if to get between my legs. J.D. held his arm, pulling him back.

'Christ, let me at her,' Melvin complained. 'This is one bitch on heat, J.D.'

'I said leave her!' J.D. barked out. 'This is the real thing, no playacting. I want to watch her bring herself off—'

That you will see, I thought. I didn't care, I only wanted the prodigious climax which I was now on the verge of. Without a shred of shame, my legs were at their widest, my toes reaching for the ceiling, my body starting to judder uncontrollably.

'And I didn't bring my camera!' Ziggy wailed. 'Jesus H. Christ on a bicycle, this would win an Academy Aware! Fuck me, look at her go! It's given me a great idea for the opening shot of my pic. This will have to go in—'

I made gutteral sounds and cries, my whole frame undulating as I was seized by great shudders and heaves, spending relentlessly for long moments until I subsided sated and weak. It was indeed a glorious come and I lay back gasping in air, my breasts rising and falling, legs apart as if to cool the burning in my pouting cunt.

'Let me fuck her,' begged Melvin.

'She's entertained us enough,' J.D. said. 'Give the lady a break. Get dressed now, dear,' he said to me, 'and thank you for a marvellous show.' He drew out a folder of banknotes from his back pocket, counting out five and placing them on the bed beside me. 'The doorman will get you a taxi when you go down—'

'Where did you find this gem of a female, J.D.?' Ziggy asked.

'French friends of mine. I can't disclose their names.'

'Hell, I want to use her in my film,' Ziggy complained. To me he added, 'I'm leaving you a script too, honey. Read it and think about it, it's worth a thousand bucks for a few days' work. It's no cheapskate production, we use colour and real sets and backgrounds. My phone number is on the title page. You call me now—'

'I'll be starring in it with you,' Melvin added. 'Guess I'll be throwing a few fucks in your direction then. Who else is cast for it, Ziggy?'

'Not decided yet,' Ziggy said. 'Someone new and fresh to play the daughter, a teenage beauty.' He went into his briefcase to hand me a slim folder stapled inside a blue manilla cover. 'Read it and let me know, please. You don't happen to have a beautiful daughter, do you, honey?'

A glance at the script's cover revealed the title, 'The Delivery Boy', and I could guess the contents. It would, I decided, be fun to read it. 'Not for what you'd want her for,' I said. I dressed, put my ill-gotten gains into my shoulder-bag, and left, carrying the script. In the lounge the three men were sitting before a large television screen, watching Ziggy's latest offering, a scene that seemed full of naked bodies writhing about on a huge bed.

I took a taxi home, needing to shower before going out on my delayed shopping expedition. Waiting for me in the foyer was a concerned Peter Gulay. I went to walk past him but he followed me into the elevator and up to my door.

'I need to know why I got the icy stare and the harsh words when you went out this morning, Mrs Saxon,' he said, genuinely anxious to appease me. 'What did I do? I thought we were friends. You're the nicest lady tenant we've got—'

'You know damned well,' I said, putting my key in the door. 'My every movement is known to the Lefarges. How much do they pay you to keep tabs on me—?'

'Christ, I wouldn't give those sleaze-balls the time of day,' Peter protested. He followed me into the apartment and my phone rang. He stood beside me as I lifted the receiver.

'Full marks for your performance today, dear Diana,' came Violette Lefarge's cooing tones. 'Your client was delighted with you. He paid you well, I'm sure—'

I hung up without answering, turning to Peter. 'That bitch knows the moment I return. She's aware of everything I do—'

'Why?' Peter asked in a whisper, holding a finger to his lips to indicate silence. 'For whatever reason—?' He looked around the apartment, drawing me to the centre of the room. 'I'd say you've been bugged, Mrs Saxon, so keep it low.'

I decided his guess was correct and I had judged Peter wrongly. I decided to trust him as a friend. 'Blackmail,' I confessed. 'I was indiscreet and they have photographs to prove it. They now demand I do as they ask—'

'Frog bastards,' Peter said meaningfully. 'We knew they were up to no good with their goddam party-giving. The management have tried to terminate their lease. You can't report this to the police?'

Sin and Mrs Saxon

'Not while they threaten to expose me. My husband holds a senior post with the U.N. I can't risk it.'

'With your permission I'm going to give this place a search for any bugging devices,' he said. 'At least that will be a start. Then I'd like to take you out to dinner later, get your mind off this trouble for a while. I go to a place frequented by actors. The food's good and you can relax.'

'I'd like that, Peter,' I said. 'Go ahead and see if you find any bugs. I've got to shower, this New York heat makes my clothes stick to me—'

'They stick to you beautifully,' Peter managed with a smile. 'Take your time while I go over the place.'

Under the cold water, the spray pinging on my breasts, I idly considered Peter as a lover. I felt I owed him something for my lack of trust. Once I had dried and dressed in my silken robe, I went through to pour us both a drink. He held out a hand and in his palm were two little button-like devices. 'Clever you,' I praised him. 'Where did you find them?'

'One in the telephone, one under this coffee table right here in the lounge. Now I think we should look in your bedroom—' We went through together and I sat on the bed while he searched behind the pictures on the wall, under my dressing table, then returned to sit beside me and lift up my bedside lamp.

'Look,' he said, tilting it for me. Fixed to the brass stem between the switch and the bulb was a little circular object which he picked off with a fingernail. Our faces touched as we inspected the bug and we turned together, our lips meeting. The first kiss was a light touch, then he covered my mouth with his, a long tongue snaking between my teeth.

Sin and Mrs Saxon

'I didn't intend that,' he apologised as we drew apart. He dropped the bug he'd found into his glass of gin. 'But then maybe I did, you looking like you do. What must you think of me?'

'That you're not the kind that would stop, once you'd made your move,' I teased him. He lowered me gently but firmly to the bed and opened my gown. Uttering a groan of pleasure at the sight of my uncovered breasts, he dipped his face between them. I held him cradled to me as his lips sought my nipples in turn. Then I felt his hand go down to stroke me between my thighs, tilting my cunt to his searching fingers. 'Fuck me, Peter,' I told him.

He rose over me, throwing off his clothes, and stood naked with a huge erection thrusting before him. It reared long and thick, uncapped and its bulbous head straining, a magnificent specimen of a prick. I sat up, unable to resist holding it, lowering my mouth to cover it. Then I was pushed onto the bed as he went down on me. A long tongue furled into my cleft, making me arch and gasp my gratitude. I pulled at his shoulders, drawing him up, wanting his length, and as if by its own accord it slid into me, going in deeply. I drew up my legs, locking my ankles behind his waist, reaching to grasp his tight buttocks.

'Don't hurry,' I told him. 'Leave it in to soak for a while. It feels so good up me—'

'Whatever the lady wants,' he smiled down at me. 'What a lovely cunt you have. May I fuck you just a little?' He made slight pelvic movements and his big cock shunted tormentingly in my moistness. 'I've wanted to do this to you since the first day I saw you, Diana—'

'Then do me now,' I urged him, the fullness within me

Sin and Mrs Saxon

making me lose control as I lifted to meet his thrusts. 'We are bad, aren't we? Naughty people doing this, with my husband away and you fucking his wife. We are beasts, but I like it and want it. Fuck me harder, love, make me come—'

'I'll fuck you anytime,' Peter said determinedly, roused by my lewd talk, his pace increasing and his prick butting into me maddeningly. 'I'll fuck all the comes you want out of you, Mrs Diana Saxon. Christ, this is my lucky day—'

Mine too, I rambled as I returned lunge for lunge, the spasms of a continuous series of climaxes making me buck under him like a demented being. With Harry away I would not want for fulfilment with his handsome stud available. Our mouths clung together as we subsided for a moment before he began shafting me vigorously again, still as stiff as a ramrod in my channel. Only when he felt that I had reached my peak and was slowing, fucked-out as the saying goes, did he allow himself to let go, uttering cries and loosing a great volley of come inside me.

'It felt so big in me, so hard,' I praised him for satisfying me so with his huge prick. 'How did you manage to last so long and give me so many comes?'

Peter leaned over me on an elbow, regarding me fondly. 'It wasn't easy, having you below me, but being an actor helps. The bugs, for instance. I once played a New York cop in a TV series that flopped, but in one or two scenes I had to act out searching for bugs that had been planted. I did the same sort of thing looking over your apartment—'

'What has that to do with fucking me so long before you climaxed yourself?' I laughed at him. 'Do you mean you were acting when we were at it?'

Sin and Mrs Saxon

'That was no act, but about the best fuck I've ever had,' he said. 'Truth is, an actor trying to make his way has to take on all sorts of roles. Like I'm working here as a receptionist—'

'So?' I asked.

'I've done porno films when I've been broke,' he admitted. 'It meant staying hard half the day for breaks in shooting like close-ups and such. I guess it trained me to hold off coming too soon—'

'I'm glad it did,' I said mischievously, fondling his limp dick. 'I bet this big chap was the star of the show. Do you still act in those sort of films?'

'If I need the money,' he said. 'Right now I've been giving some thought to recovering those pictures the Lefarges are holding over you. If I could get them, and the negatives, you could see them in hell, be free of them—'

'Someone else has promised to help me,' I said, 'but I don't know if I can trust him. How could you possibly get those pictures, Peter?'

'There are master keys to all the rooms in reception,' he said. 'The Lefarges go out a lot. I could let myself in and search the joint. If they're there, I'll find 'em.'

I could not resist kissing him fondly. 'You'd do that for me? How sweet. Wouldn't it be rather risky? I mean they'd know there had been someone in their apartment. You could lose your job and be in trouble—'

'What could they say? I'd only take the pictures if I found them. Blackmail is a serious crime. Leave it to me, I'll do it the first time they are away—'

'Then I'll help you search,' I said, feeling his prick reviving in my clasp. I had done so many things in my lifetime, burglary would be just one more—

Chapter Eight
ENGLAND

The huge naval training camp at Collingwood had been recently built and on reporting there I found myself part of a class of twenty girls. We were taking the three months' course which would turn us out as skilled drivers and motor mechanics. Once we had been allotted to a cabin with the usual double-decker bunks and lockers, we were marched to the so-called infirmary and sick bay for the traditional medical inspection. When my turn came to face the doctor and standing in just regulation navy bra and knickers for the occasion, the woman in the white coat and stethoscope was the same First Officer Mona Calthrop who had examined me on my volunteering for the Wrens. I remembered how the tall statuesque woman had felt my breasts as if fondling them while eyeing my naked form.

'I know you,' she said to my surprise. 'Mackenzie, isn't it? How are you enjoying life in the Wrens, girl?'

'Very much, ma'am,' I said.

'Slip off your bra,' I was told. I did so. My breasts felt huge. Her hands cupped and squeezed each mound, lingering unnecessarily, I thought, as her cool fingers searched for anything amiss. They caressed me so that

Sin and Mrs Saxon

my nipples rose sharply. 'Nothing wrong with those,' she decided at last. 'Quite firm and shapely, indeed. You were wearing an engagement ring when I last inspected you, Mackenzie. Have you broken off with your fiancé?'

'Fancy you remembering that, ma'am,' I said. 'I'm still engaged to a boy overseas, but I've put the ring away for safe keeping—'

'Not because an engagement ring might keep other boys away, I hope,' she added. 'Drop your knickers, please, Mackenzie—'

'Oh, I wouldn't do that, ma'am,' I said, keeping a straight face and complying with her order, my knickers at my ankles. I stood stark naked before her as she sat on a chair to be at eye-level with my crotch. 'I said I'd wait for him—'

'Yes,' she said succinctly, 'I hope so.' She peered at my pubic bush, then donned a thin transparent medical glove. 'Legs apart,' she ordered. Alone as we were in her surgery, I wondered if other girls got the same thorough inspection. Her gloved fingers parted my outer lips and she duly took a close look at the entrance to my vulva. I shivered a little and she looked at me sharply. 'Are you cold, girl?'

'No, ma'am,' I said. 'It's just, just—'

'Just what—?'

'What are you doing,' I murmured.

'I'm seeing that all is right with you,' she said sternly as her index finger entered me, probing, touching my clitoris, bringing further shudders from me. 'Stand still, silly girl,' she ordered, continuing her fingering, making me stiffen to control myself. 'Good vaginal walls, all seems in order. What is the matter with you, Mackenzie?'

Sin and Mrs Saxon

'It's – you've given me a tickly feeling there, ma'am,' I said, wanting her to continue.

'Is it arousing you, girl?'

'Yes, yes,' I muttered.

'Do you masturbate? Play with yourself at times?' she asked. 'It's quite normal to do so when one seeks relief. Is that the feeling you have now?'

'Ye-yes,' I admitted. 'It feels nice—'

'You are obviously highly sexed,' announced Mona Calthrop. 'I suppose it would be cruel not to give you relief, or would you prefer to do it yourself later?' Her finger continued to move inside me and I allowed my hips to contort in pleasure.

'You, ma'am,' I begged her. 'You finish me off, please—'

I noted the faintest smile on her lips. 'This is most unusual then,' she said, the crafty bitch. She was seducing me for her own pleasure as much as mine. 'If I do give you an orgasm, what has happened here must never go beyond these walls. Can I trust you, Mackenzie?'

'Oh yes, ma'am, yes,' I cried, my knees jerking as her fingering me continued apace. At last I gurgled out a low moan and came on her fingers, shaking life a leaf. She stood and offered her chair for me to sit down, then brought me a glass of water. I drank it gratefully, still breathing heavily, my breasts heaving.

'We will perhaps see more of each other while you are here, Mackenzie,' she said, showing me out of the door. 'There are over two thousand men in this establishment, and no doubt a fine looking girl like you will get plenty of attention. Stay clear of them, however tempted. You wouldn't want to get pregnant, would you?'

'Certainly not, ma'am,' I said dutifully.

Sin and Mrs Saxon

'Then come to see me if ever you need to,' she said. I nodded, having no doubt for what purpose. Doctor Calthrop fancied me as a young fresh thing and had made her intentions obvious.

In the weeks that followed, however, I saw little of her, being fully engaged in a training regime that left little time for anything but study in the classroom and revising at night. I learned about carburettors, big ends, fuel injection and spark plugs. I passed a driving test on the roads of Hampshire and wrote almost daily letters to Harry in Egypt saying how I missed him. Then came one duty weekend when I reported to my Petty Officer and was told I was to work that evening in the officers' mess.

It was an unpopular chore. It meant washing endless cups, glasses, plates and pots while being ordered about by the resident stewards and cooks. After my own supper at seven, I went to the wardroom and reported for duty. The Chief Steward looked a kindly man. 'What is it I'm here to do?' I asked.

'Private party, lass,' he said, 'so it's a bit of a doddle for you tonight. A few lady officers are having a do for First Officer Calthrop's birthday. Go along to the pantry and make yourself useful.'

There I helped lay a table for a dozen guests and before they arrived Mona Calthrop appeared to check that all was in order. She ignored me and the party went on for several hours, during which time I was at the sink washing up each course. When it broke up, I was left with a tray of glasses to wash, the cooks and stewards leaving me to it. First Officer Calthrop saw off her guests and came through to the pantry, bright eyed from the evening's fun and free-flowing drink.

'It was a lovely evening, Mackenzie. One shouldn't

Sin and Mrs Saxon

celebrate birthdays at my age,' she said, 'but it was fun.' She poured two sherries into a pair of tall schooners and handed me one. 'I expect you deserve this—'

'Happy birthday, ma'am,' I said, raising my glass. 'May I ask how old you are?'

'Thirty-eight. Have you been avoiding me?'

'I've been busy with my course,' I said.

'Drink up, we'll have one more,' she announced. 'I'd hoped you'd get in touch. You could have made some excuse to see the doctor—' She looked me over hungrily, came to me and put her arms around me. 'You are a sweet thing, a very pretty piece. Kiss me—'

Her lips fastened to mine and she put her tongue in as we kissed. I responded by kissing her and she hugged me close. 'Come to my cabin, love,' she whispered. 'No one will see us. I want you tonight, oh I *want* you. Will you come?'

'You're the officer,' I said wickedly. 'Is that an order? What is it you want me for?'

'You know damned well, you little minx,' she said, pressing herself to me again and kissing my mouth and face hungrily. 'No one will disturb us. God, you're a delicious thing—'

Once in her cabin she locked the door and stood beside the single bed shedding her uniform. I stood amazed at the size of her breasts, two firm fleshy spheres that thrust before her, bulging out sideways to her arms. The nipples were thumb-size, a rubbery dark brown on saucer-sized pink aureoles. There was the merest bulge on her belly, marked with the scar of an appendix operation, and her large cunt mound was profuse with hair between strapping thighs. Beside her, well-developed as I was, I felt a mere slip of a girl.

Sin and Mrs Saxon

'You must undress too, Diana,' she said. 'Shall I do it for you? Come here to me, my love—'

I obeyed, fascinated by her huge tits and buxom figure. She pecked little kisses on my eyes and mouth while loosening my tie and shirt. 'Such breasts,' she murmured, uncovering them, squashing her own mammoth mounds against them, kissing my mouth ardently. 'Too good for any brute of a man to enjoy – they're rough and don't know what pleases a woman. Such a dear little vagina too,' she added as my skirt and knickers dropped to the carpet. 'Has it ever been kissed? Tongued?'

'No,' I thought it better to say shyly.

'Then I'll give you that pleasure tonight.' She fell back across the bed, arms raised to receive me. We kissed again and again, her hand between my thighs, touching and probing me. Roused by her manipulation of my clitty, I felt her cunt, fat and lippy on the outside, moist and soft within. She gave a low moan, grasped my hand and directed my fingers to her nub, rubbing them against a big erect clitoris standing out stiffly erect. Then she pulled away from me, lying so that our heads were at opposite ends of the bed. She thrust one leg under one of mine, shuffling forward on her ample bottom until we were meshed together, cunt lips to cunt lips exactly matched.

'Give me your hands, Diana,' she ordered. 'Grip mine and pull against me. Work your pelvis—'

I reached out with both hands, grasping hers, and we began straining crotch to crotch, our cunts rubbing together tightly, rotating and clinging, exciting us to utter grunts and cries as we increased our pace. 'Heaven, heaven, work it against me harder,' I cried, feeling her stiff thumb-like clitoris actually penetrate my outer lips and enter me a maddening inch or so, making me lift and tilt to receive it. Then we were both convulsing wildly, our orgasms bringing dual uncontrolled spasms, buffeting our cunts together and gasping throaty cries until we lay inert from our exertions. I lay supine, regaining my breath, while Mona moved over me to kiss my eyes, mouth, breasts, still greedy for my body.

'You fucked me,' I told her, girl-giggly. 'I could feel you inside me—'

'Yes,' she agreed, 'but I've something longer to put into you, my dear.' She slid her face down over my belly, between my legs, pushing them apart with her palms. 'Yes,' I said as her tongue snaked into my wet receptive channel. I held her head and Mona worked away steadily, lapping and licking, using her tongue tip to flick at my clitty until I cried out that I was coming again and bucking myself into her face. Then she drew me into her bed and commenced a night of loving until I slipped from her cabin shortly before dawn lightened the sky and the bugle rang out reveille.

Mona was nothing like I had experienced before with a woman lover. Being a doctor, she knew every erogenous zone of my body and gave it the utmost sexual pleasure. With a weekend leave due to me, she arranged that we spend it together in Brighton, where she informed me good friends of the same sexual inclination were arranging to meet. To allay suspicion at the training camp, she picked me up in her car at Fareham, then she bowled along the road in great spirits, telling me we would share a wonderful weekend. How her friends would be jealous of her, she said, having such a lovely young companion!

It was evening when we arrived before the steps of an imposing Georgian house on the Brighton seafront. France was about to collapse before the invading Germans but inside the house all was gaiety. A dozen or so females drank and danced to gramophone records, holding hands and kissing. All, I noted, were in their thirties or forties, dressed in evening gowns or as officers of the women's services. As the only ranker, or more properly, rating, and considerably younger, I was cooed over and flattered, while Mona Calthrop joked that they could all look but not touch. I noted a good percentage of the women wore wedding rings. With their husbands away on active service they were no doubt having a fling.

I danced with several of the women. They gave me food from a buffet-style table, several sherries, and asked me just how 'close' I was to Mona. One woman in a flowing evening dress of silk, who was referred to as Angela, squeezed my hand as I danced with her, flirted suggestively and kissed my cheek. When I excused myself to go to the toilet and was directed to a bathroom up one flight of stairs, she followed me and put her arms around me, pressing me against the washbasin, kissing me passionately. Her scent was overpowering and her breath sweet in my mouth as we kissed, her tongue gliding over mine. I was impressed by her coiffured hair, the eye-shadow and make-up, her dress sense, being exactly the kind of older woman I intended to emulate in later years. Perhaps, too, having been surrounded by uniformed people for months, her glamour attracted me. I allowed the kisses.

'Sweet child,' she flattered me in a break in our kissing. 'Is Mona nice to you? I would be, if ever you want to spend your leave here. Do you sleep with her?'

'Sometimes,' I admitted. 'We're in the same camp and have to be careful—' As we kissed again her breasts pressed to mine and she pushed her crotch against me.

'Oh, to get you out of that scratchy uniform,' she said, 'Now kiss me again before we are missed—'

But missed we were, by my escort at least, for Mona came through the bathroom door like a shot from a gun. There was fury in her eyes as she caught Angela and I clasping each other close, our mouths fused in a long wracking kiss, both of us aroused to fever pitch. 'Angela, you bloody traitorous cow!' she screamed, making a grab for our hostess's dress by the neck and sending a string of pearls scattering over the tiled bathroom floor. 'I might have known!' As she pulled Angela away from me, it was my turn. 'Mackenzie, you little slut,' she threatened, my superior officer once again. 'Go downstairs immediately and wait for me. Do as you are told, girl!'

Angela, being swung around by her expensive gown, shouted back, 'This is not your bloody navy here, Mona! You don't give orders in my house,' at the same time twisting her body to give Mona a hearty push. In return she got a smart slap on the face and screamed in surprise and pain at the blow, pushing and striking back until the pair of them were on the landing, squabbling and grappling. To my great delight, as I found it all highly amusing, they rolled down the stairs in an undignified heap, watched by the other guests who had come out of the lounge on hearing the altercation. Sides were taken as accusations and counter-accusations were hurled and I decided, as the one who had turned the party into a brawl, to make myself scarce.

I couldn't go downstairs, now knee-deep in struggling women, so I went up, there being two more storeys in the house above me. That I could be disciplined for my part in starting the affray did not concern me. Mona could hardly say she had taken a young girl rating on weekend leave for sexual purposes.

The gilded stairway curved up and the walls were hung with splendid paintings which I admired while the hullabulloo went on below. On the very top landing I tried the handle of a door and looked into a bedroom to find a boy sitting up in bed with a cigarette in one hand and a tall champagne glass in the other. On the bedspread before him was a tray with a heaped helping of the buffet food as served below filling two plates.

'So there is a God,' he said cheerfully on seeing me. 'I was just thinking of girls.'

From the look on his cheeky face, I could just bet he was. 'Come on in,' he invited. 'What the devil is going on downstairs? I'll wager those witches below are fighting over you, aren't they? And you bolted—'

'I don't know what you mean,' I pretended.

'Come off it,' he laughed. 'I know my mother's parties, a bunch of old lesbos who'd tear each other's eyes out for a fresh young bit like you. Hide in my room if you don't fancy being the sacrificial maiden.'

'And just who are you?' I asked, going in and closing the door. He gave me a sly wink, patting the bed.

'Adrian Gurney-Ffitch, lately sent down from Harrow for being rather naughty. Hence my incarceration in this bloody bedroom until mother thinks I can behave—'

'I don't think you could behave if you tried,' I giggled, enjoying the situation and warming to the youth. 'I take it your mother is the lady called Angela?'

'The mater's no lady, I can assure you,' he grinned. 'Otherwise she wouldn't have sweet young girls brought here to seduce. Don't you like boys—?'

'Of course I do,' I said. 'I didn't know what I was getting into, did I?'

He refilled the champagne glass, offering it to me. 'Have a drink then. Eat, too, if you're peckish. What's your name?' He looked me over meaningfully. 'I can see you're a Wren—' As I took the glass, his fingers lingered over mine. 'You look pretty good to me under that uniform.'

'Diana,' I told him, taking a drink of champagne and choosing a chicken leg from the tray. 'For someone made to stay in his room, you do all right, I'd say—'

'Helped myself earlier, when my mother was getting in her glad rags for her lady friends,' he said cheerfully. On the bedcover before him was an open magazine full of naked women. 'French,' he said. 'I'd bet you'd look better than them with your uniform off, posing in the nuddy—'

'You'd run a mile if you saw a real one,' I retorted cheekily.

'Think so?' he said coolly. 'Why do you think old Adie was turfed out of the seat of learning where his father, grandfather and generations of 'em were tutored?'

'You probably seduced some poor kitchen maid and were caught at it,' I guessed.

'Seduced, yes, but no kitchen maid,' he said proudly. 'It was in fact a housemaster's good wife, all of twenty-eight and frustrated to the point of climbing the walls. Poor Candice had never known a good rogering all her life, married to a poof of a Latin professor who liked caning boys' backsides. You know how I got her naked in the empty dorm that day—?'

'How?' I asked, intrigued to know.

Sin and Mrs Saxon

'Subtly. Like this,' he said, his hands reaching out to me. My hands were full, with the glass and the chicken leg, and just for his cheek I allowed him to continue. My uniform jacket was already open, revealing my bulging shirt front. He undid my tie, undoing the buttons on my shirt from the neck down, pulling it apart and free of my skirt, giving him a close-up view of an overflowing bra and curved flesh almost to the nipples.

'Don't!' he said, as I dropped the chicken leg and made to pull my shirt together. 'A thing of beauty is a joy for ever, and in your case, two beauties. Where did you get lovely big tits like that?'

'They just grew,' I said, unsure whether to let him continue. I was getting aroused by him ogling my tits and I liked him for his carefree way. Then came a knock on the door and he signalled me to go around the bed and lie behind it.

'Who is it?' he called.

'Your mother,' I heard Angela's voice say, coming nearer. I held my breath, hugging the bedside rug. 'Where did you get that food, Adrian?' she demanded. 'You know you're being punished.'

'I'm not starving for you or anybody,' he said defiantly. 'Bad enough I'm stuck in this room. What do you want, anyway? Won't your guests be missing you—?'

'One of them seems to be missing,' his mother said. 'She came upstairs. Has anyone looked in this room in passing?'

'No such luck,' said Adie. 'Not that any of your friends would be any use to me—'

'Don't you dare say such a thing,' warned Angela. 'With your father overseas, I have to have some company. Where did that girl get to—?'

Sin and Mrs Saxon

'Probably took off down the back stairs and out through the servants' door,' her son advised. 'What was she like?'

'A young Wren. I didn't want her to go like that. However, she'll no doubt be back. Her weekend case is still on the hall stand. Don't pig yourself on all that food,' she added, going out of the door and closing it. I arose from the floor, my shirt wide open, grinning with Adrian at my narrow escape.

'Now, where were we?' he said.

'You were undoing my shirt and admiring my breasts,' I teased him. 'I suppose now you want to see them with my bra off—?'

'That would be a start,' he agreed saucily. 'This being confined to my room isn't so bad after all. See what you've done to me?' He handed the tray to me, then peeled back the bedcovers. Rearing from his pyjama trousers was a huge stiff prick, as hard as only youth can get. He stroked it slowly and fondly, making me want to hold it, rub it and take it between my legs. 'You're here for the night, I reckon,' he said. 'Let's make hay, eh?'

'That thing would make babies,' I said. 'I couldn't trust a boy like you—'

'There's a drawer full of Frenchies in there,' he said, pointing out a dressing table. I quickly found several, too far gone in my arousal to argue further, eyeing his erect cock standing like a flagpole. I stood beside his bed undressing while he whistled softly as each garment fell to the floor. By the time I joined him on the bed he had thrown off his pyjamas and I fell into his open arms, our mouths locking and tongues searching. He went on to kissing my tits, sucking hard on each nipple, his hand groping between my parted thighs. The urge to be fucked was too strong to resist. In his youthful eagerness he was all over me, trying to mount me desperately. That he would not last seconds once up my cunt was obvious, so I decided to take charge.

'No, do it my way,' I told him, pushing him flat on his back, his cock rearing upright and rigid. 'I don't believe you've fucked before – your housemaster's wife or anyone else. Let me show you—'

He nodded, impressed, his wide eyes transfixed by my breasts and the triangle of thick hair on my pubis as I loomed over him and rolled one of his fine rubber sheaths on his straining stem. I straddled him and guided his knob to my quim, pushing down, tits swaying, to impale myself on his length. Adie gasped with delight, heaving his cock up to meet me, hard as an iron bar, working his hips like a piston to meet my downward thrusts. It was no sophisticated fuck, just two randy young beings shafting at each other. He came quickly, of course, with increased jerks and a strangled groan. It made me ride on desperately, squirming my bum and rotating it against him to achieve my own relief. My climax followed, making my cry out and shudder and shake over him in its intensity.

Later, under the covers, we cuddled and kissed, fondled and played with each other, naked and enjoying ourselves as only a teenage boy and girl can when granted the opportunity. His erection returned beautifully stiff, allowing him to mount me for a long slow fuck that had me arching my back to him, sighing my pleasure. Adie had me once more on awakening around dawn, his hands exploring my bottom, cunt and breasts while I feigned sleep. Aroused by the touching, feeling his hard cock pressed to the cleft of my arse, I rolled over onto my stomach and he followed me, pushing in his shaft and missing the target by an inch or so, and penetrating the tight ring of my anus. Whether by mistake or on purpose, who knows?

He had not taken time to roll on the necessary French letter so, apart from the pleasure derived from his length sliding up my back passage, I was relieved it was where it was. I raised my rump as his belly curled over me and he fucked me there. I went mad with the feeling inside me as he slid in and out and his balls knocked my cunt lips with each thrust. By the time his load was deposited up me in long spurts I was coming myself, bumping myself back into him.

Then it was time to leave. He led the way down the silent stairs and retrieved my weekend case from the hallstand. As he saw me out of the door, we exchanged a parting kiss. It tickled my sense of humour to think the mother had fancied me and the son had fucked me.

On the seafront I found an early-morning coffee stall open for business and drank a cup. Around me workmen discussed the serious situation brought on by the collapse of France and what the surrender would mean. The trapped British Army in its retreat to the port of Dunkirk could only be rescued by sea, seemingly an impossible task. I took the train back to my base at HMS Collingwood at Fareham and reported for duty to find the camp on full alert and rifles being issued to the men. Anti-aircraft guns were sited around the parade ground.

'All training has been suspended in the emergency,' I was informed on going to the motor mechanics' course instructor. 'I expect we'll be invaded any time now that old Jerry holds the Channel ports and airfields,' said the Chief Motor Mechanic. 'You Wrens are needed as drivers, so you've all passed your training course as far as I'm concerned. Report yourselves to the drafting office and you'll be detailed to wherever you're needed most—'

So it was, thanks to the rapid advance of the German Army on the continent, that I was rated a Wren driver-mechanic and issued with a travel warrant to join HMS *Medina*, the shore establishment near Ryde, Isle of Wight, while England prepared itself for the invasion everyone was sure would soon come.

Chapter Nine
AMERICA

I know I should, but rarely do, say no. I should give a firm but polite refusal when propositioned by an attractive man or woman. But the temptation is always too strong and the urge to indulge in secretive sex with a new partner is usually irresistible. Peter Gulay took me to a jolly restaurant frequented by the acting profession and many of the clients were famous faces. Knowing the outcome, I did not turn down the invitation for a nightcap at his Greenwich Village flat to end the evening. After all, I thought, what did I have to go home to? An absent husband and an empty apartment.

So it was I awoke the following morning on Peter's sofa-bed and sat up to look through an open door into a miniscule kitchen where he stood, naked but for a butcher's apron around his waist, making breakfast. We had fucked half the night and slept entwined for the other half and I felt wonderfully alive and fulfilled. Peter had proved himself again and again a long-lasting and experienced lover, gentle and dominant in turn, his large prick, star of many a porno film no doubt, repeatedly bringing me to toe-curling climaxes. He saw me sitting up, my bared breasts lifting as I stretched my arms, and came through to admire the sight, handing me a mug of coffee.

'You are indeed a sight for sore eyes,' he said. 'Those marvellous breasts, your splendid body. Last night all my friends asked me who was the beautiful English actress I was keeping to myself.'

'Scottish,' I corrected him, accepting the coffee. 'It was a lovely evening. Thank you for inviting me—'

'Thank *you*,' he grinned, his eyes twinkling. 'Are you hungry? I'm eating. You took a lot out of me—'

'Starving,' I admitted. 'You put a lot into me—'

'The pleasure was all mine,' he laughed. 'Stay where you are and I'll bring you breakfast in bed. My apartment is crummy but the service is good. How does scrambled egg and crisp bacon grab you?'

'Terrific,' I said, sipping hot coffee, enjoying the sensation of waking up in a strange bed after a night of good sex. Peter returned to the kitchen and I reached over for my shoulder bag, seeking a comb to tidy my hair. To get at it, I pulled out the script Ziggy had given me and read the title page. 'The Delivery Boy' it was headed, 'An original screen play by Zigmund Kaplan, Filmic Studios, Yonkers N.Y.'. Intrigued, I opened it up to the first typed page. It began:

PAN IN: Julie Snow, a typical suburban housewife in her early forties, strips to take a shower in the bathroom. Voluptuously built with large breasts and rounded figure, she steps under the shower spray and soaps her breasts and between her thighs and buttocks, becoming aroused. *Camera tracks* her hands, caressing each breast together, pulling on nipples dripping with suds. Hand goes down to stroke vaginal lips. *Pan back* to her face:

Sin and Mrs Saxon

an expression of pure pleasure as she fingers herself.

CUT TO: Julie towelling herself in the bedroom, still arousing herself as she dries her breasts and the fork of her thighs. *Close-up* of her lifting each big breast in turn to dry underneath, bending her neck to kiss each nipple. Overcome by her aroused state, she drops the towel and falls back on the bed. *Overhead shot* looking down on her high breasts, one of which she clasps. *Track down* over her stomach to her crotch, where her other hand cups and strokes her vaginal lips. She tilts her crotch erotically, moving it slowly as finger is inserted. *Close-up*.

NOISES OFF: Persistent doorbell chimes.

CUT TO: Julie rising from bed, obviously annoyed. She reaches for a loose cotton housecoat, ties belt.

CUT TO: Julie in a loose housecoat which barely covers her thighs, revealing shapely bare legs, on an upstairs landing as she leaves her room to go below to answer door. On the landing is another door which is opened by a beautiful teenage girl, Julie's daughter Darleen. She is in a see-through shortie nightdress, revealing her breasts, the dark outline of her nipples and pubic hair. She looks enquiringly at her mother.

JULIE: I'll get it, Darleen. I'm expecting a special delivery. Go back to bed, dear. I'll call you when breakfast is ready—

CUT TO: Darleen shrugs, closes her door, as her mother proceeds downstairs.

CUT TO: Outside of house at rear door leading to kitchen. Youthful delivery boy presses the bell impatiently. Under his arm is large box. *Pan in* as Julie opens the door and stands before him in shortie housecoat.

Sin and Mrs Saxon

DELIVERY BOY: You all dead in there, lady? I been ringing for ever—

CUT TO: The boy's mouth remains open as he takes in Julie, his eyes lighting up. *Track camera to* what he is seeing. The loosely tied belt of her housecoat is slack, revealing the deep cleavage of her breasts and a glimpse of thigh. She notices his stare and reties the belt hurriedly. He holds out the delivery book for her to sign. She ignores the book.

JULIE: Bring in the box and I'll sign for it later. I don't want my daughter knowing her surprise birthday present has arrived. I've emptied a space for it, so bring over that stepladder for me to use—

DELIVERY BOY: (Still ogling Julie). Yes, ma'am!

CUT TO: Delivery van parked on road outside house. The black driver is a good-looking young man, a macho type. He is studying a sex magazine featuring naked girls. He glances at his wristwatch impatiently.

DRIVER: These pics sure get a man horny for a fuck. What the hell is keeping that boy of mine—?

CUT TO: Darleen's bedroom where she is lying across the bed, her shortie nightie rucked up under her bottom revealing a neat teenage vaginal mound with wispy hairs and outer lips. She holds up her Teddy Bear, talking to it.

DARLEEN: I tell you all my secrets, Teddy, for you're the only one who's slept with me so far. Dick Harriman doesn't know it yet, but he's going to take my virginity after the Junior Prom dance. Don't be jealous, Teddy. Haven't we always had fun together?'

CUT TO: Darleen pulls Teddy to her breasts, hugging him there, rubbing the little bear against them. Then she opens her thighs and pushes Teddy down to her crotch, working his nose against her vagina. She moves her crotch sensuously. She is getting turned on.

DARLEEN: I can hardly wait for it, I want it so. (Deep sigh.) I want to be fucked – by a real cock—

CUT TO: Kitchen. A step ladder has been placed below the wall units; Julie is on the top step opening door of highest cupboard while the delivery boy hands the box to her. She half-turns to take it, her breasts falling out of her loose housecoat. The stepladder wobbles as she tries to put the box in the cupboard.

JULIE: Hold the ladder, boy! Steady it—

CUT TO: Delivery boy's face, looking up and beaming at what he sees. Show his hand lifting past his head.

CUT TO: (Close-up). What the boy sees, a shot of Julie's bare buttocks, cheeks spread to show the hanging bulge of her vagina, the parted lips surrounded by hair, her anus visible. The boy's hand continues upwards, finger curling to stroke her vaginal opening.

NOISES OFF: (Julie). OH! AAAH! (Shuddering sigh). Oh, young man, just what do you think you are doing—?

I put the script down as Peter returned with a tray. The scrambled eggs were yellow and fluffy, the bacon crisp, the toast buttered, the whole thing tempting and tasty. As I ate, he picked up the script and glanced at it. He read quickly, flicking over the pages, smiling broadly. 'Jeez,' he said at last. 'One of Ziggy Kaplan's minor masterpieces. Hardly Noel Coward. I mean, look at the title – "The Delivery Boy"! But I guess he knows what his customers want. However did you get hold of it, Diana?'

'I met him,' I said, giving no details. 'He actually offered me a part—'

'More of the despicable Lefarges' blackmail?' he asked.

'I'm not sure. This Kaplan turned up at the rendezvous they'd arranged for me. He expressed surprise at seeing me, said I was right for the part – the mother, no doubt. I had a sneaky feeling Violette Lefarge had master-minded it. She'd enjoy having me appear in a pornographic film—'

'You would be ideal,' Peter grinned. 'Are you considering the offer?'

I pulled a wry face. 'The script seemed fun,' I admitted, 'and I've never done anything like that before. Act a part, I mean. But I couldn't, could I?'

'Why not? Your husband is hardly likely to see the film. It will only be shown in private movie theatres in places like Vegas and Los Angeles. As for the Lefarges, I'm working on a little plan to fix them good—'

'Tell me—'

'Later, when I've worked it all out. Ziggy Kaplan could help for what I've got in mind. I know Zig, I've worked for him before. He's straight enough. Scratch his back and he'll scratch yours. Shall I call him now—?' Peter walked across the room to fetch the telephone and sat on the bed beside me.

'I've got a feeling I'm getting deeper into hot water,' I said, 'but what's new about that? Call him—'

While Peter dialled I fluffed my hair over my shoulders, amazed as ever at my nerve. 'Ziggy, this is Pete, Pete Gulay,' he said. 'I've got your "Delivery Boy" script before me which is terrif. About the lady you want to be the mother—'

He held out the receiver for me to hear Ziggy's reply. 'I've cast that part,' came the answer. 'A broad I saw at that creep J.D. Coolidge's apartment doing a trick. She had the biggest tits you'd ever want to see. I'm hoping to get a call from her today. We're set up to shoot—'

'Then your worry is over, Zig old sport. That lady is right here with me,' Peter answered. 'I could bring her over to the studio this morning—'

'How do I know you got the same dame?' asked Ziggy. 'And if you have, what's in it for you? You her agent?'

'Just doing a favour for an old buddy,' Peter said sweetly. 'In return you could maybe do something for me—'

'There's no part for you this shoot, Peter. I got the whole cast apart from the mother.'

'Okay by me,' Peter said. 'Just remember you owe me. I'll put the lady you seek on the line for you. Her name is Sadie Gluck, would you believe? Here she is.'

I took the phone and Ziggy said, 'Miss Gluck? You the party I saw yesterday? How can you prove that? Tell me what you did while I was there—'

'I've got the script you gave me,' I said. 'I was in J.D. Coolidge's hotel room with a nineteen-year-old who looks like fifteen called Melvin. Does that satisfy you?'

'And what did you do that impressed us so much?'

With Peter beside me I swallowed hard, blushing with embarrassment. 'I masturbated,' I said in a whisper. Peter grinned and shook his head, muttering 'What a girl'.

'That's good enough for me,' Ziggy said. 'Your name really Sadie Gluck? We'll change that. Hows about Verda Laverne?'

'That would be fine by me. I'm a married woman and my husband isn't aware of – of – my—'

'Moonlighting as a hooker,' Ziggy finished for me. 'Sure, you're not the only one to earn a little on the side. We'll use make-up so your own mother wouldn't know you, honey.'

In Peter's car on the drive to Yonkers I studied the rest of the script, and was tickled by the twists and turns of the story which leads to an all-out romp in Julie's kitchen with everyone fucking and sucking. I was intrigued by the way all the characters were brought together. The delivery boy touches up Julie while she is up the stepladder which leads to her orgasming shamelessly on his fingers. They then kiss and fondle and undress each other and the pair screw across the kitchen table, uttering moans and cries while the camera closes in to give vivid shots of her cunt being shafted by the delivery lad.

Meanwhile, daughter Darleen, deciding her mother must be making breakfast, goes downstairs in her short see-through nightie. Hearing the sounds of her mother and the delivery boy fucking across the kitchen table, she peeks around the door. What she sees excites her so much that she plays with herself. Meanwhile, the young black driver waiting in the van goes to see what has kept his mate. He knocks on the front door, gets no answer and enters. Going through the hall and into the dining room, he sees the back view of Darleen peering into the kitchen and masturbating, her other hand lifting her nightie so that her pretty little bottom is bared.

I chuckled as I read on: the macho driver goes up to Darleen and sees what she is seeing – Julie across the kitchen table with the delivery boy fucking her. Turned on by the scene, the driver feels up Darleen and she, once over her surprise, allows him to continue.

Sin and Mrs Saxon

'What's so amusing?' Peter asked as I giggled. 'Ziggy doesn't miss a trick, does he? Who's screwing who now?'

'They're all at it,' I laughed. 'Now the driver is having the daughter on the kitchen table beside the mum.' I flicked over the page. 'The scene changes – they've made a swop. The delivery boy is into Darleen while the black man has the mother perched up on the kitchen counter. Good God, I've remembered that's me! do I do all that?'

'Several times over if Ziggy isn't satisfied with the take,' Peter grinned. 'As a director he thinks he's due an Academy Award. Don't worry, Di. Just be yourself, like you were in bed last night—'

'Thanks for your cheek,' I said. 'But that was with you. What about the actors today?'

'All professionals, no doubt. I don't know who the daughter will be, but you can bet Ziggy has got some beautiful but broke young actress for the part. The delivery boy is easy – a low-life called Melvin who looks a real honest-to-God kid of fourteen or so. He always gets these parts, it's the dream every guy had when he was an errand boy – classic porn – the immature lad with the mature woman—'

'I've met Melvin,' I admitted. 'What of the other actor?'

I saw Peter smile wickedly. 'A good friend of mine called Damon Butler, hoping to make it in the legit theatre or films like myself. He picks up eating money doing porn. He's black and beautiful, built like an athlete – and has the biggest dick you're ever likely to meet—'

'Is that good?' I asked, considering the fact.

'You may well think so,' Peter chuckled. 'Damon enjoys his work. He'll like you—'

123

Sin and Mrs Saxon

'But we'll be acting, won't we?'

'Sure,' Peter affirmed. 'Acting for real. Ziggy doesn't allow simulation, he demands the real thing. Some faking of orgasms takes place, of course, if the director orders one and the man or woman isn't at that stage. Then the practice is to buck and heave like the earth is moving. You were doing that last night okay—'

'That was for real,' I protested.

'So act it, if you have to,' said Peter. 'It may save an hour or two's filming. You'll soon get the hang of it. Then there are what's called "cum" shots. Ziggy will want those—'

'Pretending to come when you aren't,' I said. 'You've already explained that—'

'Not exactly, I'm just putting you wise so you'll know all the gimmicks of a skin movie. Ziggy's direction is good, you just follow what he says he wants. But then there's the out-takes as they're called. Special effects filmed between scenes and spliced into the action in the editing process.'

'The "cum" shots,' I said, trying to follow him.

'Sure. Human male ejaculate evidently isn't copious enough when a guy shoots his load on film. The punters who watch these movies like gallons of goo to flow. So it's faked, filmed later with a mix of warm water and condensed milk in a syringe squirted where required, over breasts, faces, you name it. You'll be required to pose for close-up shots that show the phoney jism being jetted over you. Male actors in porn pics always have to withdraw at the crucial moment, so the horny bastards who watch such movies can see the hot fat flying. They like that—'

'And the actress?' I asked.

'She's expected to writhe about in ecstasy, mouthing lustful utterances, and the loaded syringe is brought into play off camera to squirt gobs of thick grey liquid over her, like I said. Then the close-ups as the camera zooms in on soaked hair, or drooling mouth if it's a suck scene, drenched cleavage and dripping nipples. Always after a coupling there's the vaginal or anal shot with excess come seeping out of the orifice filling the screen. You still want to go through with this?'

'It seemed straightforward in the script,' I said. 'You make it sound so complicated—'

'Not really. Filming is all stops and starts. The guy might lose his erection. Women don't have that problem. So between times, to save time, the director will take good care to shoot other scenes, like the "cum" shots, or such as the delivery boy ringing the doorbell. Good editing of the film puts it all in the right order later—'

Seeing me looking worried, Peter patted my knee. 'Don't worry, Di,' he assured me. 'With your looks and body you'll be a natural. Did Ziggy say how much he was paying you—?'

'A thousand dollars was mentioned—'

'Think of that then. I'll make sure you get it. Now here's the studio,' he added, driving his car through a unmarked gate guarded by a security man who recognised him. 'Go in and make like a movie star.' He drew up before a wide door marked: Sound Stage One, No Entry While Red Light Is Burning.

'Red light on the door,' I observed. 'How appropriate.' I took a deep breath and swallowed hard, preparing myself to make my debut in the world of pornographic film-making. The red light blinked several times and then went out. Then the door opened and Ziggy Kaplan emerged in cravat, velvet coat and jeans.

'Great, you got her,' he congratulated Peter. 'Come right in. We're all set up to shoot the orgy in the kitchen—'

Chapter Ten
ENGLAND

As recently as the previous summer, HMS *Medina* had been a holiday camp. Now the hutted enclosure was a Fleet Air Arm base with workshops and classrooms for the training of flight engineers, aircraft handlers and armourers. With me on the ferry over to the Isle of Wight had been soldiers in full battle kit, posted there to add to the strength of that strategic island – no doubt a prime objective of the expected German invasion of Britain. I was caught up in the feeling of excitement that was general at the time, glad to be a little part of the historic events taking place. However, on reporting to my new base my arrival was not exactly greeted as a useful addition to the strength. I handed my draft papers to the surly old Master-At-Arms in his office and he raised his eyes to the ceiling.

'Christ,' he uttered. 'All we need, they're sending us little girls. What we need right now is a battalion of regular marines.'

'We could use her in the galley,' suggested his Regulating Petty Officer mate. 'The Chief Cook is going spare what with half his staff on stand-by guard duty these days. Report your nice little arse over to our C.P.O.

Sin and Mrs Saxon

Wrigley, Wren Mackenzie, and tell cheffy we sent you—'

I envisaged skivvying with endless heaps of dirty dishes and decided to stand my ground. 'I'm not taking my nice little arse anywhere near the galley,' I retorted. 'I am rated a Wren driver-mechanic, drafted here to do what I've been trained for. Where's the transport section? I'll report myself there—'

I thought the Regulating Petty Officer was about to have an apoplectic fit. He boiled with indignation. 'What's the navy coming to—' he began, but the surly old Master-at-Arms gave a mirthful laugh, silencing his mate with a raised hand.

'Seems we've got a right one here,' chuckled the Master, as such are always addressed. He glanced at my service sheet again, nodding. 'She's right too, properly rated just as she claims—'

'Christ, a split-arsed mechanic,' muttered his petty officer. 'The only "crack" troops they're sending us. So what do we do with her? Every servicable truck or car has already been taken over to move troops around this island. I still say she'd be more use in the galley—'

'I was thinking of our rather troublesome guest, Colonel bloody high and mighty Randall-Bude,' said the Master-at-Arms deviously. 'He of the Gurkha Brigade who landed himself on our navy and demands a personal servant and chauffeur like he was back in India with the Raj. He's just got himself a driver-mechanic—'

His Petty Officer's eyes lit with wicked glee. 'That should keep the bastard out of our hair. Only thing is, what do we get him as his staff car?'

The Master-at-Arms regarded me quizzically. 'How good a mechanic are you, Ginger?' he asked, getting the

Sin and Mrs Saxon

colour of my deep auburn-chestnut hair slightly wrong.

'Brilliant,' I lied, determined not to lose the chance of a driving job, crusty old army colonel or not as my superior.

'Then there's a broken-down navy utility truck of ours at Albany Barracks near Newport. You get it to work and it's all yours, lass. It was towed in there and we've never seen it since.'

'How do I get to this Albany Barracks?' I asked.

'There's a war on,' he laughed. 'Use your initiative. Take the bus—'

I found a billet in a hut inhabited by Wren cooks, dumped my kit, put my overalls under my arm, and found my way to Albany Barracks and the motor pool workshop. Several army mechanics crowded around as I walked into a hive of activity with cars and trucks being repaired. 'We're okay now, boys,' shouted one. 'The navy is here. Bit of all right, too—'

I was shown to a corner of the garage workshop where the navy utility truck had been dumped. It was a small vehicle known as a 'Tilly' with seats in the cab for the driver and one other, and with a canvas canopy above the space in the rear. The bonnet was left up as if all attempts to make it work had been abandoned. I inspected the blackened and oily engine with a sinking heart, having little idea how to get it back to life. The soldiers stood around me grinning, doubting my ability. I thought back to my base at HMS *Medina*, thinking how proud I'd be to drive the van back and have one up on those who had sent me on what they no doubt considered a fool's errand.

While pondering this, the admiring crowd of squaddies around me parted to let their sergeant through. He looked young, handsome and capable, so I gave him a winning smile. 'The navy's come to get their truck, I see,' he said. 'Do you think you can get it on the road, miss?'

'Could you, sergeant?' I asked, playing the helpless female for all I was worth.

'I could, but it's not my pigeon,' he replied. 'Use any of our tools that you need—'

There was nothing for it but to get into my overalls, ogled by the soldier mechanics until their sergeant ordered them back to work. Several hours later, after many attempts to start the obstinate thing, alone in the workshop and still struggling, the sergeant reappeared. He had with him a jug of tea, a mug and several thick sandwiches on a plate.

'No luck?' he said, watching me gulp tea and wolf into the sandwiches. 'Full marks for sticking at it, anyway. What do they call you?'

'Wren Mackenzie, Diana to you,' I said. 'I hate to think this thing has beaten me. I've done everything I thought was right. The engine just won't start—'

'I'm Reggie,' he said, looking at the engine. 'What if I stay and get it going for you? What's in it for me?'

Hope sprang eternal within me. I knew what he wanted, but I wanted the van to start even more. 'I'd be more than just grateful,' I said innocently. 'What have you in mind, sergeant?'

'Something like this,' he said, pulling me into his arms, his lips going from my neck to my cheek and then landing full on my mouth. Half expecting it, I was still surprised at the rush of excitement that shook my stomach. We kissed long and hard with his tongue on mine. I felt his erection rise hard against my crotch and gave him a little series of pushes back. 'I'd love to fuck you,' he said fervently. 'When I came in this afternoon and saw you, I would love to give *that* a length, I told myself.'

'Get the car working first,' I said, 'and you've got a bargain.' He worked solidly for the next hour, telling me what he was about and fetching new parts for the electrical system. At last, after midnight, came the magic moment when he let me turn the ignition key and the engine purred sweetly into life. I hugged him and we kissed again passionately. In my exultant state I even wanted to make love for my own satisfaction. He went away and returned moments later with several army blankets which he laid out in the rear of the van. We got in under the canopy, removed our uniforms and then fell into each other's arms.

'What tits you've got,' he said, his hands all over me. I held his prick, rubbed it to my outer lips, felt his lunge as it entered me. Thus I christened my new command, a little 3-cwt utility truck, by being fucked in its rear – and later being fucked in my rear – for Reg was a man who knew what he wanted. He told me he was married and missing his wife, rousing me through the hours of the night with randy talk of what he did to please her sexually and doing the same things to me in the process. He licked my cunt beautifully, got rampant with me sucking him and we screwed until dawn. Never had an engine sounded sweeter as I drove back to be waved in at the gate of HMS *Medina* by the armed sailor sentry.

I pulled up before the steps of the Regulating Office, once the reception foyer of the holiday camp in happier days, and the gruff old Master-at-Arms and his gaunt Petty Officer assistant came out as I tooted the horn triumphantly. 'Well, I'll be fucked,' said the P.O. in amazement. I resisted the temptation to say, 'No, but I was' and grinned cheekily at their undisguised surprise, impressed by such apparent skill in a mere girl.

The pair of old Royal Navy martinets snapped to attention as I got out of the utility truck, throwing up rigid salutes as the commanding officer of the base arrived beside us. A full captain with four gold rings of rank on his sleeves, he eyed me and the truck with interest. 'Isn't that our Tilly left abandoned with the army for spare parts?' he said. 'I thought we'd given up on that—'

'Wren Driver-mechanic Mackenzie here got it mobile, sir,' said the Master proudly. 'She's also volunteered to be driver for Colonel Randall-Bude—'

'That is the only good news I've heard this tragic week,' said the C.O. grimly. 'Now France has surrendered and our own troops are up to their necks in the sea at Dunkirk, getting shot of our Gurkha guest before he causes a mutiny in my wardroom shows that all is not lost in our darkest hour.'

'We thought you'd approve of that, sir,' said the Master, allowing himself a grin. 'That's why I volunteered Wren Mackenzie for the job. Keen girl, I knew that right away—'

I kept a straight face, remembering how I would have been endlessly washing up dishes had I not stood up for myself. As for the duty I had been landed with – driver to a peppery old colonel who was obviously not the easiest of types to be with – I considered I had a way with men. 'I'll fill up with petrol and report to Colonel Randall-Bude,' I announced, eager to impress the C.O.

'Have you had breakfast?' asked the captain.

'No, sir.'

'Then come with me and you can order what you wish in the wardroom pantry.' To the bemused Master-at-Arms he added, 'Leading Wren Mackenzie is now considered detached for special duty, driver to Colonel Randall-Bude. Log that in—'

'Leading Wren—?' queried the Master.

'She is now, I've just promoted her,' snapped his C.O. 'You can sew an anchor up on your arm, girl,' he told me. 'Whatever you did to get the Tilly operative, you showed initiative.' If only he knew, I thought.

Colonel Randall-Bude was not impressed with the Tilly when I reported to him, enquiring whether that was the best the navy could do for a senior army officer? He was more impressed by me, I was sure. He gazed at my full breasts with approval as I stood to attention beside my charge. After breakfast I had hosed it down and polished it. Now he looked it over with some disdain, peering under the canvas canopy. 'Blankets,' he said, giving me a leer. 'Most useful. Do you sleep in this vehicle?'

'I have done, sir,' I said. 'Just once. It was an emergency.'

'There may well be others,' he said smoothly. 'One never knows, does one? You know you are an extremely pretty girl. We should get on well.' He gave me a quick glance and there was a wealth of meaning in the look. 'We shall be together quite a lot, so I expect full cooperation—'

He was, I decided as I returned his glance, well aware of his intent. He was a suave lecherous type of man used to getting his wicked way with all personable females. In his early fifties, his years serving in India had left him lean and tanned; his handsome and arrogant face was adorned with a full moustache. He was, indeed, an attractive man, sitting up straight as a ramrod as we drove off to the south coast of the island. At times his hand brushed my thigh, accidently on purpose as it were. It lingered there as he grew bolder until he was almost caressing me. I allowed it, admiring him as a quick worker and not averse to his first advances.

'What exactly do you do, sir?' I dared ask, confident of myself with him. 'Apart from feeling my leg,' I could have added.

'Officially, my title is Inspector of Defences for this area. Unofficially, I nose around making sure everything has been done to make this place secure if we are invaded, reporting back to Whitehall and Churchill himself if I find all is not at a full state of readiness. So we'll be popping up all over the show, arriving at all hours of day or night to catch the unwary. You'll be on call twenty-four hours, my girl. That's why I billeted myself on the navy, I don't want the army to be aware I'm here as an official observer.'

'Pretty sneaky,' I said, giggling. His hand was now stroking my thigh, almost at my crotch. 'You're disturbing my driving, sir.'

'Then stop for a while,' he said calmly. We were on a high road on downland, a deserted narrow strip of tarmac in country overlooking the sea. Miles below we could see tiny figures on a beach stringing out rolls of barbed wire. Without ceasing to stroke my leg, he said as we pulled up, 'Excellent view of that beach from up here. I'll recommend siting a battery of guns at this spot. Where are we exactly?'

I consulted the large road map of the Isle of Wight he

had issued me. 'Brading Down, sir. Overlooking Whitecliff Bay and Sandown Bay.'

'Mark it,' he said. 'Make a pencilled ring around this bit of road.' He lolled back in his seat, looking down at his crotch. The front of his battledress trousers bulged in an impressive mound. 'Did you bathe or shower this morning, young woman?' he asked unexpectedly.

'No, sir,' I had to say, embarrassed and blushing. 'I worked half the night on this vehicle, then reported straight to you. I can assure you I wash regularly—'

'I'm sure you do, don't take it as a reprimand,' he smiled. 'I like it, the scent of a woman. Terribly randifying, don't you know? Sweat and cunt is what I smell, the sweetest perfume known to man.' He reached out to stop me winding down the window. 'Don't! It takes me back to India, where the heat made the female body ripe. Do you fuck, Mackenzie?'

'What a question to ask,' I said. 'You don't waste time, do you?'

'Life's too short. I've always found the direct approach best. I have the most urgent hard-on, as you can see. A simple yes or no will suffice.'

The bulge in his trouser front lifted the khaki material as if to urge my compliance. 'Let me see it then,' I agreed, weak as ever in such situations. 'I really don't think we should be doing this, sir, do you?'

'I entirely agree,' he laughed shortly, unbuttoning his fly and drawing out a thick and rearing prick of considerable length. 'I have a wife in Poona, and you no doubt have a boyfriend somewhere. That makes it all the more deliciously wicked, doesn't it? I think we should resume this conversation in the rear of this vehicle and make use of the blankets there.'

He had put my hand on his cock, wrapping my fingers around its girth, noting how I gazed upon it. The stout staff was rigid and the bulbous pink knob glistened. 'You want it, don't you, my dear?' he said invitingly. 'It's so tempting. In the back with you now, no argument—'

I crawled into the rear of the truck in a fever of arousal so easily attained by the unexpected offer of sex. Randall-Bude joined me and began casually taking off his uniform, urging that I do the same. 'Nothing like getting down to the skin for romping,' he said, sitting up on the blankets and watching me divest myself of my uniform. 'Gad, I haven't rogered a young girl like you since Allahabad, daughter of my adjutant actually, out for the school hols and prime for fucking. What fine breasts you have, girl, I'd forgotten what young skin does to a man. You are a beauty! Come, let me enjoy you.'

'It's not all one-sided,' I pointed out. 'I want some enjoyment too—'

'And so you shall,' he promised, 'for my main pleasure is in giving it.' He clasped me to his bare chest, my tits flattening as he hugged me. He covered my mouth with his, his tongue protruding wet and warm deep into my mouth. He laid me flat and looked me over, his large hands covering my tits, thumbs flicking my nipples before going down to suck upon each in turn. When I sighed, thrusting up to him, his suction increased, pulling tit flesh into his mouth as well. Then he was sliding down over me, his lips on my belly, tongue tip in my navel, and finally clamping his mouth fully over my cunt. I groaned my approval, raising my knees and grasping his head. His thick moustache tangled with my pubic bush; he began to lick and lap my cunt expertly.

His searching tongue reemed me in every corner of my

cunt channel, at times his teeth nipping my clitoris or his lips sucking hard on its prominence. I gurgled my pleasure, bucked into his face, and came and came several times over before he ceased. He sat up on his knees before me and directed his turgid prick to my lips.

'Suck on it nicely,' he ordered. 'Relax and take your time. Enjoy it. It should be savoured, not gobbled.' I nodded agreement, as best I was able with a full mouth and sucked on the swollen stem like a child with a lollipop. 'Good, very good,' he said. 'I can see we'll get on very well. You must swallow it all when I come, it's the only way to complete the act. Suck harder now, bring me off—'

I did so and listened to him grunt out his pleasure as he worked his hips, fucking my mouth and finally losing control. He jerked in rapid spasms and his hot emission filled my throat. Even as I was swallowing, he reached into his battledress pocket to hand me a small silver flask. I drank, feeling the warm glow of neat whisky in my stomach.

'You did just what you liked with me,' I told him. 'I believe you intended to have me as soon as you saw me this morning.'

'You had that look about you,' he said. 'I'm never wrong when I judge a filly needs to be put to the cock. You've done this sort of thing before—'

'A little,' was all I'd admit. 'Shall we get dressed now, sir?'

'I don't think so. We've only just begun. We're not liable to be disturbed or invaded by the Germans this very day. Never be ashamed of having heightened sexual feelings or denying them either, young woman. I know you enjoyed what we did. Admit it.'

'It was nice—'

'Nice?' he said sternly. 'It was fucking good. Sex between male and female is the strongest aspiration of this planet. I have shagged females of every creed and colour, man and boy, never tiring. Gad, but you've got fine tits on you, girl. Have those delightful things ever been fucked? Known as a titty-ride in regimental circles. Yours would make a delightful mount—'

'You don't mince words.' I had to laugh at him. I mean, with the pair of us lying naked together under the canopy of the Tilly there was no time to appear shocked. I was rather enjoying the situation and his open talk, taken too with his hard lean body and his now limp but still impressive prick. As he appraised the size and shape of my breasts, he leaned over to caress them almost idly, toying with them, enjoying their feel. 'And did you titty-ride your adjutant's young daughter on her trip out to India in her school holidays?' I teased him.

'Of course,' he said naturally. 'I would have been neglecting my duty if I had not. Being keen but unversed as she was, I took it upon myself to service her properly, front, back and wherever. It was the way of things in the Indian Army, generally agreed that young gels be taught the rudiments. Make 'em fit to be proper wives later in life, you know, with no silly inhibitions if their future husbands demand satisfaction—'

'Front, back or wherever else?' I suggested saucily.

'Exactly,' he nodded cheerily. 'You understand me. Were you brought up in India, by any chance?'

'No,' I laughed. 'You really are the limit. No doubt you feel it your duty to teach me the rudiments though, Colonel. Not always on the hard floor of this truck, I hope—'

'We'll find an hotel tonight,' he promised lewdly. 'In the meantime, young lady, roll over on your front. I'd like to admire your bottom. Tits are splendid, but there's nothing like well-rounded buttocks for the real connoisseur. By Gad, yours are magnificent, girl,' he exulted as I turned myself over. 'Twin moons of marbled flesh, firm as flint with the most delightful crease between them. What pleasures are hidden in there, would you say?'

'No doubt you intend to find out,' I taunted him. 'I don't think you are nice to know, sir—'

'Quiet, girl,' he ordered. 'This is no time for levity. I have worshipped fine arses from Madras to the Hindu Kush. Yours would match any I've enjoyed. This is serious business.'

'Keep speaking like that,' I had to tell him, 'and you'll have me in a fit of giggling—'

His response was to fetch me a hard sharp smack across both raised cheeks. 'Behave,' he warned. 'It would not be the first time I've walloped a spirited girl into submission. Do you require your backside warmed?'

'No, sir,' I said meekly.

'Pity. It often increases the ardour,' he commented. 'Lie still now, girl.' I felt his hands glide sensuously over my bottom cheeks, smoothing, patting, fondling, the effect making me expectant and aroused. I awaited his pleasure. His face pushed between my moons, snuffling and sniffing at my core.

'Essence,' I heard him mumble. 'Reach back and part yourself, open those cheeks for me.' I did so, straining my neck in turning my head to see what he was up to. His tongue rasped the space between my anus and cunt, probed both orifices, lapped at me like a cat drinking

Sin and Mrs Saxon

milk. The tickling made me give a little moan and a leap and I was admonished by getting a further sharp slap across my bottom. Then his weight was over me and I felt the round bulb of his resurrected prick nudge between my thighs. I wanted desperately to hold it and direct it into my cunt. I was unable to do so because I was using both hands to part the cheeks on my buttocks.

'Fuck me,' I told him savagely. 'Put it up me and fuck me! Go on, it's what we both want. Fuck me do—'

'With pleasure,' he said meaningfully, his shaft sliding up into my eager recess beautifully, deep and thick and filling. I reared my bottom, feeling his hard stomach pressing into me, his balls slap-slapping in my cleave as he fucked me slowly and deliberately. He thrust in to the hilt then withdrew maddeningly to make me beg him to 'thrust it up my cunt harder, give it to me'. 'All in good time,' the lecherous sod promised, his hands going under my belly to grasp both my tits. 'First, I want to hear you squeal for it. Tell me how you love it and you'll let me fuck you whenever I want to. Say it!'

'You can fuck me anytime, only fuck me harder now,' I heard myself whine. 'Please, please, ram it up, keep it up!'

In truth he was playing with me like a hooked fish, with me squirming on the end of his hook, the rampant cylinder of flesh keeping me on the verge of my climax. To try to beat him at his game I worked my buttocks furiously into him, getting yet one more firm slap for disobedience. Then he settled his thrusting into a steady rhythm, poking me to the hilt. 'Go now, girl,' he ordered and, as if on command, I came in a series of wild undulations, crying out in relief. 'There now,' he said as my heaving body subsided somewhat. 'Wasn't that worth waiting for?' He was still hard within me, gently rubbing my outer lips with his stalk in slow movements.

'You didn't come,' I said, amazed at his prowess.

'Never until I'm ready,' he said matter-of-factly. 'It's a matter of will, taught to me by an Indian guru. Hindu women like and demand full satisfaction—'

'Well, don't waste it, fuck me again,' I offered, on my elbows and knees for him, his cock a tormenting inch or two up the entrance to my cunt. 'I wouldn't mind, in fact I'd like it. You've made me want it so—'

'Then we'll try something different,' he said. 'With such a nice bum on you, young woman, the temptation is great. Have you been buggered before – corked? It's a special pleasure—'

'Yours would be too big,' I complained. 'Fuck my cunt—'

'Nonsense. Don't lie now, girl. Have you been plugged?' I felt the knob of his cock leave me and trail upwards the inch or so required, pressing against my serrated anal ring. It gave inwards and his crest entered, just the bulbous head parting my rear hole. I gasped and remained still, getting a further inch or two eased gently but firmly up my back passage. The itch it gave me made me squirm and groan, then more was worked up me until I was fully contained, warmth and mass filling me. Aware of the throb in his shaft, I was terribly excited. For long moments he remained still inside me, then he started a slight movement which I reciprocated by moving my bottom back to meet his first tentative thrusts.

'How does that feel?' he asked. 'Good, I think—'

'How do you suppose it feels,' I grunted in reply, 'that huge thing up my back passage. You're a beast—'

'And you are a little minx who loves it,' Randall-Bude

Sin and Mrs Saxon

chided me. 'Not for the first time either, I'd say. Shall I take it out then?'

'No, no,' I said quickly. 'Now that it's in, leave it—'

'Good girl,' he praised. 'Admit it. Have no false modesty. My fondness for bum-tailing knows no bounds and I don't care who knows—'

'You are not on the receiving end,' I gasped. 'I feel full to the stomach—'

'Corked to the hilt,' he agreed, 'and taking it like a true maharajah's favourite concubine. The ladies of the regiment got a taste for this, fucking without the consequences of being made preggy while their husbands were away on frontier duty. I shall now thrust harder, girl. Are you ready?'

'Oh, yes,' I agreed, and his pumping into me commenced. My head rose on my neck and I brayed with the pleasure and the depravity of the act. I thrust hard back into his curved lap, balling my arse, taking his all. 'Beast, beast,' I croaked. 'You're fucking my bum, fucking my bum, you swine. You'll split me—' Then I was bucking wildly and he was shooting his volley deep inside me. When he withdrew it was like a cork popping from a bottle. I remained on my hands and knees, my head drooping, fucked to a frazzle as they say.

Back in the driving cab he was once again Colonel Randall-Bude, businesslike and disciplined, reprimanding me for grinding the gears and calling me nothing but 'Mackenzie'. This from the man who had just taken me front and back, and I realised I enjoyed the hold he had over me. I like strong men, and knew I was his for him to use and abuse as he wished. At least it made for interesting service as a humble Wren – or, rather, Leading Wren I remembered with pleasure.

Chapter Eleven
AMERICA

Novice at film-making as I was, I had assumed that the shooting script would be followed from the first scene to the last. This was not the case. I had come prepared to do the opening scene in the shower, but was informed that would be shot later in Ziggy's apartment, using his bathroom and bedroom to save building a set. Other scenes had already 'gone into the can' as the film-makers called it – such as outside shots of the driver in his van and his approach to the house plus any other exterior scenes. Time was money, and the sooner an actor's part had been filmed and he was paid off, so much the better. As Peter had pointed out, Ziggy's expert editing, cutting and splicing would finally bring it all together from start to finish.

The studios in Yonkers had been a large warehouse in its time. Now, as I was led in by Peter and Ziggy, I saw that areas had been 'boxed off' into sets, one of them a perfect replica of a typical suburban kitchen where the real action was to take place. All around were cameras, boom microphones and overhead lights, with the film crew busily arranging their equipment. On canvas chairs awaiting their call were my fellow actors: the juvenile-

Sin and Mrs Saxon

looking Melvin, who grinned wickedly at me, a lovely girl in her late teens and a handsome black man I took to be Damon Butler. All were wearing dressing gowns as if prepared to strip to order. I was quickly introduced to them in turn, Damon offering his huge hand, rising to well over six feet in height and proportioned to match. My stomach fluttered to think that almost right away this complete stranger, a perfect specimen of the negro race, was going to fuck me before the assembled crew.

'Off to the make-up department with you, honey,' Ziggy said impatiently, cutting short the introductions. This, I found, was a table full of cosmetics, two old barber's chairs and a large mirror fastened to the wall. The make-up man indicated I should sit down and wrapped a cloth about my neck. Then he stood behind me, hands raised like an artist surveying an unfinished portrait. Ziggy decided for him. 'Black wig and spectacles,' he ordered. 'That's all that's needed—'

'Shame to cover up that glorious burnished hair,' argued his make-up man. 'It will look great shot in colour—'

'She looks too damn good to be a frustrated housewife,' Ziggy opined. 'Black wig and big round glasses, that's all we need here. When he's through, honey,' he added to me, 'get out of your clothes and join us. You want a coffee or a shot of something—?'

'No,' I said, my hair being tied up and the black wig fitted over my head.

'Good. Now where's that goddam continuity girl?'

'Here, Mr Kaplan,' said a tall thin girl with her hair tied up in a top-knot, dressed in a jacket and skirt and a silk scarf knotted at her neck. She carried a copy of the script, flipping it open and standing beside me as the make-up man pencilled my eyebrows to match my wig.

'You know we're about to shoot Scene Twenty-seven?' she enquired of me. 'I guess you have if you've studied your part, but I'll go over it with you. There'll be no rehearsal, Mr Kaplan will explain what he wants between cuts. Basically the scene opens with you and the delivery boy making out on the kitchen table. He's on top to start with, but you change positions later and are mounting him—'

I gulped and nodded, hoping the flush I felt did not show on my face. She spoke as if directing me to a bus stop, very businesslike, as though discussing 'making out' and such was perfectly normal. The make-up man did not falter in his work either, using a soft brush on my cheeks. 'Yes,' I said, finding my voice and sounding strangely hoarse.

'Good,' said the girl. 'Then you are joined by the black driver who leads your daughter into the kitchen. You look at them in momentary surprise, but are too engrossed with the delivery boy to halt or protest. The arrivals then make out right beside you on that table. I hope it can stand it all right. Props says it will. Mr Kaplan will probably come up with some new ideas about all this, but that is the scene so far. There'll be some breaks in filming, of course—'

'Yes,' was all I could say again.

'Then we go into the switch,' she announced. 'The delivery boy moves over to have the daughter. The driver will lift you on to the kitchen counter and take you in that position, with you sitting and him standing in front of you. Sometime in this scene you'll hold on to his neck and he'll lift you up, pull you clear of the counter and bear your weight, still coupled with you. Your legs will be around his waist, of course. Damon is very strong, you get the idea?'

'Vividly,' I admitted.

'That's right on, then. Hand cameras will be operating close, taking in your action and that of the other couple. We hope to can it in one long take. Damon will lower you before the sink, turning you so that you present your buttocks to him. You will hold on tightly to the faucets while he's inside you. Do you allow anal penetration in your work?' She gave me a brief smile. 'Mr Kaplan has probably mentioned that to you for this action at the sink—'

'No, he didn't,' I said.

'Well, you can discuss that matter with him. Then it's orgasms all around, cum shots added, and that's it. The two men dress and leave, with mom and daughter remaining naked and completely sated in the kitchen as we fade out. You got all that?'

'No doubt I will—'

The girl smiled briefly again, walking away towards the kitchen set. The make-up man drew the sheet from my neck and handed me a pair of large round spectacles. 'See what you think, doll,' he said and I stood up to see a strange face in the tarnished mirror – black hair with a fringe, owl-like glasses, my fresh complexion replaced by a light tan.

'The lady next door,' he said proudly. 'No one would know ya.' From the pocket of his white overall he brought out a flat bottle of Jack Daniels whiskey, offering it to me. I took it gladly, tilting the bottle to my lips and swallowing a long draught to gain courage for my acting debut. The strong spirit burned my throat, heated my belly and emboldened me tremendously.

Sin and Mrs Saxon

We were joined by an agitated Ziggy. 'What the Jesus is going on? We're waiting on the set and you two are drinking on the job.'

'Just giving the little lady a booster, Mr Kaplan,' said the make-up man. I winked at him, raised the bottle and he nodded, so I took another long swig, growing mellower and more relaxed as the liquid fire suffused my innards. My whole being glowed. Ziggy took the bottle from me and led me away to the set.

'You should be out of your clothes by now,' he complained, directing me to a door in a box-like structure. 'Your dressing room, Miss Gluck; get in there and undress, pronto. I want you on call right away. Jesus, this production is costing big bucks, I expect cooperation—'

'And you'll get it, Ziggy, you old dirty film-maker,' I told him, made cheerful by the whisky, beginning to enjoy the experience. 'Fucking, sucking, you're the boss. You want me with my clothes off, you got it. Anal penetration too, I understand. That's naughty—'

'Get in there with you,' he laughed shortly. 'I'm expecting great things from you. Just a minute or two now,' he warned.

In the dressing room the dark-haired young girl who was to act the daughter was sitting and smoking a hand-rolled reefer. 'Hello, mom,' she smiled. 'I guess we're in this together, Julie and Darleen. What we do to earn the bread to try to make it as actresses! Have you seen what Damon's got?'

'The young black actor? No, I haven't.'

She held her hands apart a good twelve inches, like a fisherman describing a catch.

'You're exaggerating,' I responded, liking the girl. I

Sin and Mrs Saxon

stepped out of my dress so as not to disturb my wig. She watched me unhook my bra, pursing her mouth as if impressed.

'Not exaggerating one inch,' she giggled. 'I've already done the scene where I'm peeking through the door into the kitchen, watching you and the delivery boy fucking. Damon comes up behind me to feel my cunt and I get his dick out. I can tell you he is *huge*. In this next scene we've cast off our clothes, a see-through nightdress in my case, and come through to join you on the kitchen table—'

'So I've been informed,' I said, standing naked before her. She rose to walk around me, admiring, coming back to face me and reach out to hold one of my breasts gently.

'God, but you are a beautiful woman,' she said. 'I wish I had tits like yours.' She pulled apart her dressing gown, revealing neat pear-shaped breasts with unbelievably long nipples. 'Don't touch them,' she asked as I couldn't resist wanting to give one a pinch. 'They're false. Ziggy Kaplan thought my nipples weren't prominent enough, so had the make-up man paste these over them. Long, aren't they?'

I chuckled at the idea. 'I've heard of false fingernails, false eyelashes, padded bras, but that's a new one on me. They look so real,' I said, inspecting them.

'You don't need them,' the girl said softly, both her hands at my tits and gently pinching my nipples. 'You have such gorgeous breasts and long nipples. Do you mind this? Are you gay?'

'A little merry,' I admitted. 'I've had several good long swallows at the make-up man's bottle of Jack Daniels to relax myself. Does it show?'

'Gay,' the girl laughed, her curls tossing. She was indeed a pretty thing and temptingly close with her dressing gown open, revealing her neat slim figure, her pointy breasts with the false nipples and dark patch of hair at her crotch. 'Gay is what we call ourselves now in these so-called swinging sixties. We're coming out of the closet, saying what we are. Lesbians, homosexuals.' Her cool hands cupped my breasts, squeezed them sensuously. 'Are you with us?' She looked at me slyly. 'I've made your nipples erect doing this, haven't I?'

'Much as I'd like to continue, my dear,' I said huskily. 'I think Ziggy would prefer us on stage. If you are that way entirely, doesn't making these porno films go against your own sexual preference? I mean having to let men—'

'Fuck me?' nodded the bright young thing. 'I'm an actress so I go through the motions. I prefer doing lesbian scenes, but beggars can't be choosers. I would like to make love to you very much. Do you know the gay women's bar in Greenwich Village? Why don't you come along there one evening—'

Any response I might have made to this offer was interrupted by Ziggy banging on the door. 'Are you broads still alive in there?' he shouted. 'Get your arses out here—'

'He's so refined,' laughed the girl, pressing herself to me quickly and kissing my mouth. 'We could make such lovely love together, mom. I'll give you my number—' Her breasts flattened against mine and she rotated them against my globes.

'Watch out for those false nipples,' I warned her.

'You haven't seen anything yet,' she giggled. 'Wait till you get a load of Damon.'

Sin and Mrs Saxon

I did shortly afterwards on the kitchen set. He wore just a dressing gown as he took directions from Ziggy who was sitting in a director's canvas chair. Melvin and I waited while the props man made last-minute adjustments to the scene: putting the stepladder in place before the high cupboard and laying the delivery boy's uniform on the kitchen floor along with the short houserobe I'd supposedly been wearing on going downstairs. I felt naked as never before with the eyes of at least a dozen people on me. Melvin gave me a lewd wink. 'You look great, fit to fuck,' he said, grinning. 'Just let me at you, we'll make a great movie—' In the crowd of faces behind the director's chair I saw Peter Gulay, giving me a thumbs-up sign.

A sound-effects man in earphones and a microphone on a long pole hovered near. This was it. 'Right,' bawled Ziggy, sounding relieved. 'This is a shoot. Sound man keep your mike out of the frame, any noises we want we can add later on the soundtrack. You two up there, Melvin and Miss Gluck, get in a clinch and make it hot. The delivery boy has felt you up on the ladder, the pair of you have thrown off your clothes. Take it from there. I want the two of you at each other like sex maniacs and then fucking across the table. Convince me—'

Melvin shrugged off his dressing gown, ready for action. Between his legs reared a huge erect prick, impossibly thick and long for his boyish frame. He strutted about with it bobbing before him while I covered my mouth to prevent bursting with laughter. 'They wanted a well-hung delivery boy,' Melvin grinned. 'This is fantasy land, pussy cat, there are no small dongs in skin-flicks. You like it?'

I was not unaquainted with false pricks but this looked

entirely the real thing and grossly out of proportion on Melvin's youthful body. False nipples, so why not false dicks, I reasoned, bending to inspect the thing. It was indeed a masterpiece of the make-up man's art, fixed over Melvin's own equipment with no joins showing, a rearing monster of a shaft and heavy balls perfectly matching the tone of his skin, the plum head complete with eye. 'Give the balls a little squeeze,' Melvin invited. I did so and was surprised when a jet of thick goo exactly like male come spurted out.

'This is a goddam shoot,' Ziggy bawled again and Melvin grabbed me. A clapperboard man shouted 'Scene Twenty-seven, Take One,' snapped his clapper in front of us and hopped off the stage. Melvin immediately drew my mouth to his, forcing his tongue between my teeth, his hand grasping at one of my breasts. Remembering to act the part of a lust-crazed older woman, I moaned loudly and returned the wet slobbering kiss as if desperate to go along with the randy boy's urgent desires. I pushed his head down forcefully as if seeking his mouth on my nipples. Veteran of many such films, no doubt, Melvin rubbed his face between my cleavage, giving my breasts little bites, then suckled on me with tremendous force, pulling the flesh into his mouth. His hand was between my thighs, his fingers inserted in my pussy. My writhing was no act. I was aroused for real.

As he finger-fucked me, still nuzzling at my breasts, I was forced back until my buttocks pressed against the table set in the centre of the kitchen. My hand had gone down instinctively to grasp his prick. The dummy he wore was thick and lifelike though lacking the warmth and throb of the real article. All the same it was long,

Sin and Mrs Saxon

hard and cylindrical, the next best thing in my wanton state.

'Fuck me, boy!' I cried, lolling back on the table, parting my legs and raising my knees. 'Fuck me with your big prick right now! Fuck it all into my cunt! Do it, do it!' Even in my excitement I noticed a man with a shoulder-held camera crawling on the floor towards us, the lens pointing directly up between my open thighs for a close-up of my cunt. As if made lewder by the thought, I reached down and parted the outer lips with my fingers. Then Melvin was moving over me, up on the table with his knees on either side of my waist.

His eyes and flushed face, showed me he was no longer acting a part. He gripped my breasts at their sides, pushing them tightly together to make a channel for the big dildo he wore, moving his hips as if fucking my tits. 'Suck!' he ordered, the crown of the dildo pushing up above my cleavage and nudging my chin. I dutifully inclined my head forward, so eager for a prick in my mouth that for a moment I forgot it wasn't the real thing. The shape was certainly the same, if larger than life, but the plastic shaft was dry and tasteless. I recalled that I would be taking its length up me in the scene and lubricated it with my saliva. Then I gave the life-like balls a squeeze in my excitement and in turn received a mouthful of condensed milk and warm water. It filled my throat and dribbled from my lips, sticky and sweet, covering the huge dildo's crown and dribbling into the cleavage of my tits.

'Fill me with *that*. Fuck, fuck!' I heard myself begging. As Melvin drew back over me I reached between his thighs and guided the plastic prick to my pussy lips. One heave of my pelvis and it was embedded deep inside me,

Sin and Mrs Saxon

my legs automatically curling around Melvin's waist, ankles locking across the small of his back. My hands reached for his taut buttocks, aiding him in his thrusts by hauling each cheek forward as he fucked me with vigorous inward strokes. I was on the verge of a terrific come, wanting to continue, when I heard Ziggy's voice bawling out a direction that we change position. Melvin rolled sideways and I mounted him, still impaled on the dildo, then Damon and my supposed daughter were on the table beside us, her legs over his shoulders and moaning each time he lunged into her.

Director, camera crew, the man below us taking close-ups from his vantage point under the table, all were forgotten as I rode the monster dick, squirming down and rotating on Melvin's thighs, moaning, keening, my head thrown back and my tits flying, bobbing, leaping on my chest. I shuddered violently in a continuous spasm of climaxes, then the girl acting my daughter was sitting up beside me riding her big black stud. As we fucked together on our mounts, as if by agreement thrusting down in perfecting timing, she reached across to pull me close. One hand clasped my right tit as her mouth clamped over mine, kissing me lewdly, unable to restrain herself.

This was not any part of the script but, beyond all reason now, I returned her mouthing lewdly. Our tongues entwined and lapped, our wet lips sucked and crushed together. Ziggy's next shouts went unheeded until I realised Melvin was pushing me off and pulling my daughter to the table to mount her. In a daze, unsure of my next move, I was lifted bodily by Damon, the athletic young black. He carried me over to the kitchen counter and plonked my bare bottom on the formica top with a

Sin and Mrs Saxon

slap. I steadied myself by putting my arms around his neck, my face to his handsome features, breasts flattened to his chest, legs wide apart. Before he fixed his lips to mine, I glanced down to see his hugely engorged black prick with its egg-sized purplish knob poised to penetrate me.

'Oh, oooh yes,' I murmured against his mouth, tilting my eager cunt to feel the plum head part my outer lips. He needed no enhancement, wielding a weapon of enormous girth and length. It was as rigid as blue steel after his bout with my daughter. As he moved his hips I thought what was entering me would reach my throat. I groaned as the magnificent stalk filled me up, nudging my cervix, driving me wild with its sensuous hot mass. I jerked to his thrusts, undulating my hips, then he was pulling my legs around his waist, lifting me clear of the counter, standing upright with me clinging and bobbing on his cock. His large hands were cupped under my bottom cheeks, a finger pressing into my rear hole. I whined in a fever of pain/pleasure, grinding my rear down on the invading digit. I was pierced at both orifices and jerking out of control, cunt and arse boiling over with the heat spreading up to my belly. Then Damon lowered my feet to the floor, turning me to face the sink, pushing me forward.

The script was superfluous in my condition. I wanted that prick up me again desperately. I was begging for it. To grip the taps before me, the faucets as they are called there, seemed entirely the natural thing to do. Damon's hand was between my buttock cleft, stroking and poking, a finger and thumb inserted in cunt and bum. To aid him I reached back, grasping a cheek in each hand and pulling them apart to their fullest.

A glance over my shoulder showed Melvin and the girl screwing away on the table top and Damon poised behind me with the inevitable close-range cameraman hovering; another lay flat on the floor behind us. 'Steady, honey, this is it,' I heard Damon breathe into my neck. 'Take a good grip on those faucets—' I drew in my breath, and tried to relax my hindquarters, then his knob was at my serrated ring, pushing gently but insistently, forcing its entry. My groan as the extended length slid up my back passage was no act. Filled with hot flesh taut as an iron bar, I flinched and drew in my flanks. 'Oh, no, babe, you're taking this right up,' I heard Damon say harshly, giving me a smart slap on my hip. If he was acting, I was a Dutchman!

His thrusts against me were no act either, I concluded, for once embedded in me with his balls slapping in the valley of my arse, he went full throttle, regardless of my cries, squawks and throaty entreaties. 'You beast, that thing is right up my poor bum. You're splitting me!' I cried but I was getting used to the hot mass up me and settled into a rhythm with his thrusts. I balled my rump back into his lap and my cries changed to pleasurable grunts as I urged him on, the pair of us humping like dog and bitch. My bottom was going like the proverbial fiddler's elbow in my throes. He gripped my hips tightly, rose on tip-toe and fucked away . I felt his quickening pace, he gave a loud cry and shot wads of hot unction into me as he lost all control. For long moments I lay across the sink, sated and fucked to excess, not caring what spectacle I presented. Damon withdrew his cock from me with a plop like a cork coming from a bottle and moved away to gather up Melvin's discarded delivery boy's uniform. The pair of them left the scene.

I couldn't move, which was just as well as the cameramen came in close to capture me with hanging tits, buttocks tilted and widely parted, my insides still spasming with the feel of Damon's great prick and my abused anus gaping and trickling out his copious discharge. On the table nearby the girl playing my daughter lay supine too, arse up and fucked out to all intents and purposes. But when Ziggy shouted 'Cut, that was a take!' she immediately rose like the professional she was and came across to me solicitously. I straightened up nodding when she enquired if I was all right. Damon and Melvin reappeared too in their dressing gowns, coffee cups in hand.

'Of course she's fine,' said Ziggy admiringly. 'You all did great. One long take too. You guys shouldn't expect to be paid for that romp. From where I was standing you were all having a ball—'

'Talking of being paid,' Melvin said, 'hows about an advance? Seeing as how we did so well, something up front before we pack in for today—'

'That goes for me too,' Damon said. 'I'm sure these girls would like to see some folding money for their labours. Make with some dough, Zig, or you got half a movie on your hands—'

'I'd love to,' Ziggy protested. 'But as Toulouse Lautrec always said, I'm a little short. You people will get paid, have no fears.'

Peter Dulay brought me a coffee as I sat listening to this talk, amused by the Americanisms of the conversation. After the break other shots were taken, short takes to fill in the gaps – my letting Melvin in at the back door and talking to daughter Darleen at her bedroom door – then Peter took me to Ziggy's apartment for the shower and masturbation scene. It was late evening before he drove me home to my apartment, one thousand dollars richer for my day's work. Peter had made him pay up.

'You did great,' he said. 'Ziggy wants you for other epics he's got in mind. I also put to him the little scheme I've worked out to get back at the Lefarges and he agreed. More of that later. Right now I'm due on night duty at the reception desk.'

As I left him after parking his car, I slipped a roll of notes in his hand. 'For services rendered,' I said. 'No argument, Peter. It was a fun day, but I've done it and will retire from the porno flick scene while I'm ahead. I've a feeling my husband has been phoning me, so I'll be there if he calls again.'

'Christ, this is five hundred bucks,' Peter said, protesting.

'Pay me back when you're a big movie star then,' I laughed. 'Right now I need my bed, it's been a hectic day. Damon is a big boy, I need sleep.'

'He enjoyed having you, lucky swine,' Peter said. 'Even the girl fancied you. That scene where you were kissing and fondling when going at it on top of Melvin and Damon, wow! Ziggy got his money's worth there—'

'She's invited me to a club for lesbian ladies,' I told him. 'Do you think I should go—?'

'Honestly, Diana,' he laughed. 'I'm sure you will. I've never met a woman like you. Your husband is one lucky guy.' He took me in his arms and kissed me fondly, then passionately. 'One lucky guy,' he repeated.

'One *absent* guy,' I said wickedly, aroused by his kissing, his hands at my breasts. 'What time do you get off duty in the morning, young man?'

'Six,' he grinned. 'Would you care for an early morn-

Sin and Mrs Saxon

ing call? We could discuss what I've got in mind to get your own back on the Lefarges.'

'That,' I said, turning to leave, 'is not exactly what I had in mind—' Back in my apartment I had a call from my sister Jennifer in Scotland, excitedly announcing she would be flying in to New York the following day. Soon after, Harry called from Rome and about to leave for Africa.

'I rang you several times today, love,' he said. 'I take it you were out. I'm glad you're not stuck at home alone. Did you have a nice day?'

Looking back on the day's events after we had talked, told each other how we were missing each other, I decided it had been a very satisfactory day. Paid handsomely for being pleasured so greatly appealed to my sense of humour, wanton woman that I am. I went to bed looking forward to Peter's visit next morning and then meeting again with my favourite sister after so many years.

Chapter Twelve
ENGLAND

Glorious sunny weather continued throughout that summer of 1940 and I drove Colonel Randall-Bude to every corner of the island. I shared his bed at night in the cottage he had rented on the outskirts of Carisbrooke. By then his presence as a trouble-shooter, ensuring that the local defences were on full alert, was well known. Gun sites and concrete fire positions dotted the island and his arrival at any outpost was hardly unexpected. I was given meals by the army and on most nights was tucked up in bed along with the colonel, whose appetite for sex in all its forms never diminished. A man who liked his vice-versa, you could say, my bottom got little rest from his attentions.

When the first big daylight air raid occurred at the end of June, he was actually up me, unable to resist having me under the canopy of the truck after a picnic lunch taken at a quiet spot on the downs. I was on my knees as usual, facing out of the rear of the Tilly, being buggered when dozens of aircraft passed over, chevron after chevron of them in vee formations, anti-aircraft shells bursting among them. The gallant Randall-Bude, like Drake with his game of bowls, continued sodomising me

Sin and Mrs Saxon

until we were both groaning out our helpless pleasure and vibrating in our climaxes. 'It has started,' he reckoned as we both finished. Over the next month or so the Battle of Britain took place in cloudless skies over our heads as we drove around the island defences.

Aircraft of both sides were shot down frequently. Once a German bomber flew over in flames and the crew parachuted out. The colonel ordered me to drive foot down on the accelerator to where they had landed. He leapt out, pistol to hand, to round them up, then the three surly German airmen were packed in my truck's rear and taken to a nearby village pub where Randall-Bude telephoned for the Military Police to collect the prisoners of war. It was lunchtime and the local farm workers were enjoying a pint and bread and cheese as a break from the harvesting. I noted the Germans looking about with surprise, expecting to find a population in panic. 'In two or three weeks,' the arrogant pilot said to me, 'our army will come and we will be free again.' But the summer passed into autumn and the Germans never came and my job driving for randy Randall-Bude came to an end.

In September I drove him to Albany Barracks for a meeting with a brigadier who was his senior officer. Dropping him there, I took the Tilly into the motor pool, the covered workshop where I had first encountered the faithful little truck. Emerging from a small closed-off office, Sergeant Reg Courtney came out to greet me. 'So how has it been running?' he asked. 'Could use a new set of tyres, I see. I'll have a look at the engine too. Same arrangement as last time?' he asked cheekily. 'I've had no leave this summer and haven't dipped my wick for ages. Fancy a fuck?'

Sin and Mrs Saxon

'You're such a smoothie, Reg,' I told him. All the same I liked the idea of a good ride with the young man as much as getting new tyres and an engine overhaul. We worked together for several hours, then I went to the women's barrack and took a shower, returning to find the workshop empty except for Reg leaning against the Tilly. We got under the canopy, kissing and fondling, wriggling out of our uniforms, eager to get at each other. Naked and very erect, he held up a condom, which I rolled over his rigid shaft. 'You should be having this done by your wife,' I teased him. He did have a big one. 'What would she say if she knew I was putting this Frenchie on you—?'

'Knowing her, somebody will be stuffing her cunt,' Reg said easily. 'Wouldn't have her any other way either. She loves the prick same as you. Christ, you're lubricated, wet as a damp sponge,' he added, feeling my cunt. 'You can't beat a good juiced-up quim to get stuck into. On your back—'

That made a nice change from the colonel, whose favourite expression both for drinking and fucking was 'bottoms up,' invariably taking me on my elbows and knees, buttocks raised, whether employing my arsehole or cunt as a receptacle for his insatiable lust. Sergeant Reg took a less direct route, fancying himself as a great lover, God's gift to women. He gave full attention to every bit of me, long tongue-probing kisses while caressing my tits, nipple sucking, sliding down between my open thighs to lick me out expertly, making me utter groans of sheer pleasure and urging him shamelessly to shove it up, fuck me, make me come. I loved it all. I had a grasp of his prick, trying in desperation to haul it between my legs. All the time he spoke to me in the crudest terms, insisting I reply in similar vein.

'You horny little cow,' he said as I lifted my cunt to his fingering and jerked my pelvis wildly against his hand. 'Don't you just fucking love it. I can feel your fanny throbbing to take my dick. Beg for it, say you want a good fucking—'

'I do, you know I do, so fuck me, fill my cunt!' I pleaded, wanting his prick up me more than anything in the world such was the frenzy of my excitement. Receiving it, feeling the long hard length penetrate me, brought an immediate gasp of relief from my throat. I cradled him in my thighs, locked my legs around his waist, hauled on his arse, and fucked back at his thrusts, climaxing in helpless shudders. Still I craved more of his prick. Beneath the army blankets on which we lay, the hard floor of the truck rubbed my shoulders as I lifted my whole body to take his all. Then Reg was grunting and mouthing that he was coming, coming up me! His flanks thrust rapidly in his last throes, balls and belly slapping against me. Our exertions slowed down till we both lay sprawled out, sated.

'What the devil is this, then?' I heard an irate voice snap officiously. Looking up, I saw Colonel Randall-Bude standing by the lowered tailboard eyeing us, face set and moustache bristling. Beside him, looking on with interest, stood a full Brigadier-General, brass hat, Sam Browne belt and briefcase, the complete War Office warrior.

The sight of two very senior officers confronting us was too much for Sergeant Courtney, regular soldier that he was. He scrambled out of the rear of the truck, bollock naked from our session, standing rigidly at attention before his superiors with the now crinkled and soiled French letter dangling from his limp dick. Despite the apparent seriousness of the situation I had to stifle a giggle at the sight. More decorously, I wrapped my nakedness in one of the army blankets and got out to join the sergeant, facing the wrath of Randall-Bude for my obvious lack of discipline – and for fucking with someone else apart from him. The Brigadier-General, I noted, was attempting to suppress a sly grin, amused by the situation.

'Sergeant Courtney, 525667, Hampshire Regiment, SIR!' spat out the unfortunate Reg, reporting himself, attempting to click his bare ankles together. 'I was servicing this here truck—'

'And my bloody driver, too, while you were at it, *Private*,' said Randall-Bude summarily. 'Get some clothes on, man, and remove that slimy object from your tool. Out of my sight before I throw the book at you. I'll deal with this young woman later—'

'What charge did you have in mind, Colonel?' asked the Brigadier-General, smiling. 'Being out of uniform? I must say I've rarely seen anyone more out of uniform.' Sergeant Courtney grabbed his discarded uniform and fled, leaving me clutching the blanket, trying to keep it over my tits but not being very successful. 'So this is the navy driver you've been telling me about,' he added, stroking his moustache, eyes regarding me lewdly. Men!

'Into the back of the truck with you, Mackenzie,' ordered Randall-Bude, 'Brigadier-General Sir Bernard Cloote will be my guest tonight at the cottage, so I shall drive. When we arrive you will prepare supper for us. Regarding your quite disgraceful conduct of this evening, I shall consider suitable punishment appropriate to the event. Demotion, loss of your Leading Wren rating perhaps, if reported to your base at HMS *Medina*. Think on that, young woman—'

I did think on it. I was proud of the anchor badge sewn to my sleeve and reluctant to lose the promotion. That, however, I doubted, knowing full well that the carnal colonel would have something more to his taste in store for me. As the truck bounced about to his speedy driving on the way to the cottage, I tried to dress myself, fumbling with bra and knickers while being thrown around in the rear. On arrival I rushed indoors, still half-dressed, going upstairs to get into uniform and report myself ready for all eventualities later. I made a cold meat salad, served the two of them, cleared away the plates and ate my meal in the kitchen while hearing them guffawing over their port and brandy in the dining room.

That they were discussing me I had no doubt. 'Game little filly,' I heard the Brigadier-General say. 'A beauty too. Fine tits and arse on her from what I saw. You've no doubt put her to the cock, Randall-Bude, being with her all summer. I'm well aware you Indian Army johnnies roger anything that has an arse. You *have* buggered her, I presume – fully corked the little piece?'

'Once or twice,' admitted Randall-Bude modestly. 'I have thrown the occasional fuck in her direction, both front and back, of course. She's all for it, as you were made aware this evening. Takes it like a trooper, enjoys the tradesman's entrance as much as the regular route. Fine girl—'

'Cunt and gunpowder,' said old Cloote, 'with the odd arse to plug just for variety. What more could a soldier want?'

I tapped at the door of the dining room and entered,

Sin and Mrs Saxon

presenting myself. 'If there's nothing else you require tonight, sir,' I said. 'I shall go to my room—'

'First there's the little question of suitable punishment for your outrageous behaviour today,' Randall-Bude said snidely. 'I have no wish to blot your service record over the lapse witnessed by both the Brigadier-General and myself, but you must agree to some act of contrition for your conduct.'

'What would that be, sir?' I asked apprehensively.

'Damme, yes,' said Cloote, almost rubbing his hands together at the thought. 'Let's hear it, Randall-Bude—'

'A good bottom warming,' said my superior officer. 'Drawers fully down and the posterior presented smartly to receive its due, six or so of the best while the recipient bends forward over a chair. In India it was found most effective for taming wayward girls, daughters of the regiment and even wives when necessary, painful duty though it was—'

'For the females especially,' I dared say. 'If I agree then, would that be me off the hook—?' I unhooked my blue serge navy skirt, letting it fall to the floor. There was a mounting excitement in my loins.

'The matter will be closed,' Randall-Bude said unctuously. 'Grip the arms of that chair, Mackenzie, and bend forward. There. Brigadier-General Cloote will remain as witness to ensure the punishment is not unduly severe.'

Pompous buggers, I thought, knowing they were both eager to see my bare bottom. I felt Randall-Bude ease my knickers down over my knees to the carpet. Bum up, I awaited the first blow, tensing my bottom cheeks. 'Gad, what a splendid arse on that girl,' I heard Cloote say in admiration. 'Such round cheeks, so matched and

Sin and Mrs Saxon

perfect. I could think of better things to do than thrash it, Colonel—'

Randall-Bude undoubtedly intended to have the best of both options. I howled out and clenched my backside as his trouser belt, wrapped around his hand with a foot or so of its end hanging free, cracked across both cheeks. I counted six, then seven, flailing my bum and heating it like a fire before he stopped. 'To your room now, girl,' he ordered, and in a daze of hurt pride, humiliation and a glow spreading from my arse to my cunt, I picked up my skirt and knickers and ran from the room. I went to a spare bedroom and inspected my red bottom cheeks in the wardrobe mirror. Then I climbed into the big feather bed stark naked and awaited the arrival of the no doubt aroused colonel. I played with myself idly, anticipating.

It was dusk before he appeared, having no doubt finished off the port and brandy with his general before retiring. 'So here you are,' he said, 'I wondered where you'd got to. How is your bottom, girl?'

'Still warming me up,' I giggled wickedly. 'You had better do something about it—'

'Do what you like,' he said, pulling off his uniform shirt and trousers, tugging off his shoes. 'For once I feel like sleeping – must be getting old.' He pulled aside the sheet and lay beside me naked and yawning.

'Too much port and brandy,' I said, determined to have my way with him for a change. 'Don't you dare sleep, damn you, getting me worked up, making me show my bare bum to you two lechers—' It was one of those autumn nights, not dark and still hot with the heat of day when bedcovers were stifling. I leaned over to kiss his mouth, probing my tongue to his throat, tasting the port and brandy fumes. Next I draped my breasts over

Sin and Mrs Saxon

his face, my hand reaching down and finding a welcome hardening of his large prick. I rubbed gently, feeling it stiffen and lengthen in my grasp. I heard his pleased sighs, felt his hand pushing my head downwards to his crotch. My cheek resting on his flat hard stomach, I pulled the upright cock to my mouth and sucked, desiring it in my cunt once my lips and tongue had raised it to full rigidity.

'Mount me, girl,' he mumbled. 'You do the work tonight. Sit on it, squat over my prick, impale your body on me. Feed it in your cunt, use me—'

I straddled his thighs, my tits falling forward to his cupped hands, delving between my parted thighs to hold and direct his knob to my cunt lips. I pressed down as it gained entrance, squirming to accept it all, feeling its length and girth sliding up me until the heavy balls nestled in the fork of my crotch. It felt so good in my aching channel, like a complete blockage way back to the pit of my stomach. I sat bolt upright so that it reared straight up, a tormenting but delightful feeling in my belly.

My bottom moved back and forth, jiggling the big stalk inside me and he pushed up against me, hoisting his pelvis to penetrate deeper if possible. 'You're fucking me, girl,' he groaned. 'Raping me—' The idea obviously appealed to him but I wanted a submissive body under me. I slapped hard at his hip, ordering him to lie still, then continued my motion alone, shifting to get a subtle difference in the angle of penetration. I raised myself on the balls of my feet until only his crest was in me before I ground down over the whole length. 'Oh, you lovely dirty little bitch,' my mount grunted as my bottom thrust down repeatedly on his crotch. 'Using me like this—'

Sin and Mrs Saxon

'Getting my own back,' I told him sternly, 'and don't you dare come until I tell you.' He pulled me forward, his mouth reaching for my juddering tits, seeking a nipple. His hands tightened on my hips as I felt the surge of an impending explosion in my cunt. I was bent over him, riding like a jockey on the final run-in. Then I felt a presence behind me, an extra weight on the bed. Turning my head, I saw Brigadier-General Sir Bernard Cloote kneeling up at my rear, out of uniform and short of breath in his agitated state. Leaning over Randall-Bude as I was, fucking with quickening movements, my bottom was on offer to the new arrival. His hand went in my cleft, stroking and fingering the length of my parted buttocks, exciting me more with the thought that two men were at me. A finger pierced my arsehole, adding to my wild writhing as I bucked and came fiercely, urging them to continue.

Then Cloote was over my arched back, a hard prick nudging between my cheeks. 'I must, I just must, so help me!' gurgled the general, seeking my tight serrated ring by directing his knob to it. To aid him, I reached back to pull my cheeks wide apart and felt the plum head enter my behind, to be followed a moment later by a long thin cylinder of flesh, making me groan loudly. The two men in me, front and back, were now almost face to face over my shoulder, conversing too. 'I'm right up her, to the hilt, by Gad,' cried old Cloote. 'Tight as a fish's arse. A nun's bum!'

'Then plug the little trollop's bottom hole properly,' enthused Randall-Bude. 'Reem her out, cork her arsehole, sir! Fuck her rigid from behind while I roger her quim for her. By the deuce, I can feel your cock nudging mine in there. Have you ever enjoyed such a

Sin and Mrs Saxon

bout with a game little bitch before—?'

'Never!' was the reply as the general buggered away at me while my cunt was now being pounded lustily by the aroused Randall-Bude. It was true, too, that their pricks were meeting in their inward thrusts, just a thin membrane inside me separating the two cocks. The feeling I received was indescribable, making me thrash about wildly between them. I raised my head and neighed like a horse, gabbling the most unintelligible sounds as I came in a long spasm of climaxes, both my arse and cunt seemingly on fire.

Then all three of us ceased our thrusting and heaving. We rolled apart on the bed and gasped for air. On my back, I felt goo trickling out from my back passage from the buggering I'd received. My stomach and breasts were sticky and wet with Randall-Bude's emission where he had heaved out of me at the last second to jet his come harmlessly over my body.

We were fucked-out and spent and fell asleep in moments. When I awoke it was to find myself half-draped across Randall-Bude, my breasts on the upper thigh of his left leg, his big flaccid prick beside my face. My bottom was upward, my cunt pressed to the wrinkled sheet below me. In a moment of naughty impulse I reached out with my tongue and gently licked the curled cock resting on the balls of the sleeping man. To my great delight and amusement it gave the merest jerk, lifting slightly, inviting further kisses and licking. Behind me I felt warm breath in the split of my arse, the cheeks being parted, and the tickle of the Brigadier-General's heavy moustache and wet mouth pressed to my rear-directed cunt. A long tongue rasped over my outer lips, the tip probing. Then the avid mouth was sucking

Sin and Mrs Saxon

vigorously at my core, drawing in outer lips, inner lips, soft moist flesh. It was heaven.

'Suck it up, suck it dry,' I mumbled. 'Lick it clean! Eat it, reem out every nook and cranny—'

The effect was to make me grind my tits hard against Randall-Bude's thigh, grasping his prick and tilting my neck to get it in my mouth. It grew rigid over my tongue with my first hungry sucks, then he awoke and gripped my loosened hair, pulling me to his hardened shaft. 'Claris,' he muttered, no doubt imagining his wife was pleasuring him as of old. My raised rear was churning against a face, a tongue, and even with my mouth full I gurgled my pleasure. 'Swallow,' Randall-Bude demanded, and in his thrusting I gulped down his come juice, spurt after spurt; I was coming myself in wild jerks and shudders and old Cloote was slavering in cunt juice from the very recesses of my slit.

The two men left me used and abused but wonderfully fulfilled. I rose later to take a bath, dress in my uniform, and report to them below stairs. Both were spruce in their military dress. They sat at the table with tea and toast. I was made to sit and pour tea and offer them toast, but no mention was made of the torrid threesome we had indulged in. Later that morning I drove them and their luggage to the ferry at Ryde. Randall-Bude's tour of duty now complete, he was returning to London with his senior officer. He boarded the little steamer without a glance back at me, but on returning to the cab to drive to my base I found an envelope on the seat. On the outside was the simple message 'Thank you,' and inside were five crisp white five-pound notes. For services rendered, no doubt and cheap at the price.

Back at HMS Medina I was informed my presence was

required as a driver at the Admiralty in Whitehall, no less. I was to chauffeur Very Important People about, so I packed my kit, turned in the faithful little Utility truck that had seen so much action that fateful summer, and left for further amorous adventures. I was certain there would be some in store.

Chapter Thirteen
AMERICA

As naked as nature intended, and what better way to receive a lover, I let in Peter Gulay when he called next morning. He slipped through the door and took me in his arms as I led him through to my bed. There we had one of those long slow fucks, changing positions occasionally, telling each other in the usual lewd terms just what we liked most until the heat of the bout got out of control and we went at it until spent. My appetite for sex satisfied, I was ravenously hungry, so I left him in bed to prepare breakfast. While in the kitchen, surprised to note our love-in had lasted over two hours and it was nine o'clock, I heard the door bell sound.

I wrapped myself in a robe, intending to quickly be rid of whoever was calling. On opening the door there stood my sister Jennifer with a bell-boy and her luggage. 'Diana,' she cried, hugging me to her ample figure, 'you have kept your looks, lucky thing. How long has it been—?' Her body was warm, cushiony pliant, her Scottish accent broad. She was a handsome and voluptuous woman herself. With her deep chestnut hair and emphatic curves, she was a slightly more fuller version of myself.

'Must be twenty years and more,' I muttered, still

shocked. 'You weren't due until later—'

'There was a seat on the night flight,' she said cheerfully, 'and I couldn't wait to see you again.' She tipped the bell-boy and entered the apartment, looking about with interest. 'This beats the old cottage we were brought up in, eh? And New York, all those tall buildings I saw from the taxi – what a change from Auchenmuckle, a kirk, post office and pub and a row of farm cottages. Here, I hope you haven't changed into one of those snooty females who look down on us poor folk—?'

I hugged her in return, laughing at her words. As for being one of the 'poor folk', Jennifer was anything but, having married Archie Macpherson of Clachan Farm, one of the largest and most profitable acreages in Ayrshire and world-famous for its stud bulls. 'I'm making breakfast,' I suddenly remembered, bolting for the kitchen. The bacon was crisping under the grill and the eggs were ready. I turned off the cooker and returned to Jennifer. She was not in the lounge, so I hastened through to the bedroom where Peter and I had made love. She was standing beside the bed smiling down at him, while he hastily drew a sheet over his nakedness.

'Thought I'd take a look over this palace,' Jennifer said, 'and it seems I've disturbed your husband.' She thrust out a hand. 'So this is the Harry Saxon I've heard so much about, who swept my little sister off her feet.' Peter shook the hand numbly, looking at me for guidance and remaining silent. 'I'm Jennifer. You know that our father used to be employed by your old man? I knew him quite well—'

She certainly had. I was aware that Mr Saxon had fucked her often enough as a girl. That fact, and remembering the high-spirited oversexed lass Jennifer had been in her teens, made me decide that a full confession might well be received with approval. 'This is not my husband, Jen,' I had to say. 'Not the Harry Saxon you expected. He's in Africa again. This,' I said awkwardly, 'is Peter Gulay. A friend.'

'Some friend!' Jennifer chuckled wickedly. 'No wonder he's still in bed at this time of day. I thought he looked very young for the Saxon boy. How do you do, Mr Gulay? Very well from the look of it—'

'Call me Peter,' he grinned self-consciously. 'And you are a very understanding lady. Welcome to New York.'

'Does this lad have a brother?' Jennifer said turning to me. 'I could use one like him. My Archie is no the greatest lover, you ken. I think he's forgotten how—'

'That then,' Peter said gallantly, 'is an inexcusable waste of a lovely woman. A crime. I hope while you are here I may be allowed to show you the town—'

'He knows all the best places,' I said.

'So I see,' Jennifer laughed, looking down at my rumpled bed. The doorbell rang again. 'You're a popular person, Di,' she said. 'Who are you expecting now?'

'Whoever it is,' I said, 'I'll get rid of them. You'd better shower and dress in the bathroom, Peter. This place is busier than Times Square this morning.'

Jennifer remained where she was, much taken with Peter and intrigued by his presence. So I left her with him as I went to the door. This time the arrival was the suave Miguel Martinez dressed in cravat, blue blazer and slacks. He regarded me lustfully as I opened the door with my hair loose and the silk robe doing little to disguise my figure.

'Did I get you out of bed, Diana?' he asked. 'I would much rather get you in it. Aren't you going to ask me in?'

He walked in anyway, reaching for my breast as I

Sin and Mrs Saxon

stepped back to avoid his hand. 'If you've something to tell me about your promise to retrieve those photographs from the Lefarges,' I said meaningfully, 'then I'm glad to see you. If not, then leave. I'll bet you haven't even tried—'

'I plead guilty to that,' he admitted, smooth as ever. 'I did consider it, but it's only harmless fun—'

'It's blackmail,' I protested. 'They've used me as a prostitute to amuse their important friends—'

'Yes,' he said smiling wickedly. 'And I'm one of those friends. It occurred to me that while they have this hold over you, I could be a beneficiary, for want of a cruder term. Like now, for instance. You look very desirable, Diana. Shall we go through to your bedroom?'

'Over my dead body, you creep,' I snapped. 'On your way!'

Martinez shrugged, drawing a long envelope from the inside pocket of his blazer. 'Addressed to your husband's office,' he announced, 'and containing copies of photos of you indulging in the lewdest sexual excesses. Would you like me to mail it?' He showed it to me, stamped and ready for posting, addressed to Harry, care of Food and Agricultural Organisation, United Nations, Somalia. 'Be cooperative, Diana,' he urged, 'and you can tear this up afterwards. There are other pictures, of course, but you shall have these, I promise.'

'My sister is here in the apartment,' I told him. 'She's just arrived. We can't do anything with her here—'

'I don't see her.' He considered the situation. 'Where is she?'

'In a bedroom—'

'Overnight flight? Then she'll be resting and won't miss you. I have the most urgent need to fuck you. I

Sin and Mrs Saxon

always do when I see your body. We'll use the Lefarges' apartment—'

The envelope was replaced in his blazer pocket and he led me off by the arm. 'You are the lowest type of beast,' I said but he laughed and replied that fucking a reluctant and angry woman was one of life's greatest pleasures. In the Lefarges' ornate lounge Violette was sitting beside a plump older woman on a settee. She looked up as Martinez dragged me in by the arm.

'Miggy, darling, what a nice surprise,' she enthused. 'Gloria and I were just deciding what to do to amuse ourselves this morning and you turn up with Diana. Might I surmise the purpose of this visit?'

If I expected to escape my fate because of the presence of another woman, I was sadly mistaken. 'I need the use of a bedroom to fuck Diana,' he said boldly. 'I knew you wouldn't mind. Her sister is visiting.'

'How delightful,' Violette said, as if Martinez had announced he had popped in for a normal visit. 'That is something that Gloria and I will enjoy seeing. How are you intending to take her? Front or back—?'

'Considering her superb bottom, I think with her on her hands and knees,' he decided. 'Diana is evidently not in the best of moods this morning, as you will have noticed. Therefore she declined my polite offer rather spiritedly at first, making it necessary to bargain a little—'

'To blackmail, you bastard,' I said heatedly. The plump woman, Gloria, regarded me with shrewd interest.

'Tell me,' she asked coolly, 'does she suck?'

'She does if we say so,' Violette Lefarge said with a cruel smile. 'Diana's spirit does not become her. Such petulance deserves punishment, humiliation to curb her unwarranted defiance. I take it you would like her to – pleasure you – Gloria?'

'Now that I have seen her, very much so,' Gloria nodded.

'Then I'm sure Miggy wouldn't mind sharing her with you,' the vile Violette cooed salaciously. 'That would be rather fun. You at her head and Miggy at her tail. First I think we should warm her up a little, beat some of the insolence out of her. Do we all agree?'

I stood burning with helpless fury. I realised their calm and calculated conversation was deliberately intended to wound, to brand me as a sex object entirely in their power. But there was also a growing excitement in my loins, despite my anger. I felt a masochistic urge to give myself over to them completely. I hated it, but I was aroused by the thought. I was not outwardly agreeable to their intent, but that too was part of the pleasure of erotic humiliation. I hung my head as if in dark despair, awaiting my orders with the utmost reluctance.

'Take your robe off, Diana,' ordered Violette. 'We want you naked. Let us see your delightful breasts and cunt—'

'I don't want to,' I protested.

'Then Miggy will do it for you,' I was told. 'Really, your obstinacy will only add to your humiliation.' I felt the silk of the robe drawn from me and cast aside, leaving me completely naked to their gaze. The dark woman reached for my crotch and fingered my cunt arrogantly. It was hers to do with as she wished. She was rough in her probing, making me cry out.

'Soft and moist,' she declared. 'I'd say she's been had this very morning—'

Sin and Mrs Saxon

'With her husband abroad, tut tut, Diana,' Violette said. 'Who was the lucky man?' I remained silent, glaring at her. 'We can beat that information out of you, you know, *chérie*. Do tell us—'

'Go to hell,' I swore at her. She rose and slapped me across my breasts, making me cower. A snap of her fingers brought her maid to her side, smiling in her enjoyment of my shame. In her hand she held a leather strip divided at the end into several six-inch thongs like shoelaces. Violette took it, shaking it out, watching my fearful glance. Martinez, I noted, was taking off his clothes beside us, his huge prick already rampant. My lower belly fluttered at the sight, my cunt trembling in anticipation.

'Let's proceed, Violette,' he urged. 'I'm aching to get this up her, so whip her if you must and let me at her when her ass is hot.' His hand was already fondling both cheeks of my bum, middle finger probing. 'There's a load in my balls I have to give her. I'm boiling over. I have a letch to fuck sperm into the surly bitch, to flood her—'

'In good time,' promised Violette, 'and that we want to witness. Gloria, you wanted her to lick you. Get yourself ready. She can bend to you while I punish her. Tell me if she doesn't do as you please – I'll make sure she does—'

Still being fondled by Martinez, his finger and thumb in the crack of my buttocks, curling to meet and only parted by the membrane of my cunt and arse, I writhed on tiptoe. Before me Gloria rose from the settee to raise her dress over her hips and lower her wide French knickers, kicking them aside with a rustle of silk. Her face was impassive as she gathered up her dress and sat back on the settee, her plump thighs held wide apart. A

Sin and Mrs Saxon

hand at my back forced me to kneel before her, my face close to the dark cunt lips protruding from her fleshy mound which bulged at the fork of her fat thighs. How hairy she was, I thought, a forest of thick black unruly hair. I could smell her sex, it was pungent and strong and tempting.

'Lick!' she ordered, parting her deep cunt with her fingers. So I knelt before the strapping white thighs of a strange woman, forced to serve her with my tongue and lips. A swish from behind me brought the first slash of the thonged leather across my bottom and I howled in surprise more than pain. To beat Violette to a second blow, I pushed my face into Gloria's thighs, seeing in close-up the wet pink furrow and prominent clitoris. As Violette continued to flog me, I lapped with my tongue and fastened my mouth over mound, lips and entrance, alternately sucking and tonguing her cleft. She moaned as if restraining her pleasure, reaching down to clasp my tits and squeeze them tightly. With each strike across my clenched bottom I gave a little leap, my cries muffled in the warm juicy cunt I lapped and licked. I gulped, swallowing the excess flow, as she quivered, moved her hips against my face.

'How greedy she is for it,' Violette observed. 'She has Gloria going berserk.' True, the combination of my excitement, heightened by Gloria's grunting and bucking, had made me want to bring her to a climax. The flogging had now ceased and hands were on my hips raising my bottom higher. Then Martinez was there, curled over my back, thrusting in his great length to the hilt and shafting me vigorously. A wild threesome ensued, we were fucking, licking and moving like wantons in our lust.

Sin and Mrs Saxon

Martinez had not lied when he boasted that his balls were full, for he came in what seemed endless spurts, jetting a full load deep within me, the force with which he shot his fluid striking my cervix. He gripped my hips, fingers digging in my flesh, roaring out that he was coming, he was *there*, coming! His tremors went on and on, haunches jerking wildly, my cunt walls gripping his prick, reluctant to lose the oh-so-pleasurable feel of its penetration. Before me, the plump Gloria cried out in her throes, falling back on the settee with legs apart. On hands and knees, mouth and chin slathered with her juices, cunt leaking thick clinging grey jism from Martinez's copious climax, I must have presented a fine sight. I lowered my head, my hair cascading to the carpet, breathing deeply while trying to regain some composure. I dimly heard voices speaking, words were spoken about some women's eagerness to suck and be fucked; how easily they submitted. They were discussing me and it was true.

When I got up, naked and pink from the heat of several climaxes, breasts enlarged and nipples upstanding, I tried hard to regain my dignity. 'You've had your way with me,' I said tersely, 'so I hope you are all well satisfied with yourselves. Damn you for the dirty beasts you are—'

'But you loved it, Diana, every moment.' Violette laughed at me. 'It was so plain to see. Even the beating. We want you to be our good friend—'

'It's obvious she's a woman who requires a good regular servicing,' Gloria added. 'Look at her breasts, swollen with her excitement, and such erect nipples. She has a greedy mouth on her, too, sucking so avidly at my cunt, making me quite faint. I do hope we can repeat this meeting.'

I pulled on my robe silently, deciding I had no defence against their opinions of my nature, holding out my hand to Martinez, who handed over the long envelope as he had promised.

Back in my apartment, sister Jennifer had made herself at home. She was freshly bathed, wearing a comfortable dressing gown and nothing else, her large breasts exposed at the opened neck as she sat at the kitchen table eating breakfast.

'Where did *you* get to, Di?' she asked. 'You took your time with guests here. Your nice young man had to leave but said he'd be in touch. He tells me he's an actor. I made him a good breakfast, thinking he needed it,' she chuckled naughtily, 'as the one you made had spoiled. And I had a bath and made myself bacon and eggs. I was starving. It must be the holiday feeling I've got, now I'm free of Archie's farm and all the work – I know I'm going to enjoy myself here—'

'I'll make sure you do, Jenny,' I said. 'I'm sorry I had to leave you like that. I was needed in the apartment opposite – we have a sort of business agreement—'

Jennifer was no fool. She looked me over carefully. 'Are you feeling all right, Di? You *do* look hot and flustered.' She poured me a cup of strong tea and eyed me shrewdly. 'What about these neighbours of yours, the French couple? Your friend Peter warned me not to get friendly with them. Are you in some kind of trouble? Money worries perhaps? I've got plenty and would be glad to help—'

'I'm fine, really,' I smiled to assuage her concern. 'No financial problems either, anything but—'

'Remember,' Jennifer said, 'I'm the sister you had to share a bed with, who grew up with you in thin times.

Archie is a millionnaire a good few times over, though you wouldn't think so to see him in his overalls with dung on his boots. It's all he thinks of, the farm and making money. It's none of my business, but you will tell me if you're in some kind of difficulty, won't you?'

'I'm fine,' I repeated. 'My married life is fine, everything is fine. Harry is a good husband. What you saw this morning, Peter being here with me, doesn't mean I don't love Harry—'

'Oh that,' Jennifer dismissed the matter of Peter in my bed. 'I say a bit of what you fancy does you good. I've been at it since my tits first started to grow and I got hairs on my fanny. Archie has been no fun in bed for years, so I wouldn't like to count how many rolls in the hay I've had with his farm hands. Young lads too, they like a good comfortable body under 'em—'

As ever, Jennifer's outrageous honesty made me laugh aloud. 'I remember you were the most popular girl at school with the lads,' I said fondly thinking back to the young shapely Jenny. 'If father had known about you behind the bicycle shed he'd have done an "Annie Laurie" or walloped your bum—'

'He didn't know the half of it, nor did you,' Jenny said with glee. 'Father' – she pronounced it faither – 'would have laid doon and dee'd right enough. I was just fond of it, that's all, same as you are, Di. We're sisters and two of a kind.'

'You taught me to masturbate,' I reminded her, giggling. 'To use my fingers or take the bunched-up pillows between my thighs and rub against them. That's how I had my first comes—'

'Do you know,' she asked suddenly, 'who took my virginity? I mean *really* took it with a prick up my pussy

Sin and Mrs Saxon

the whole way? You'll never guess—'

I was sure I could, but wanted to let her say. 'It wasn't Archie Macpherson when you married him,' I ventured cheekily. 'Tell me then, as I'm sure you're bursting to—'

'Your father-in-law, the posh Mr Saxon who our father worked for, and whose son you married,' she said, leaning back in her chair and laughing at the thought. 'Can't you remember I always had some money for you and I to go to the cinema? It wasn't on the tuppence a week I got for pocket money, stupid. Mr Saxon gave me half-a-crown a time to go to his house and pop into bed with him. What do you think of that—?'

'Not very much,' I had to tell her, wiping my eyes with my own outburst of mirth, 'for the randy devil took my virginity too. When you left to go into service I took over where you left off. He told me he'd known you and what he was doing to me made me guess what he'd been doing to you. What a pair we were! Mother would have killed us. As it was I had to run away from home when I was caught in what they call a compromising situation with his son. Ma wouldn't tolerate that—'

'Saxon, the crafty old lecher,' swore Jennifer, highly amused. 'Then he had us all, ma and two daughters—'

'Never,' I said. 'Surely not mother? Not her!'

'I saw them!' said Jennifer. 'Remember she used to take vegetables there from our small-holding? One afternoon coming home from school I saw her bike at the back of his house, so I thought I'd wait to go back with her. I looked in the kitchen window to see if she was there. I saw it! She nearly saw me, she was facing right at me, but her eyes were closed—'

'Heavens,' I was forced to chuckle. 'And remember how she used to complain when dad wanted her? We could hear her going on to him about it through the bedroom wall.'

'They say a change is as good as a rest,' Jennifer claimed, highly amused. 'But I guessed even then it was for the money. Remember how hard up our family was, hardly a penny in the house after Monday? She was a good mother. I've admired her for it—'

'Let's hope she enjoyed it too, then,' I said. 'How were they doing it?'

'Like I said, her face was right up at the window when I looked in. He had her over the sink, gripping the taps for dear life as he shagged her. In the moment or two I saw, she was bumping back to him all right—' While I shook my head at the thought of one man having us all in turn, Jennifer continued. 'That wasn't all. Do you remember our coalman, Geddes the Kirk Elder?'

I had good reason to as he had fucked me frequently in his shabby car. 'I remember Geddes,' I said. 'It was rumoured he let hard-up women customers pay for their coal delivery "behind the door" as it was said. Don't tell me that he and mother—?'

'Not behind the door either,' Jennifer admitted. 'Poor ma, what she did to feed us and keep a fire burning. Mind you, not that I think she didn't get enjoyment out of it. When I caught them at it, she was groaning out how good it was.'

'Tell me more,' I laughed. 'How come you were so adept at catching her—?'

'Pure chance,' said Jennifer. 'You recall old Miss Cole, the cookery teacher at school? That day in class I threw a cake at Moira Sneddon for annoying me. Cole sent me to report to the headmaster, but I just walked out of the school and went home. It was early afternoon and that old car Geddes had was outside the cottage. I went in and in the living room I heard the big brass bed rattling—'

'Like it did when ma and pa were at it,' I said.

'Only this time it wasn't pa,' Jennifer smiled. 'The door to the room was open an inch or two, so I peeked in. I nearly shrieked with surprise. There was this big round white bum bouncing up and down over something and it was our mother riding Geddes for all she was worth. I could actually see his big cock going in and out of her as her bottom cheeks lifted. In the mirror across the room I could see her big titties bouncing too and then I left them at it—'

'You never told me what you saw,' I complained, laughing.

'You were too young,' Jennifer teased. 'This has been a day for revealing family secrets, hasn't it?'

'There's one more to tell,' I said, deciding to admit all. 'The people in the opposite apartment are blackmailing me. They have a certain hold over me and use me for sexual purposes. Like this morning they called me over and made me do certain things. With the help of Peter Gulay I'm hoping to get back at them. He's working out some plan to trap them—'

'Good God!' Jennifer exclaimed. 'We really are in America. I thought such things only happened in the pictures. Could I pay them off? Whatever kind of hold could they have over you?'

'Photographs,' I said. 'Taken by the French couple when they had tricked me into what is known as group sex—'

'I'm well aware what group sex is,' Jennifer stated. 'I quite enjoy it. Were the pictures very naughty—?'

'Very,' I admitted. 'And they threaten to send them to Harry and his United Nations people if I don't do all the things they want while they hold the evidence. You know my husband loves his work. He's in the running for a knighthood. I can't risk ruining that—'

'So at present you do their bidding?' Jennifer mused. 'Like this morning. What were you asked to do, Di?'

I shrugged, deciding there was no point in beating about the bush. 'I was made to lick out another woman—'

'I've done that often enough,' Jennifer observed.

'—while getting screwed at the other end as I was kneeling before her.'

'By that tall dark man who led you away,' Jennifer said. 'He looked a randy brute. Did you come during all this? I know I would have—'

'I couldn't help myself,' I admitted. 'They whipped my bottom first, or rather the French woman did, then I was made to go on my hands and knees. That part I can put up with. It's the blackmail threat that irks me. Somehow, some way, I must get those pictures back—' I remembered the envelope in the pocket of my robe, taking it out and handing it to Jennifer. 'These are some of them,' I offered. 'See for yourself—'

She tore open the envelope, inspected the contents, looking at me in surprise. 'These are just blank,' she said. 'Every one a blank piece of thin card. What does it mean?'

'The bastard!' I shouted in fury. 'The big dago bastard! It means I've been conned! He didn't have any pictures at all! I can just imagine him laughing his head off—'

I would get my own back on them all, I decided, but as

Sin and Mrs Saxon

my anger subsided somewhat I saw the funny side of it, especially with Jennifer grinning all over her face at my being taken by such a low piece of trickery. 'So I was fucked,' I admitted wryly. 'Next time I'll do the fucking. Whatever Peter Gulay has in mind, I'll go along with it, even if it includes armed robbery.'

'Just what does Peter mean to you, Di?' Jennifer enquired. 'I mean is he someone special — someone you want to keep for yourself—?'

'Of course not,' I said. 'I've got my husband, Jenny. It just happened with Peter. Nice but only a substitute.' My eyes took in her full figure in the loose dressing gown, the ample sweep of her large breasts. 'Don't tell me,' I laughed. 'You and Peter, while I was out of the apartment! Goodness, did you leap on him—?'

'Got into the shower with him,' the naughty Jennifer admitted proudly. 'He was a bit surprised at first, but once I suggested he soaped my tits he perked up quite considerably. Seven or eight inches or so, I'd say. After that, well, things just happened. I didn't want to go behind your back, Di, but I did so want that big cock of his. We had it off across your bed—'

'Good for you,' I said. I could well imagine Peter loving all of my sister's succulent flesh. 'He's something else we've shared then, like our childhood and Mr Saxon. Feel free while you are here!' As she reached across to kiss my cheek, the telephone rang. I answered, surprised to find Tako, the Japanese butler of the blind and immensely wealthy Milo Circassion on the line.

'Are you the lady who visited my master at his home?' he enquired. 'The lady with the chestnut hair?'

'That's me,' I said. For a moment there was silence, then Circassion was on the line.

'Diana,' he said. 'You have not visited me again. I have waited for your return but you have not come. Could you tell me why—?'

'I've never been asked to,' I said, mystified. 'I only go where the Lefarges direct me—'

'I have requested you frequently. They said you were no longer available to me. Why should they say that?'

'Nothing that I said,' I answered. 'I can only think they don't want you and I to get too friendly. I mean, in case you wanted to help me in a certain situation—'

'Which is?' I heard steel in his voice.

'A long story,' I said.

'Then I should like to hear it,' he said. 'Will you have lunch with me today? I'll pay double what you received on your last visit. Do come. We will eat beside my pool. There are a nice party of friends I'd like you to meet.'

'I have my sister from Scotland staying with me,' I said. 'I've promised to take her out—'

'Bring her,' Milo said instantly. 'Is she like you?'

'Very.'

'My car will call for you around eleven. Will that be suitable?'

'I'll look forward to bringing her,' I said.

'What was that all about?' Jennifer asked as I replaced the telephone. 'Are we invited out?'

'Only to have lunch with the richest old man in the whole world,' I said happily. 'He likes his naughties too. I take it you won't be shocked if anything goes at his party?'

'Try me,' Jennifer laughed. 'Really, Di, you do live an exciting life compared to me on the farm. Whatever he's like, we aim to please. I said I was going to enjoy this holiday.'

'He could also be a help in getting back at the Lefarges, so let's keep in with him,' I said. 'We'll get our war paint on and dress up to knock 'em dead. The Mackenzie sisters ride again—'

'With any luck at all we will,' said my game sister.

Chapter Fourteen
ENGLAND

At the time of my arrival London was not the best place to be stationed, being bombed nightly. I was assigned to the Admiralty to chauffeur any senior officer who had business at the War Office or went on inspection tours. This often meant waiting long hours to return them to Whitehall with air raids in progress. One duty night during a heavy attack, I was called up from the basement where I was sheltering to drive the Prime Minister back to Downing Street. I held the car door open for him as he got in the rear, a long cigar clamped in his mouth, accompanied by his secretary. On arrival, with the sky lit by flames and the thud of bombs shaking the buildings, he looked at me as I held open the door. I couldn't help staring back at the famous man, surprised at his small stature.

I wore my navy cap with the HMS ribbon because the helmet issued was so heavy and uncomfortable. Besides, I thought that if a bomb had my name on it a helmet would not save me. He noticed, however. 'Have you no tin hat, girl?' Churchill asked me gruffly. 'Are you afraid it will disturb your hair? Wear it in future, we can't afford to lose service personnel killed through vanity.'

Sin and Mrs Saxon

With all the problems he had, it tickled me that the stern old man should show concern. 'I wouldn't like that very much myself, sir,' I ventured to say, for old men are fair game for young girls. 'I'll wear my helmet in future.'

'Scottish, eh?' he said, recognising my accent. 'You had better come in with me and shelter. Have you had supper? Go to the kitchen and tell them that the Prime Minister of Great Britain says you are to be fed.' So it was that I was invited to No. 10 Downing Street and was served a good supper by the order of Winston Churchill.

The billet where we Wren drivers lived was bombed flat, fortunately while I was elsewhere on duty. Issued with an address from the Red Cross for new lodgings, I went to the allotted house and the door was opened by a plump woman in her forties. She was a faded blonde in a sheath dress, the curves of her hips and breasts accentuated by the clinging material, her hair up in a bun, her handsome face stark without make-up. 'I'll show you up to your room,' she said, having introduced herself as Mrs Dorothy Snaith. The bedroom was clean and well furnished, with a feminine bathroom next door on the landing. Then we went downstairs to her living room to discuss what turned out to be very reasonable terms. They were ridiculous really as the navy would be footing the bill for my civilian billet.

It was a large house and I concluded that Dorothy Snaith was not short of money. To my surprise I found in the living room a sort of four-poster double bed with supports made of steel, as was the overhead canopy. 'I can't be bothered leaving the house during the air raids,' she explained, 'so I had my bed brought down here. It should withstand the roof and ceiling caving in.' Jammed into the rest of the room was a piano with silver-framed photographs on top, a sideboard with more photographs, a radiogram and armchairs. I studied the pictures out of interest and also because she hovered beside me, delighted to explain who they were. Most of them were of a fat boy and, later, a plump young man with thick spectacles.

'My Gordon,' she said fondly of her son. 'I had him evacuated to the country in Wiltshire for safety, dear boy.'

'How old is he?' I asked dumbly, for I knew of children being evacuated. He looked old enough to be in the army.

'Twenty-seven,' said his mother, 'but Gordon is special, highly strung and of quite nervous disposition. He couldn't go into the services or anything like that—'

I could guess where he got his nervous disposition, I thought, while nodding agreement. 'What does he do?' I asked.

'Sketches, writes poetry and music,' she said proudly. 'Of course I hate not being with him but there are too many valuables in the house to just leave it.' She picked up one photograph and kissed it. 'He's such a mummy's boy and I know I'm to blame for that. Being away will be good for him, although we both hate it. He's led such a sheltered life with me. He needs someone like you, dear, to bring him out. I do believe he's afraid of girls—'

'What of Mr Snaith?' I said, noting no pictures of him.

'A brute. I threw him out years ago,' she said sharply. 'He is never mentioned in this house. Now, shall we have a cup of tea—?'

Over the following days I was kept busy with runs to Dover and Portsmouth, only eating the occasional meal and taking a bath in the house, sleeping out. When I was

Sin and Mrs Saxon

there I noted her eyes on me, flicking away if I caught her staring. I was not quite sure what it was she found so fascinating. Then came the first night I was off duty. I returned late and tired, had a bath and went to my bed. Almost immediately the siren wailed and bombing commenced. I lay there with the covers pulled up to my chin, feeling very lonely upstairs by myself and vulnerable. Then came a knock on my door and Mrs Snaith looked in on me.

'Would you care to come down to my bed, Diana?' she asked solicitously. 'It's so much safer, and it would be company—'

She was fully dressed in a woollen frock and, with the noise and danger outside, any thoughts of her suggesting I go to her bed for sexual purposes seemed out of the question. I welcomed her offer but as I always slept nude I hesitated to get out in front of her. 'I've nothing on,' I said. 'It's how I sleep. I haven't a nightdress here—'

'That is how I sleep too,' she said quickly. 'With clothes rationing I don't waste coupons on night attire any more. Pop down to my bed, dear. You'll find it very cosy and safe.'

Safe from bombs, perhaps, but I wondered about Mrs Snaith as I got out of bed and stood naked before her. Her eyes, reflected in the bedside lamp, glowed with approval as she took in my breasts and thighs and the triangular pubic patch of hair on my mound. 'You are such a lovely girl, Diana,' she said, her voice sounding strained. 'How I wish my Gordon had a friend like you. Come quickly before you get cold—'

I got into her bed while she undressed. She made no pretence of disrobing discreetly, chatting away as if to keep my attention while taking off her clothes. The human body, male or female, has always intrigued me. Her breasts were large but very pointed, pear-shaped, with a slight pendulous droop from their weightiness. Her thighs were well rounded and very white, accentuating the dark forest of hair at the fork. When she turned to place clothes over the chair by her bed, I was surprised at the rounded fullness of her broad arse, the cheeks tight with packed flesh. She was a handsome woman in her prime and, as if she knew the effect on me, she remained naked in full view for long moments while winding the clock deliberately slowly. Then she put out the light and slipped in beside me. As I stretched out an arm in a tired yawn, my hand slid under a pillow and met silk – no doubt the nightdress she usually wore!

She cuddled up, clasping me as if for human companionship while the guns and bombs roared outside the house. Our cool flesh warmed quickly, her pointy breasts and sharp nipples digging into my tits. If she was going to seduce me, I decided, it would be fun to see how she would go about it, so I made no move. I played the little innocent allowing her close contact for comfort. It's funny, isn't it?, how in those days womanly love was considered so rare that many doubted its existence, while it flourished in secret every bit as much as today. Mrs Snaith pecked a light kiss on my cheek, muttering how cosy this was, assuring me it was quite natural for females to be so snug and cheer each other up, all the while continuing her kisses.

'It is nice,' I conceded, when she asked if I was comfy. 'No, I have never been with a man, Mrs Snaith,' I lied in response to another whispered question. 'Dear girl,' she said, and, as if unable to resist, kissed my mouth lightly. As I did not turn my face away, I was kissed again, quite passionately, her lips glued to mine. As my sexual life had been negligible since coming to London, her smooth plump body to mine, her kiss with the first hint of her tongue seeking mine, had made me lustful. Wishing she would hurry up with her seduction, I muttered it was sweet, *sweet*, her nice kisses, and sort of went soppy, relaxing my body against hers. I parted my thighs as if naturally when I felt her hand glide down between my legs. '*Yes!*' I sighed helplessly as her fingers stroked my outer lips gently and provocatively.

She was a skilled seducer, taking her time, not intending to frighten off or disgust a supposed novitiate at the game. Telling me softly how *nice* I was, too tempting to resist, she kissed my eyes, mouth, neck, nipples, sucking each one in turn, all the time fondling my cunt's entrance without any attempt to enter me, reducing me to a state of high arousal, wanting, *needing* to be finger-fucked by her. To let her know, I groaned my helplessness, lifting my bottom off the bed and thrusting my cunt into her hand. As we were face to face at that moment, I clasped my arms about her neck and kissed her with an open mouth and probing tongue, as if unable to resist her advances any longer. To acknowledge my eagerness to comply with whatever she wanted of me, her fingers slipped into my quim, rubbing and pinching my erect clit. I bucked like a stallion, then I was sharply ordered to be still. She slid down in the bed and fastened her mouth hungrily over my cunt.

It was, of course, no new experience, but her avid licking, lapping, tonguing and sucking had me screaming out, clutching her head, coming time and time again against her face. Then she was over me, on top of me, positioned between my open thighs, her hands below me cupping my buttock cheeks, rubbing her cunt to mine furiously. I anchored my legs behind her back, clutching her big wide cushion of a bottom, meeting her thrusts with mine and matching them. Our breasts flattened against each other, our pubic mounds and hair mashed together. Finally my sobs of pleasure and her low grunts subsided. She kissed my mouth lingeringly, patted my cheek, and told me to sleep.

Air raid or not, on the following nights I went to Mrs Snaith's bed and we made love. She was a 'tit woman', as opposed to a tit man, loving to get mine out at all times and fondle them, sucking hard on my nipples prior to us stripping and making each other come strongly, often in the early evening when we couldn't wait for bedtime. Another pleasure she enjoyed was to make me lie back with legs over the bed and eat my cunt. As I was kept busy both night and day with my driving duty, it was an excellent substitute for a man to have her so keen to be at me. It seemed to her I'd taken to sex with another woman in the manner born. Never once did she ask me to reciprocate, to suck her nipples, lick her cunt or masturbate her. She liked to be the 'man' and dominate, until one night at bedtime she showed another side of her nature.

I was naked beside the bed when she came from the bathroom carrying a short leather strap with a hand-grip, a cut-off section of her ex-husband's razor strop I learned later. I thought here goes, she wants to wallop my bottom now I've agreed to just about everything else. Instead, she had a hang-dog look on her face, offering me the strap. 'What we do together is lovely, I know,' she said, 'but some may consider me wicked, seducing an innocent girl like you, dear Diana. Sometimes I have this guilty feeling for what I've done and I know I should be punished for it. If I begged you to thrash me with that strap, would you? I do feel it would make me feel better, take away some of the guilt—'

Standing before me in her Rubenesque nakedness, tits hanging and cunt thrusting, I could not conceive of her needing a belting to salve any guilt. I had to keep a very straight face at the thought, for she was a kind woman. As if certain I'd agree, or to tempt me, she bent over the bed, legs apart on the carpet, big buttocks raised, showing the deep cleft of her arse with its puckered hole and the hanging fig of her cunt, the whole festooned with thick dark hair, surprising for a blonde woman. She urged me to start, so I gave the strap a flick across both cheeks. 'Harder!' she urged. 'Don't spare me! I want it hard, as hard as you are able. Thrash me, mark me, beat the wickedness out of me—'

Her upraised solid moons did look tempting to belt and the urge to do so was overwhelming. I cracked the belt down time after time, seeing her flinch and clench her cheeks, reddening them, but the only sound she made was to implore me to continue, strike harder, beat her! Then her bottom was jerking, pistoning her crotch to the bed, and she did cry out, cry out loudly that she was coming, COMING! Her agitated motions increased and her bottom shuddered and rippled, and she rolled over in bed to face me, eyes glazed and mouth open, completely spent. My arm ached and the belt hung from my hand, seeing before me a woman who had had a tremendous orgasm by being severely beaten. When she crawled into bed it was to turn away from me, sated and exhausted. Left to my own devices, strangely aroused by the situation, I had to masturbate to gain my own relief while lying beside her.

Sin and Mrs Saxon

So my stay at Dorothy Snaith's continued, sleeping with her in the big bed with the steel canopy, enjoying the sex she supplied, doing the necessary whenever she brought out the belt at night. Then came the night we were in bed together, kissing and fondling during the usual noisy air raid over London, when the doorbell rang. I could only think it was someone requiring me for duty, but Dorothy put on her dressing gown and returned from the door with a plump young man who strangely resembled her. I sat up as the unexpected arrival came into the room, covering my breasts with the sheet and wondering how she would explain having an obviously naked girl in her bed.

I need not have worried, she being more concerned at her precious Gordon turning up in the middle of a heavy raid, all the way from Wiltshire. She sat on the bed and hugged him and they both sobbed while Gordon told how he missed her. He had been insulted at the small village hotel where he lived by a guest who had suggested he at least join the local Home Guard. 'The beast,' swore his mother. 'They don't know your sensitive nature. We'll find another place for you to stay tomorrow, darling. Meanwhile, you must remain here with me tonight for safety. You can sleep in my bed—'

In that case it looked like I would be returning to my room upstairs. I suggested that darling Gordon left the room so I wouldn't shock him with my nakedness when I got out of bed. 'You don't have to move, my dear,' Dorothy said. 'It would be foolish and dangerous to be upstairs tonight. The bed is large enough for us three and the safest place in the house.' Gordon, the presumably meek and sheltered mummy's boy, nodded agreement

Sin and Mrs Saxon

and smiled at me. 'Diana won't mind, will you, dear?' said his doting mother.

It was true I did not fancy returning upstairs to a cold and lonely bed, the windows rattling with bomb blasts. Still, the situation was one I had never encountered, sharing a bed with a young man and his mother. 'Why not?' I said, as always amused by the unusual. 'Would you like the light off while he undresses?'

'Goodness, no,' said Dorothy. 'I've seen Gordon in the bath since he was a boy, and we've taken naturist holidays together. Undress, Gordon, and get into bed, dear. I'll make you a hot drink, then in the morning I insist you go back to Wiltshire. We'll find somewhere suitable for you.'

I watched with sly interest while Gordon undressed. He was a young man with a slight paunch but a bigger-than-average prick hanging down between fat thighs. As he didn't mind showing what he had, I let the covers fall from my tits and smiled at him, seeing his cock lift in the stirrings of an erection. Then he scrambled hastily into bed beside me to cover his embarrassment, sitting up and offering his hand in introduction. His mother returned moments later with two mugs of steaming cocoa, the situation made even more bizarre by our sipping the drink side by side in bed. Then Dorothy took off her dressing gown and got in, with Gordon in the middle. We handed her our mugs when finished and she placed them on the bedside table, but did not put out the lamp.

'Isn't this cosy?' she asked of us. 'I'm so glad you've met Gordon, Diana, even if he has been very naughty coming to London. It's so lovely to see him.' She gave him a hug and kissed him. 'Now *you* must kiss him,

Diana,' she said. Gordon duly turned his face so, for the hell of it, I kissed him, one hand steadying his shoulder. The other hand, under the bedclothes, went down and brushed an erect penis. I giggled and Gordon jumped. 'What is it?' asked his mother.

'Nothing,' he said, but his own hand captured mine and guided it back to his prick. Gordon, it seemed, was not so slow. The light went out and we settled down, the air raid still continuing and me thinking that if a direct hit landed on the house, what a find it would be for the rescue squad – three in a bed. I turned away from Gordon, immediately feeling his soft stomach against my back and a hard stalk of a prick nestling at the cleave of my bottom, nudging its way in deeper until the round head butted my nether hole. Does he know just where he is? I thought, while Gordon lay still as if feigning sleep. It seems he did, for as I sighed and lay as if in slumber myself, his hand stole across my waist. He gave both my tits a friendly squeeze, then felt down to my crotch and insinuated a finger in my cunt. He moved it slowly, as if not to disturb his mother on the other side of him, and I had to contain myself from moaning out loud as he found my clitty. Then a slight movement forward, as if getting comfortable in bed, made the crown of his prick push my arsehole ring inward, allowing an inch to enter. I remained still and silent, wanting very much to throw all caution to the winds, to urge him on to fuck my bum.

It became absolute torture. I was penetrated a maddening inch and my back passage itched to receive more, to be corked fully. Bit by bit he edged in, inch by inch penetrating until his warm balls nestled up to me. His fingering had me on the verge of a come, my arse desired movement, my back passage squeezing the shaft embedded there. At last, with a strangled groan, it became too much for him. He thrust at me and I rolled on to my face, tilting my bottom to take his thrusts. Bump, bump went the bed as he shunted into me, my hoarse cry loud enough to wake the dead. My hand reached out and felt another hand, Dorothy's rubbing wildly at her cunt as she lay on her back with Gordon and I fornicating beside her. Then she was groaning, Gordon was gasping and a flood of hot sperm was saturating my innards as I climaxed myself. The operation complete, we settled down without words, my arse palpitating and leaking, but warming my lower belly through to my cunt. I fell asleep in a haze of satisfaction.

Dorothy took her boy back to the wilds of Wiltshire by train next day, returning late in the evening to say she had settled him in a village hotel safe from harm. 'He didn't want to go, brave young man that he is,' she announced. 'Said he wanted to stay here. Of course,' she added slyly, 'that was because of you, Diana. I could hardly not have been aware what went on between you two—'

'Gordon is a bigger boy than you give him credit for,' I said, remembering the blockage I had felt while entered by his prick.

'I think perhaps so,' she admitted. 'I telephoned his previous hotel to say he would not be back and the horrid man who answered said he had better not, for his sake. It would seem Gordon and the man's wife were caught in a rather awkward situation in Gordon's bedroom—'

'He was discovered, fucking her!' I laughed, delighted. 'As I know very well myself, Gordon can look

Sin and Mrs Saxon

after himself. You are the one who thinks he can't—'

'I shall try to do better, Diana,' she promised. 'Do you think that I deserve to be punished for being a clinging and possessive mother?' she added hopefully.

'Definitely,' I said sternly. 'Bring the strap at once and stand naked beside the bed. You won't escape lightly. I owe you one for what that son of yours did to me, everything but get me pregnant. That wasn't possible—'

'Naughty Gordon,' his mother said proudly. 'Surely not *that*? His father was so keen on that—'

'Yes, *that*,' I said. 'So off to the bedroom to pay for your son's bad behaviour. Tonight I'll thrash your bottom until even you beg me to stop—'

'Oh, yes please,' Dorothy begged, hanging her coat in the hall and making a beeline for the bedroom. But it was to be one of our last sessions for the navy came up with a billet in the Admiralty building itself and ordered me to move in. Shortly after I'd left, Dorothy's house did take a bomb blast that brought down her ceiling but the trusty steel four-poster that had seen so much action of a different kind protected her until she was dug out unharmed.

Chapter Fifteen
AMERICA

A chauffeur held open the door of Milo Circassion's Rolls-Royce and Jennifer and I were whisked away to meet a small gathering of his guests in the garden of his mansion. The men present were middle-aged and distinguished, greying at the temples and with the look of wealth and power stamped on their features. The women were younger, gorgeous and sophisticated types with the slim bodies of models. For all that, as my sister and I were led into the house by the Japanese butler, the men's eyes followed us with interest, mentally undressing Jenny and I as we passed by the tables set by the pool where drinks were being served.

'This beats being down on the farm,' Jenny observed. 'You certainly seem to move in the right circles, Di. All those handsome men too. I bet I could prise any of them away from those skinny girls. Men like something to hang on to, something like you and I have. You know, with a few drinks in me, I just might fancy a romp with one – or three – of 'em later.'

'You may well have to,' I told her, 'it's that sort of party. You can bet that Milo Circassion is throwing it to entertain people important to his business empire—'

'And has he had *you*, Di, seeing as you got a special invite with a chauffeur-driven Rolls?' Jenny queried saucily. 'I don't think you were invited for your business brain; more likely for your big tits—'

'Thanks a lot,' I replied but I laughed with her as we were led up to Milo's room. 'You're probably right, but no, he hasn't. He's a nice man, but blind and impotent too. Evidently he can't get it up—'

'Never?' Jenny said. 'So what does he do with women? 'What did he do with you if he can't see or fuck you—?'

'He lets his hands do the business,' I said, 'and very skilled hands they are too. I came off strongly, I must say, standing there with a blind man fondling me.'

'That sounds bloody marvellous,' Jennifer enthused, 'and a new one even for me. I wouldn't mind trying that myself. I bet I'd make him hard, I've never failed—'

We were at Milo's door and the butler tapped gently. 'You take my place then,' I whispered conspiratorially, tickled by the thought. 'Quiet as a mouse now when we go in. Just do all he wants me to do.'

The butler stepped back as we were ushered in, the deep pile of the carpet silencing our steps. Milo was in his wheelchair, dressed in the silk robe, the table beside him holding an ice bucket and champagne with crystal glasses. 'Diana,' he said, 'I've eagerly awaited your return. You will enjoy a drink with me and tell me why I was told you would not be back to visit.'

Jenny stood back, listening while I gave Milo a brief explanation of the Lefarges' hold over me. He nodded at times, smiling bleakly, and finally informed me that I could be assured he could fix the French couple's game and ruin them financially if necessary. 'Leave it to me,' he said grimly. 'They'll be a sorry pair and your pictures and negatives will be returned to you. Now that I know you are not really a call-girl and were forced to do the Lefarges' bidding, perhaps you don't care to – indulge – in the pleasant little entertainment you provided for me before?'

'I don't see why not,' I admitted, delighted with his offer of help. 'I enjoyed it. Shall I take off my clothes?'

'That would indeed be a pleasure,' he agreed. 'Then we will join the others in the garden. Did your sister come with you, as you said—?'

Jenny was standing beside me with a glass of champagne I had slipped her. She put a hand to her full-lipped mouth to suppress a giggle. 'She's around somewhere,' I said lightly.

Milo flexed his fingers, much as a concert pianist would, and Jenny, game for anything, handed me the empty glass and at once began undressing. With her clothes strewn about her on the carpet she presented a picture of magnificent nude womanhood. Shapely big breasts hung nobly from her chest, the brown nipples big as thumb tips. Below, a narrow waist flared out to rounded hips and comfortable thighs formed a prominent vee, the curved bulge forested with the same reddish-chestnut hair as my own. Bare-footed, she stepped in front of the wheelchair. Speaking over her shoulder, I announced that I was ready.

Milo's hands reached out, gliding over her hips, under her arms, then around to clasp the two fleshy breasts. He squeezed both, took the erect nipples between his fingers and thumbs and pulled on them. Down from her breasts, his slim manicured hands roved over her flat firm belly, then one cupped palm covered her mound, the middle finger entering her cunt. I watched Jenny's

Sin and Mrs Saxon

face, saw her bite her lips to contain a groan of pleasure and widen her legs to facilitate his fingering her clitoris. She pushed her crotch to his hand, wanting more, moving her hips, feet planted firmly and leaning back to tilt her cunt to him.

'Magnificent, superb,' Milo praised. 'Such breasts, such an eager vulva gripping my finger. But not Diana, I think. You have played a delightful trick on me, you girls. Yet the similarity is strong – dare I ask if this is Jennifer, your sister?'

'It's me all right, but don't you dare stop,' Jenny giggled in her broad Scots accent. 'You'll have me coming off for sure with much more of that. Oooh, yes, *there*, keep your finger moving there! OH!' she squealed, her hips jerking wildly, 'I've just come! Lord, I'm going to come again – can you make it to the bed, Mr Circassion, where we'll be more comfortable? I'm a woman who likes to lie down for it. Keep your hand there while we go across—'

They crossed to the big four-poster bed together, Milo's hand at her cunt, then Jenny was on her back with legs spreadeagled, big tits lolling on her chest while he was over her sucking at each nipple in turn, his hand working in rapid jerky motions at her cunt. The urge to join them proved too much and I shed my clothes and got on the bed with them.

'On his back with him, so we can work together,' Jennifer said urgently. 'We'll see if he can fuck or not! Give him your tits to suck, Di, while I go below—' Milo was most unceremoniously rolled over and I draped my breasts over his face, moving my shoulders to swing them across him back and forth, my rounded tits becoming elongated, the stiff nipples striking his nose and

Sin and Mrs Saxon

mouth. He stilled them by grabbing them, pulling a nipple to his mouth like a starved baby, sucking so greedily that nipple and flesh was drawn into his mouth. Glancing below, I saw Jennifer holding his flaccid prick upright, licking the shaft, tonguing the split crown, before engulfing it in her mouth and sucking eagerly.

Beneath us Milo gulped on my breast, eyes wide with lustful pleasure, his body shaking and lifting to our treatment. Then his mouth left my tit to open wide in a loud gasp that became a groan. Looking down to his crotch I saw Jenny with her cheeks full of cock, Milo's knees raised and his pelvis heaving. Jenny drew her mouth away, grinning wickedly at my questioning glance.

'Got my finger up his bum, right up,' she said proudly. 'And he likes it. Look!' I did look, seeing in the moment before his prick went back between her lips that it was quite erect and stood stiffly upright. Then Jenny stopped her sucking, straightened her back and threw a leg across him. With the fork of her thighs poised over his crotch, she directed his prick to her cunt mouth and pushed down so that I saw its length slide up until her hairy mound rested on his pubic bone.

'Oh, yes, yes, please yes!' Milo moaned, raising his hips. My sister was firmly mounted on the blind billionaire and reached behind her back to titillate his arsehole. She rode him gently, hardly rising from him, savouring the feel of his prick up her and staying upright to get the full depth. Milo's face was a picture of ecstasy, his features twisted, mouth agape.

'Told you we could do it,' Jenny cried triumphantly. 'Don't just sit there gawping, Di. Squat over his face, feed him your quim! Let's make it one he'll remember—'

Sin and Mrs Saxon

I needed no encouragement and neither did Milo object. Indeed he reached for my bottom cheeks and parted them as I hefted them over his face, feeling his tongue curl out to taste my cunt, to lick and lap at it furiously. Facing me, Jenny had increased her pace, rising so that the prick in her was being pistoned by her urgent up-and-down motions. She reached out to hug me, tit to tit, her mouth clamping to mine, and then we were bucking over Milo helplessly, climaxing to prick and tongue, crying out as the convulsions shook us. The blind old man below was thrusting gamely as he came into Jenny.

For long moments afterwards the three of us lay sprawled and sated, chests heaving. I wondered if we hadn't overdone it with Milo and asked him if he was okay, fearing a heart attack or stroke. He lay back, grinning a huge grin. 'That,' he declared delightedly, 'was worth a million dollars to me, the finest thing that's happened for years. You lovely sisters gave me what no Park Lane quack could prescribe and I'm duly grateful—'

'You fucked me beautifully,' Jenny praised him, 'and Di seemed to be well pleased at your other end. That's thanks enough for us—'

'Have you heard of Santigue?' Milo asked mysteriously.

I never had, but Jenny surprised me as usual. 'It's an island in the Caribbean, a paradise for the very rich. I've tried to get Macpherson to take me there, he could well afford it, but my husband's idea of a holiday is a day out at a cattle show—'

'I own that island,' said Milo, 'and my private plane will fly you two there whenever you like. Now I think we had better join the others. Use the bathroom next door, then I expect you will both be ready to eat—'

When we arrived in the garden, as giggly as young girls over our sex romp with our host, one or two of the men and young women were using the pool. The afternoon sun was hot and the water tempting. An enquiry of Tako the butler, engaged in serving food from a buffet table, assured us of a selection of swimming wear in the pavilion nearby. Jenny and I found a closet full of costumes hanging on a long rail. 'Do you think we could risk bikinis?' she laughed. 'With our tits and bums—? Let's do it, and put those skinny models to shame.' She chose a purple one, filling it or rather overflowing it, once again making me see what a splendidly shapely woman she was. I was used to bikinis, always wearing one in Uganda. The two-piece I picked was white and scanty and showed off the tan I still had from my years in Africa.

Our appearance at the pool drew admiring glances from the males and resentful looks from their female partners – but wasn't that why Jenny and I had picked two such brief outfits? Our breasts bulged, barely contained in the bra cups. Down below, the inadequate triangular patches over our mounds accentuated the prominences there. We were soon surrounded by men offering to bring us drinks. Jenny was in her glory, loving every moment, flirting and teasing her admirers. 'Och, I have a pool at home,' she told one who asked if she swam or was just a beautiful decoration at a poolside. 'I use it all the time and in less than this bikini too. With no one around, I go in bare buff. It's such a feeling of freedom.'

'*That* I would like to see,' said her questioner. 'The

pool is there before you, why not do as you do at home?' There was a general mutter of agreement from the other men around, making Jenny laugh aloud at their eagerness to see her naked. She made a pretence of unhooking her bra, large tits wobbling as she shook with amusement at the admiring audience gathered around us. At that moment our host arrived in his wheelchair, with his butler behind him guiding the electrically operated machine. Milo was smiling, no doubt still in an elated mood from the rare fuck he had enjoyed with my sister and me. His sharp ears had caught the sound of hilarity from our group and he had directed Tako to take him to the laughter. Such was his presence, all fell silent as he joined us.

'I'm glad my guests are enjoying my party so much,' he said. 'Don't stop on my account, please. May I enquire the reason for such merriment? Who is there?'

'Carlo Bonetti and others, Mr Circassion,' replied the handsome man in Bermuda shorts who had challenged Jenny to swim nude. 'We've been joined by two surprise guests you kept up your sleeve. If you have brought them here to cause a sensation, then you've succeeded—'

'For want of a better word to describe such perfect specimens of women, Milo,' said a distinguished-looking man in a foreign accent, 'I think your American term for them is *stacked*. You've been keeping them to yourself, you sly dog.'

'It would seem you have met Diana and Jennifer,' Milo smirked. 'I can think of no others that fit your rather crude but factual description as perfectly, Ambassador.'

I squeezed Milo's hand. 'So much for the so-called

gentlemen you associate with,' I teased him. 'They are standing around us with their tongues hanging out. The one called Carlo even suggested that Jenny swim in the nude. Was that nice?'

'It would be if she did,' called out Carlo, getting encouraged by my frivolous manner with Milo. 'Five hundred bucks if she does—'

'I'm worth far more than that,' Jenny laughed. 'You've got quality and quantity with me—'

'Yes, you cheapskate, Carlo,' agreed Milo, enjoying the fun, his usually bleak features relaxed. 'Your offer is an insult — peanuts. You make five hundred every waking hour out of my business interests. Think big.'

'I am, oh I am,' Carlo said, ogling Jenny in her brief bikini. 'If the lady is willing, one thousand dollars—'

'Two thousand,' offered a voice beside me, 'just to take off that goddam top. God, I've got to see those breasts—'

'That is more like it,' Jenny agreed, unclipping the hook of her halter but restraining the cups as they fell forward to rest on her nipples, showing a great deal of the sweep of her lovely tits. 'Any further bids? Let's make it for charity, the New York Salvation Army. Who wants my top—?'

'Ten thousand,' said Milo sharply, 'and I can't see the result. You heard the lady, any advance on that?'

'Double it and my sister will remove hers,' Jenny piped up cheekily, including me in her scheme without asking. 'You'll get to take them off as well. Did I hear twenty?'

'Twenty,' Carlo said as several hands went up. 'I always like to start what I finish.' He drew Jenny's top from her breasts, stepping back to admire a fine upstand-

Sin and Mrs Saxon

ing pair of breasts pulled slightly apart by their mass and weight, white as marble and perfectly matched. 'Christ,' he said, his hands poised as if to grasp them, 'worth every cent.' I noted nods of approval all round, even covetous glances from the women who had gathered. He turned to me and I thrust out my chest in invitation. He reached behind my back, unhooked and stepped back with the bikini top in his hands, leaving my tits bare. All present stared.

I had always been proud of them, their size and shape, their uplift and thrust, the thick uptilted nipples. Standing bare breasted beside my sister, the act of exhibiting myself as ever made excitement flare in my stomach and the fluttering infiltrated to my cunt, moistening it, causing a definite throb. 'Now who is going to bid for our panties?' my sister demanded briskly. 'You'll get to pull them down too.' The thought of a complete stranger taking off my bikini bottoms, revealing my cunt, drove a bolt of excitement through my already turbulent loins. Beside me, Jenny was showing all the signs of her highly stimulated state, her magnificent tits like ripe fruits, pink and swollen with arousal.

'Thirty thousand,' said a calm voice and a wiry little man stepped forward to confront us. He went down on one knee, reaching out and drawing Jenny's panties over her full thighs and rounded calves. Staring intently at the uncovered hairy split, he held her hips and kissed it reverently to murmurs of approval from the others. Then he moved sideways to confront me, pulling at the side straps and lowered my bikini, allowing it to drop to my ankles. His face pressed to the fork of my legs and I felt a darting tongue probe my outer lips.

'What a pair of exhibitionists,' said a tall willowy

blonde witnessing the scene. 'Anything they can do, I can do better.' She stripped off her bikini top, showing neat but small pear-shaped tits, then drew down her briefs to reveal a wispy little cunt. 'All of you,' she said turning to the other girls. 'I want you all to take off your bikinis. That's what we're here for, isn't it? This is for free,' she announced grandly to the men.

'Nothing is for free, Velma,' said Milo Circassion drily, hearing her voice. 'You and your girls have been paid most generously to attend my party and perform. As for doing it for charity, the only worthy cause you support is your own. Isn't it time you and your girls went to the pavilion to earn your keep? I'm sure my friends are ready for you now you've been wined and dined at my expense—'

Jenny and I watched the girls go off to the pavilion with a posse of men following. Carlo Bonetti hovered back, eyeing our nakedness. 'You two ladies make Velma's girls look like boys,' he said. 'You're good sports, join us.'

'I'd at least like to see what goes on,' Jenny said eagerly. 'Who knows, I might learn a few things, if that's possible. Will you escort me?' She took Bonetti's arm held out in invitation, going off towards the pavilion with the bare cheeks of her bottom wobbling provocatively as she walked. It was, there was no doubt, turning into the holiday of a lifetime for her and I was pleased. Beside me Milo Circassion caught my hand while his butler came up to guide his electric chair.

'Will you join them, Diana?' he asked.

'I think I should keep an eye on my sister,' I said. 'She might prove too much for your guests—'

'Let me know when you wish to go to my island,' he

Sin and Mrs Saxon

offered. 'You'll be honoured guests. Now I have an appointment with an investment broker who'll help me make the Lefarges sorry they ever bothered you—'

Alone, I wandered over to the pavilion, glancing in to see a heaving mass of bare bodies on cushions scattered on the carpeted floor. One or two men stood watching, others were engaged in group sex with the women either below or above them in the tangled mass. Everyone seemed to be doing something to someone else, sucking while fucking or groping, buttocks heaving, flanks thrusting. I saw Jenny sitting astride a man, riding him with her hips thrusting while another man stood straddle-legged before her and she sucked greedily at his prick. On the floor beside her, the man fucking the girl below him was reaching across to grapple her free-swinging tits. Her head was thrown back as if in sexual hysteria, crowing out her delirium.

I felt a hand on my wrist and was drawn into the throng, pushed down on my back in a narrow space between bodies, a large cushion under my bottom. The man who had brought me in was too slow and was pushed aside by the bulk of another, the distinguished foreigner I had heard addressed as Ambassador. He withdrew his long glistening prick from the cunt of the girl he was mounting, moving crab-fashion to get between my thighs and thrust his thick length right up me almost in the same movement. I gasped and reared at the suddenness of the fierce penetration, feeling the solidity of his body as his large hands slid around to cup the orbs of my buttock cheeks. I felt raped, filled with the mass of his hardness, moving to adjust to the angle of his thrusts. I felt the hands of the girl he had left grip my breasts between our bodies, a mouth and tongue at my

Sin and Mrs Saxon

lips. Giving myself over completely to the assault, my now gaping, pouting cunt tilted to meet every buffet and followed as he withdrew to thrust again.

'Oh no, no, yes, yes, fuck me, fuck me!' I heard myself urging as the great cock shafted me. Then someone's buttocks were spread above my face, lowering so my nose and mouth were covered. I licked, finding a succulent cunt moist and pungent on my tongue, directly over me. The woman called Velma cried out, 'Suck, bitch, lick me clean, lick me out. Lick!' as she worked her arse into my face. The Ambassador, whoever he was, cried out and increased pace, fucking me with long hard strokes, shooting a volley up my begging crack as I convulsed with him. Unceremoniously, I was rolled over by several hands, face down. 'Fuck the cow in the ass,' I heard Velma cry, no doubt revelling in my degradation.

Whoever it was above me, growling with lust, spread my cheeks apart while someone else gave me several hard spanks. A finger probed my bottom hole, provoking a squeak of pain from my compressed lips. As the finger moved I groaned and was forced to move my arse with it, the pressure both arousing and humbling. Held down by other hands, I begged for mercy in a dozen silent ways, glancing sideways in my prone position to see faces all around me and cocks being masturbated over me. 'She likes it,' someone commented, 'just see her arse move.' Then came the weight on my back, someone covering me and directing a bulbous knob to my anus. At the first push the tight hole caved in, allowing an inch to enter.

The wet warmth of it inside me spread through me to my lower belly and cunt. A little jiggle from whoever was buggering me eased in a further inch or so. Maddeningly it held still as my buttocks rotated on it. I desired more desperately. 'You want it?' a voice demanded. 'Ask for it, babe,' my tormentor went on. 'Beg nicely. It's yours for the asking—'

It was too much to resist. 'Yes, I have to have it. Fuck me there, please.' I saw the faces around exchange knowing glances. The prick up me was thick and frightening, sliding up all the way, beginning to shunt, its crest plumbing my innards. Heavy balls buffeted my bottom as I was regally fucked then inundated with come. I jerked and wriggled showing my own increasing pleasure as I was brought off. Then I was left alone, my bum numb, my hair, neck and back sticky with the goo shot over me by those wanking and watching while I was taken in the rear entrance so spectacularly.

I went outside, cunt and arse still twitching from their rude penetration, more than fulfilled for once. The pool looked so inviting that I dived in, swimming down to the bottom and twisting and turning as if to cleanse myself. I climbed out feeling wonderfully alive and refreshed, admitting to myself it had been an exhilarating romp, one I had enjoyed all the more for its apparent humiliation and abuse of my body. The linen-covered tables before me, deserted now, were laden with choice food and wines. Still naked, enjoying the warming sun on my skin, I heaped up a plate and helped myself to champagne. I was joined by my sister, who emerged from the pavilion looking delighted with herself, if worse for wear.

'Now that's what I call a party, Di,' she enthused. 'The kind of get-together where the guests really *do* get together – and how!' I saw you getting it from both ends between times. I should have looked you up years ago.'

Sin and Mrs Saxon

At home in the apartment that evening, bathed and relaxed, reminiscing about the afternoon's orgy, once again I had an unexpected guest. It was Manny Levinson, whom I had first met at the Lefarges' party.

'Strictly a business call, Diana,' he said apologising for disturbing us as he saw Jenny and I in our dressing gowns. I made the introductions and he sat down with us, accepting a drink and admiring Jenny and myself.

'You're so alike, I thought there could be only one Diana,' he said flatteringly. 'I'm here on behalf of Milo Circassion whom I met today on business concerning certain photographs held by others. I'd never seen the old moneybags in such good humour. You two ladies certainly are his favourite people right now—'

'I can't think why,' I said, tongue in cheek, Jenny enjoying the joke beside me. She refilled Manny's glass and her own, intrigued by the situation.

'Do I get to see these famous photographs before they are destroyed?' she chuckled. 'Are they so good—?'

'Good and lewd,' I admitted, 'with Manny and I and a French maid doing all sorts of naughty things. I wouldn't want my husband to see them—'

'You too, Manny!' Jenny exclaimed delightedly. 'God, how I've been missing out these past years. I should have visited Diana when she was in Africa. Did you get into such situations there?'

'All the time,' I had to confess. 'It just seems to happen to me. I don't try—'

'Looking like you do, you don't have to,' Manny said gallantly. 'Meantime, old Milo would like you and your sister to accept his invitation to live it up on his paradise island of Santigue. When you return those pictures will be all yours and the Lefarges will be sorry they ever heard of you—'

'What will you do to achieve that, Manny?' I asked.

'Heard of insider trading?' he queried. I had not, waiting for him to continue.

'Works both ways,' he said. 'It can make millions or lose them. I tip the wink to the Lefarges that a certain billionaire is about to buy shares in a company that in reality is about to fail. The Lefarges will borrow from a bank owned by Circassion himself to get in on the deal. If he threatens to demand a return of the loan, or denies it to them after negotiation, they'll go broke. Milo has done it before and the Lefarges know it. They'll be delighted to hand over those pictures to save their skins—'

'I wouldn't want them ruined, just frightened a little,' I said anxiously. 'Enough to get my own back on them—'

'You'll do that in spades,' said Manny confidently. 'So off you two go to Santigue Island and let Milo and I do our snow job on those French bastards. Now I'll leave you ladies—'

'Not so fast,' Jenny chipped in. 'The night is but young and we are beautiful, to coin a phrase. I take it as a young man about town that you know of some good night spots?'

'I've been known to frequent some,' Manny grinned. 'So do I have the honour of showing you ladies 21 Club or Ciro's this evening?'

Suffice to say, after a wild night out on the town, visiting the best watering holes, I awoke next morning in rather an alcoholic haze beside Manny who was fucking my sister. I snuggled back down, content that it would me my turn next. Once again it seemed that all was well in my world.

Chapter Sixteen
ENGLAND

Quartered in a small room with a bed and locker deep in the bowels of the Admiralty, I was one of a pool of girls called upon to drive senior officers as required. I took Winston Churchill to and from Downing Street on several occasions, as well as the French leader, General de Gaulle, the King of Norway and others of varying importance. One of these was Commander Leopold Walenski, a Polish Navy officer serving in the Admiralty in Strategic War Planning, a most secret department. He was a horny little creep, and the Wren drivers did their utmost to avoid driving him about on his duties to inspect dockyards and depots.

Whenever I drove him he sat beside me making suggestive remarks and feeling my thigh. He asked me to accompany him to night clubs and for drinks in the flat he rented in Chelsea. All of these offers I turned down on the excuse that mere ratings and other ranks did not mix socially with officers. The real reason was that I couldn't stand the rat-faced midget who was pompous and arrogant with lesser beings – except females who attracted him. Worse, he began to ask for me personally when ever he required a driver, which pleased the other

Wrens but meant I constantly had to fight off wandering hands. His favourite ploy was to go on duty trips where we had to stay overnight. Much as I enjoyed a man in my bed, the door would be locked against him and he'd knock, plead and order me to open up to let him in, becoming furious at my refusal.

I could have reported his behaviour, but felt well able to handle the situation and I enjoyed frustrating the weedy lecher. But other girls had complained of his groping and suggestions, so the day came when I was ordered to report to the office of First Officer Gayle, commanding officer of the Wrens detachment. I found her sitting behind her desk with a very worried look on her face, the tall figure of the Royal Marines colonel in charge of security standing to one side. 'I think you had better sit down to hear what we have to say, Leading Wren Mackenzie,' she said, indicating a chair. 'You've met Colonel Moffat before, haven't you?' For a moment I wondered what kind of trouble I might be in, searching my mind for any breech of discipline. I had recently allowed one of the Royal Marine guards to spend the night in my room. Presumably the boy had boasted of it and word had reached his colonel.

'What do you think of Commander Walenski, the Polish Navy officer you've driven at times?' Moffat asked suddenly. 'Don't beat about the bush, girl, tell us your opinion. We've had complaints of his conduct from every Wren driver but yourself. Why is that? Do you enjoy his advances—?'

'Colonel—' began my Wren officer, but she was stilled by his raised hand. Her complaint was silenced.

'Let the girl speak,' he said harshly. 'Have you or have you not been intimate with this officer?'

Sin and Mrs Saxon

'Certainly not!' I replied hotly, annoyed by his manner. 'I didn't report him because I can handle the – the officer—'

'What were you about to call him?' Moffat said, amused.

'Slimy toad with more arms than an octopus, sir,' I said, making the Wren officer grimace. 'I detest him as much as the other girls—'

'Would you consider having an affair with Commander Walensky?' asked the colonel. First Officer Gayle gulped and stood up to protest, saying that to suggest such a thing to one of her girls was outrageous. Again the colonel silenced her with a glare. 'Would you do that for your country's security?' he asked me. 'In the highest national interest? Of vital importance to our war effort?'

Lost for words, I said, 'Why me?'

'Firstly,' said the colonel roguishly, 'you are without doubt the most comely and attractive of the Wrens who serve here. Walensky has an obvious lech for you; that we know from our observations. But apart from being an obnoxious bounder, and this must remain top secret, we have reason to suspect he's an agent of Germany, engaged in espionage—'

'A spy—?' I said amazed.

'A very clever one. His papers are in order, he's a genuine officer of the Polish Navy but planted there by the German secret service years ago as a cadet. With the collapse of Poland, they aided his escape to this country, no doubt, and so he carries on his work here. Friendly little fellow, isn't he?'

'Why not arrest him?' I said dumbly. 'I mean if you know that much about him—'

'We want to know what he's up to, where he keeps his secret radio transmitter or passes on info to other agents.' The marine colonel gave me a friendly smile. 'He'd love to take you home to his flat; pretty girls are his one weakness. Once there, we'd have someone on the inside, as well as our outside surveillance—'

'And I'd be in that nasty creep's bed,' I said. 'What makes you think I'm that kind of girl?'

'I know you're a lively, intelligent and patriotic one,' the colonel said, 'and most certainly not afraid of a bit of danger as you've proved by driving throughout the London blitz. Besides,' he added cunningly, 'we did run a test on you. First Officer Gayle, would you mind leaving the room?'

'I think I had better,' said the Wren officer, rising to leave. 'If Leading Wren Mackenzie volunteers for this duty, that is her choice—'

Left alone with him I said I hadn't observed any test made on me. 'On your sexuality,' he said casually. 'Some girls do, some don't, others positively enjoy it. To find out your category I ordered Marine Stevely to chat you up, as the saying goes. He gave you full marks for performance.'

'You rotten devil,' I said, senior officer or not. 'You made Steve sleep with me to find that out—?'

'He's a lucky fellow,' Moffat allowed. 'It's a duty I should have relished myself if younger. Will you now agree to help trap Walensky—?'

'Then you'll arrest him?'

'Perhaps not for a while,' said the colonel. 'Once we know his methods, he'll be a useful feed. We'll give him false information, mislead the Germans into thinking we'll be doing what we're not. Then we'll nail him when he's no longer of use. You, of course, would not have to put up with him that long. We'd get the navy to move you as soon as we know all we want to.'

I nodded my agreement, got a solicitous pat on the back for my sacrifice, and that evening on the duty notice board I saw that I had been appointed personal driver to Commander Walensky. He had obviously noted that too and was pleased that his request had been granted. Anxious not to let him suspect I regarded him differently, I repeatedly moved his hand from my leg as I drove him to deliver a message to the War Office. He was back out in moments, saying I was to drive him to The Black Cat Club, one of the elegant night spots still operating in wartime London. It was a venue for officers, black marketeers and expensive whores. I mentioned to Walensky as we arrived there that I'd heard there was no shortage of choice food or drink inside.

'Come and see for yourself,' he said in his excellent English. 'Never mind your uniform, plenty of service girls come here and Mario keeps evening wear for them. Have a nice evening as a civilian, Diana. Be my guest.'

'I don't think I should, sir,' I said, wavering. 'What about leaving the staff car here?'

'Tonight call me Leopold,' he said ingratiatingly. 'Look up the street, see how many military vehicles there are. You know it's my birthday? Celebrate with me—'

I was sure it wasn't, but I entered the club with him and went into the foyer, a brightly lit area dazzling on the eyes after the dark of the blackout. A fat man in an evening suit made a great fuss over our arrival, guiding me up a narrow stairway to a room where a selection of women's evening wear hung on racks. 'Mario,' he intro-

Sin and Mrs Saxon

duced himself, offering a pudgy hand and his eyes taking in my figure. 'Girls like you are welcome here any time, my dear. Pick yourself a nice evening gown, something special for Commander Walensky to admire you in, lucky fellow.'

I couldn't help be aware that I was on a mission, unlike the several other service girls around who were chattering away excitedly as they chose their long dresses. 'Does Commander Walensky come here frequently?' I asked innocently.

'He drops in from time to time,' said the club owner carefully, 'but never with such a lovely girl as you. Now I must return to greet the new arrivals. I shall look forward to seeing you out of uniform, my dear.'

I just bet you will, I thought, seeing the lustful gleam in his eyes. I found a long dark red dress that suited my colour, and went back downstairs to the crowded foyer where fat Mario threw up his hands as if seeing a vision. Beside him Walensky was chatting up the cloakroom girl, drink in hand, but he turned to see me and positively licked his thin pale lips at the sight of me. The gown was cut low in a deep vee at the neck, showing the full upper sweep of my breasts and the tight cleavage. A little too small perhaps, the silk gown clung to my waist and hips, accentuating my curves.

'Perfection,' Walensky said, taking my arm and leading me into a smoke-filled arena with tables set around a small dance floor. A five-piece band of truly professional musicians played the hit tune of the period and but for the horrible little man who accompanied me, I could have revelled in the gaiety, light and music.

I knew I would have to pay for being shown this side of life and did not relish the thought as I sat opposite

Sin and Mrs Saxon

Walensky. I saw his sly eyes take in the crowd, many of them handsome young officers I would have been delighted to spend the night with. He drank glass after glass, his hand groping me under the table, once or twice taking my hand to his crotch. To show willing, after pulling my hand away several times, I finally gave him a squeeze and felt a surprisingly long tubular object through his tailored navy trouser front. Several men came up and asked me to dance, at which he gripped my wrist to hold me to the table, glaring at those who dared to ask. I realised I was with a mean and possessive partner, one who could easily turn nasty. As if to prove this, he touched the back of my hand with his cigarette, just enough to make me wince and protest.

'When you're with me,' he said, 'you stay with me, no one else. Didn't I bring you here? Remember that and you will do well. Drink your wine, there's plenty more.'

'I'd like to dance,' I said. 'Dance with me—'

He rose to his feet, pulling me onto the dance floor which was so small and crowded that we were jammed together. Hardly moving our feet, he began rubbing his prick against me, pushing it in sensual motions against my mound. It rose hard and long, its heat penetrating the silk of the borrowed gown. 'Let's go,' he said suddenly, taking my hand and pushing through the dancers arrogantly. I was almost dragged through a door, along a passage, and out into a yard. It appeared I was to be raped in the service of my country.

In the black night I found myself pushed against the front of a parked car and draped back over the curved bonnet. His hands pulled aside the vee of my gown, exposing my breasts. I had left off my bra as the straps would have shown. He grasped both my tits agonisingly,

Sin and Mrs Saxon

making me cry out. He slapped my face and told me to be quiet before lowering his face and chewing rather than sucking my nipples. I tried to fight him off, which brought a wild Polish oath of elation from him, then I was thrust back onto the bonnet of the car.

A hand groped between my legs, pulling and tearing my panties. 'Please,' I begged him. 'I'll let you, I want you to do it, only there's no need to be so violent—' In truth I felt like kicking and screaming at him. To take me by force was obviously to his liking, however. He dragged up the long gown to bare my upper thighs, his hand at my cunt grasping the whole mound as if to tear it off. Two fingers probed me intently. Then he was splaying my legs, climbing up onto me, his feet on the front chrome bumper of the car to give him height, fumbling to direct his hardness into me. When it entered he fucked me rapidly with no thought of my pleasure. As his throes increased I thrust him away and heard him fall back to the ground even as he croaked out he was coming, coming—

He rose in the gloom, straightening himself, wiping his prick with a handkerchief. 'You've torn this gown I borrowed,' I said, my only protest at his treatment of me. 'What will that man Mario say?' He gave a curt laugh, saying what Mario might think about it didn't matter a damn, the man did as he was told.

When I had changed back into my uniform, I was ordered to drive him to his Chelsea flat and was dragged indoors, thrown across his bed and stripped naked. He crouched above my prone body, his wiry nude body in strange contrast to the very long thin prick he masturbated before my face. As in the yard of the night club, everything he did was in desperate haste, without finesse, using me as I knew he would all women as an object to subdue and humiliate, to satisfy his lust. Hardly able to raise an erection, for he was totally drunk, he fed his flaccid slug of a penis into my mouth, ordering me to suck.

I did so, wanting to bring him to orgasm so that he would fall off me and sleep, his position on my chest flattening my breasts painfully. But once hard in my mouth he withdrew and actually tried to penetrate my nose with his prick, directing it to a nostril and thrusting. This was a completely new sexual deviation to me, an old Germanic-Polish custom perhaps, but certainly not welcome. I protested loudly and twisted my face away, but he grasped my head firmly and proceeded to try and fuck the earhole turned up to him. His knob nudge-nudged the entrance, then he was groaning and shuddering, unloading spurts of sticky warm sperm into my ear, the overflow running down my cheek to my neck. Then he fell back. For long moments I dared not move until assured by his heavy breathing that he was in a deep and drunken slumber.

I went first to his bathroom and washed off the result of his attentions. Then I examined the medicine cabinet and the drawers around the built-in washbasin, finding nothing remotely sinister. A look into the bedroom assured me that Walensky was still dead to the world, so I daringly went to his living room, and opened drawers in a sideboard, finding a revolver, bottles of whisky and gin and cartons of cigarettes, all goods hard to obtain at that time of war. His bookshelf revealed little. Naked, shivering with cold and nervousness, I tiptoed back to the bedroom, dressed silently and put out the light as I left. When they've done with you, I hope they hang you,

you bastard, I said to myself.

Back at the Admiralty, Colonel Moffat came out of his office as I passed by, bidding me enter and leading me to a deep armchair. Not usually a nervous type, suddenly I was shivering in a delayed reaction to the night's events. Moffat fetched a large brandy which I swallowed gratefully, shaking myself as if to steady up. The wall clock showed it was four in the morning. 'Good girl,' said the security officer. 'First phase evidently accomplished, much as I hate to put you through all this. Off to bed with you now, you've had enough for one day. We can talk in the morning—'

'You waited up for me, sir,' I said, pleased by his concern. 'I can't sleep the way I feel. I'd like to talk—'

He smiled and I thought that beneath the stern military exterior was a kind man – a handsome one too. Tall and well built, smart in his khaki uniform with a row of medal ribbons, around the early forties mark, I wished my orders had been to let him make free with me instead of Walensky. I was handed another brandy with the warning to sip it this time. He noted that I looked at the framed photograph of a lovely woman he kept on his desk. 'My wife,' he said. 'Evelyn. Stationed in Ceylon as a Wren officer, so that makes it difficult for us to get together. I've no doubt some young lieutenant or other is keeping her company. Why not?'

I realised his talk was to make me relax before being debriefed about my time with Walensky. 'You don't mind that, sir?' I said, the brandy warming me and making my head light, all the better to chatter and tell him all later. 'I mean that your wife—?'

'—Takes lovers, Lord no,' he said easily. 'Keeps her

happy. She writes and tells me about it. Better that than some sordid affair behind my back. She's been away since the start of the war and neither of us are celibate creatures. I have my moments too, which she knows all about. She encourages me to write with all the lurid details. Does that shock you?'

'I think it very honest and sensible if you are both that way inclined. Without jealousy or being too possessive,' I agreed. 'Sex without guilt, I seem to have read somewhere—' The brandy made me giggle. 'If you feel that way about it, I wonder why you didn't sleep with me yourself in your sexuality test, sir.'

'Would you have minded, Leading Wren Mackenzie?' he asked.

'Perhaps not,' I admitted tipsily. 'It is wartime and people get lonely – like your wife. She's actually written telling you that she sleeps with other men?'

'Complete with a description,' he said. 'I also find you damned attractive, young lady, but as a senior officer I reluctantly delegated the pleasure of having you in bed to Marine Stevely. Nothing personal, you understand. I should have loved to—'

'Instead I got Commander Walensky,' I grumbled. 'He took me to a night club first, acting like he owned me. He acted like he owns the man who runs the place too—'

'Mario,' nodded the colonel. 'We keep an eye on him. No doubt he picks up tit-bits of information from the officers he entertains there, passing it on to friend Walensky, but he can be used too. Our main man is the German posing as a Pole, with access to more vital secrets here at the Admiralty. We had a man at The Black Cat tonight, and one watching outside his flat. He saw you leave there and telephoned me. How did you get on? Was it so bad—?'

'The whole story?' I asked. 'He raped me in the backyard of the night club, then did things to me in his flat. He's nothing but a sadist and sex maniac. That much I discovered—'

'Then I can release you from this mission if you wish,' Moffat said sympathetically. 'Just say the word, Diana.'

'No,' I answered emphatically. 'It will be worth it all to help you catch him out. The dirty beast gets his thrills degrading girls and hurting them. I'm still sore and have a mass of bruises from his treatment on our first night—'

'Do you want me to call the Wren medical officer to attend to you?' he asked.

'Then they would want to know how I got roughed up and who did it, wouldn't they?' I said. 'Walensky will no doubt enjoy seeing the marks he left on me. If I'm to continue to go with him, obviously the kind of girl he wants has to be completely submissive to his demands. I'll be that if I have to be. Through it all I'll remember how he'll be punished in the end.'

'Good girl,' he said. 'I hesitate to ask, but would you allow me to tend to your injuries and make sure you haven't suffered anything too serious? I am fully trained in first aid to treat sprains, bruises and cuts. I can recognise broken limbs and internal injuries. There's also a pretty comprehensive medical kit in my desk. I'd be happier knowing you were all right—'

I had the feeling that Colonel Moffat, despite his apparent concern, wanted to undress me and the idea was immediately arousing. During my time with Walensky I had been felt, fondled and fucked, all without pleasure at the hands of an uncouth sadist. I required

Sin and Mrs Saxon

gentleness to restore my faith in human kindness and Moffat was kind, even if I suspected an ulterior motive in his offer. I nodded, as ever in the right circumstances, always willing to exhibit myself.

'He was so rough with my breasts,' I said, 'hurting them deliberately, the beast. They're still quite sore—' Looking up at him I saw his face set, as if to contain his quickened emotion at my words. In a moment the atmosphere in his office had changed, becoming charged with sexuality. The excitement affected us both. 'You may inspect them if you wish, sir,' I said, my voice suddenly quiet and strained.

'Sit on my bed,' he indicated, his tone sounding like he was swallowing deeply as he said the words. I went to the made-up single bed in the corner of his office, noting that he took the precaution of locking the door. He produced a first-aid case marked with a red cross on its lid and sat in the chair beside the bed expectantly. He could certainly not inspect my tits without seeing them uncovered, so I took off my uniform jacket, shirt and tie. Finally I removed my bra and sat up with my two beauties thrusting out proud before his face. As ever, my nipples were taut and stretched, perking up invitingly.

'My God!' exclaimed Moffat, but more at the sight of two perfectly matched orbs of firm flesh than at the dark bruises on the curved undersweep of each one, I considered. 'The brute,' he went on, his hands reaching out to cup them gently, lifting them slightly. 'Does that hurt?'

In fact it was rather nice, his cool hands soothing and tender. 'Squeeze them a little harder and I'll tell you,' I said shyly. 'I don't think they're too bad—'

'Too bad—?' he said admiringly. 'I shouldn't say this, young lady, but they are bloody marvellous. Such a perfect shape and size.' His hands lingered, fondling more than inspecting them for any apparent damage, thumbs brushing my stiffened nipples. 'God,' he said again meaningfully. Sitting up before him, bare to the waist, shoulders back to thrust out my chest, I was excited by his touching.

'Colonel,' I said weakly. 'I believe you are playing with my titties. It makes me excited. Should you be doing this? They don't hurt, I just like it—' I smiled to show him I was in full agreement of his handling me so. 'Does your wife like *her* breasts felt the way you are feeling mine?'

'Evelyn?' said he. 'Very much so, they are her pride and joy, full and firm like yours.' Emboldened, as I had intended, set on a course now to allow him anything, he kissed both nipples, pressing his face to the pliant fullness of my tits. I wanted crude talk from this hitherto reserved gentleman and was intent on encouraging him. I put my arms around his head as he delved his nose and mouth to the divide of my breasts, nursing him as he found a nipple to suck on.

'Tell me,' I said. 'Tell me about her. I want to know. About her breasts. Do you suck them, have you done other things—?'

'I've sucked them, fucked them and soaked them,' he muttered against my bosom. 'Just as I wish to do to you. Just as she writes to tell me her latest lover does to her.'

'And does he fuck her?' I asked perversely, well aware I was on to his quirk, his fetish about other men having his wife. 'What does she write to you about that—?'

He stopped suddenly, pulling his face from me, and I wondered if I had gone too far. 'What a randy little piece you are, Leading Wren Mackenzie,' he observed. 'And

Sin and Mrs Saxon

how delightfully refreshing to meet one of your kind. As a somewhat senior officer, you know I could be in serious trouble dallying like this with a female rating. Before we continue, if you agree, I must be assured what might happen never goes beyond this room—'

'Of course, sir,' I agreed. 'After the mauling I had tonight in the line of duty, well, I needed something nice to happen to take my mind off it. Besides,' I added quite saucily, 'you were inspecting me for injuries received. I think there may well be bruised areas between my – other places I think you had better see—'

'Yes, I should,' he smiled sardonically. I brazenly stood before him, removing skirt, stockings and finally the panties Walensky had torn in his haste to get at me. Naked and proud of myself, I enjoyed the way Moffat gazed at the triangular thatch of hair between my thighs on the plump mound, my shapely legs. 'Lie on my bed,' he said, his eyes showing his approval of me. 'I think a very thorough inspection is called for.'

Before I got on his bed I wanted one more thing of him. 'I feel so exposed,' I giggled. 'Should I be the only one out of uniform? I think you should be too—'

'That would be appropriate,' he nodded. Undressed, he presented a firm athletic body, a thick and lengthy penis stoutly erect and curving up to his belly. Thick hair covered his chest.

'It's got a bend on it,' I said in surprise.

'All the better to poke around inside a receptive fanny,' he promised, a finger parting my outer lips. 'How moist you are,' he observed. 'It looks perfectly fine in there. There is a bruise on your right thigh and an impression of finger marks. How lovely you are stretched out like that, those perfect tits parted on your chest, that delicious quim so inviting. You know that I shall have to fuck you—?'

'Do you say such things to your wife?' I teased him.

His mouth was at my cunt, covering it, sucking in my lips. 'Back to her, are we, you salacious little minx?' he said affably, raising his face. 'It arouses you when I talk about her, makes you randified —'

'No more than it does you to tell me,' I challenged wickedly. 'You enjoy other men having her, reading about it and talking about it too! Tell me while you lick my cunt out—'

He gave a short laugh, his breath warm on my crack. 'We're three of a kind,' he uttered, 'and how I would love to have you and her each side of me in bed. She would love that too, not being averse to what I'm doing to you right now – eating cunt. Have you ever been with a woman?'

'Ooh, yes,' I had to admit, his tongue curling into me. 'I'd like that too. Have you watched her with another girl?'

'Of course, variety is the spice of life,' he said quite naturally, pausing in his tonguing me, making me draw his face back between my thighs. 'As I've watched men riding her, hearing her cry out, "Your wife is being fucked hard, Gerald, there's a big hard prick up your wife's cunt" and other crudities. And I've seen her switch to the mounted position herself in invitation and I've entered her rear to sandwich her, plugged her bottom—'

I drew him up over me, cradling my thighs, cunt drooling to receive him. 'Fuck me now,' I begged. 'You've made me want it so, you horny sod. Fuck me and think of your wife—'

'Oh, but Walensky is wasted on you, little bitch,' said Gerald Moffat decisively as his long curved prick slid up me to its full measure. He knelt up, taking my legs over his shoulders, penetrating me so deeply, his balls slap-slapping my raised bottom cheeks, that each thrust had me grunting out expelled air. 'Grip me with your cunt,' he ordered me, 'like Evelyn does. I shall write and inform her all about this, how I sucked you, fucked you. Have you a photograph I can send her? I want her to see the girl I fucked and will fuck every damn chance I get. Is it safe to come up you, girl?'

'Yes, yes, let it go,' I urged him in my throes, having already climaxed and on the verge of another. 'I had a pessary fitted in me so Walensky wouldn't get me pregnant. Shoot into my cunt, I wouldn't care – I want it all up me—'

Colonel Moffat let out a loud groan of anguish, heaving his flanks as he emptied his big balls into me, spurt after spurt, thrusting mightily and pushing my knees back to my ears. He rolled off me and returned with two glasses of brandy. He handed me one and smiled. 'You are some girl,' he said. 'I raise my glass to you. More than a match for Walensky, I'd say, but you must be careful with him. What we just did was no doubt a severe breech of discipline on my part, but the best damned briefing of an agent I've ever known.'

'It was also a terrific fuck, sir,' I said, smiling at the thought. 'As good as your wife?'

'She would have been proud of us, applauding and urging us on had she been here,' he grinned. 'Like wild animals, weren't we? Have you any regrets?'

'Only that it's nearly dawn and I'd better go before

everybody's around,' I admitted. 'I wouldn't mind staying—'

'There'll be other times,' I was assured. 'You'll be reporting to me after every meeting you have with the odious Walensky. I'll try and make it up to you, having to put up with him—'

'Debriefing me as you just did, sir?' I enquired mischievously. 'I'd rather like that—'

So once again, without trying really, I had a lover, par for the course for me it seemed. Two lovers, I supposed, if that rat Walensky counted. As I dressed and departed to snatch an hour or two's sleep, I wondered if there would ever come a time in my life when I wasn't getting any. I doubted it.

Chapter Seventeen
AMERICA

The prospect of flying off on a sunshine holiday to the millionaire's playground isle of Santigue had Jenny and I shopping for beachwear and packing excitedly. On the day before Milo Circassion's private jet was to whirl us off to the Caribbean, Peter Gulay phoned me from the foyer. 'Is it okay for me to come up and bring Ziggy Kaplan with me, Diana?' he asked. 'This is the day we nail the Lefarges. Let me see you and explain—'

I told him that plans were afoot to foil the Lefarges already but that he was always welcome. He appeared at my door with Ziggy carrying a shoulder-held movie camera and with two Polaroid cameras hanging from his neck. 'Could you,' Peter asked, 'get the Lefarges over on some pretext? Any reasonable excuse will do. Say your sister has expressed a wish to meet your neighbours and you have reluctantly agreed—'

'And if I do?' I said, mystified. 'What have you in mind, Peter—?' I looked at Jenny, noting her interest. 'I could invite them over for drinks, I suppose, making it clear I do so only because my sister asked to meet them. But you know the Lefarges, they would turn the afternoon into an orgy, like they always do—'

'Well, sounds good to me,' Jenny laughed. 'I wouldn't mind—'

'What would the object of the exercise be then?' I asked. 'We can be sure they'll expect nudity and group sex—'

'Exactly,' Peter agreed. 'Get them all over, both Lefarges, Martinez and their French maid. During all the activity, I'll call you on the telephone—'

'Whatever for?' I had to ask.

'Because I'll be in their flat making the call while I search the place for your incriminating photographs.' He held up a master key. 'You answer the phone, then fetch your sister from the bedroom, saying it's from her husband in Scotland. While you are both out of the room, they'll continue with the orgy—'

'—And I capture it all on movie film and on my instant cameras as they go at it,' Ziggy chipped in. 'I'm told that your bathroom has a magic mirror, a two-way job that looks right into the bedroom. I'll be there, taking in the scene on film, hoisting them with their own petard as the saying goes—'

'Even better,' Peter exulted. 'I intend to slip back to their apartment and replace your photos with the instant ones Ziggy will take. How d'you like them apples, girls?'

'Great,' I said laughing, 'if it comes off. I must say you've got it all planned. It will be worth putting up with that crowd for an afternoon to try out. I'm willing to go along. Need I ask you, Jenny?'

'Count me in,' she said. 'I'm ready to sacrifice my body for such a cause, hard though that might be. Call them up now, Di, say I'm dying to meet them. I can't wait.'

I phoned the Lefarges' number, getting Violette on

the third ring. 'Diana,' she said snidely, 'we were just talking about you. Friends of yours are with Marcel and I right now. Miggy Martinez has been saying what a delightful fuck you are. Gloria Stazak, too, whom you so kindly cunt-licked on your last visit. We were about to give you a call. No refusals now, you know we wouldn't like to make public those photographs—'

'You'd do it in a moment,' I said. 'Actually I've been asked against my will to invite you to my apartment for drinks and a snack. My sister Jennifer is visiting and is interested in meeting my French neighbours—'

'How very sweet of her,' cooed Violette. 'And is she like you, Diana drop-drawers, ready to fuck and suck with all and sundry? I should like to meet her. So I am sure would Miggy Martinez and Gloria – they are so adept at seducing unwary women. When shall we call?'

'Come over in about an hour,' I said, as if doing something against my will. 'Bring Martinez and that Gloria woman if you must. Perhaps you'd bring your maid as well, to serve us. I've never got around to employing one—'

'We'd all be most honoured,' Violette said, sniggering. I heard her talking to the others, her voice high with excitement. In my apartment, Jenny and I made up snacks and neat little triangular sandwiches and filled a trolley with bottles of spirits and glasses. Ziggy Kaplan made himself scarce in the main bathroom, setting up his camera on a folding tripod before the two-way mirror. All was set and Peter sidled out. Jenny and I were made-up in our war-paint and best dresses, awaiting our guests.

They came *en masse*, bearing champagne, exclaiming on Jenny's wholesome beauty and her resemblance to

Sin and Mrs Saxon

me. Martinez making no effort to disguise the lustful look in his eyes at her full figure. The drink flowed and so did the suggestive talk. Jenny was thoroughly enjoying herself and, much as I disliked my guests, I had to admit it was the kind of party I loved – certain to end with a bang, to use an old cliché. Martinez had already parked himself on the settee next to my sister, his hand idling along her thighs, liking what he saw down the low-cut neck of her dress: twin hillocks of rounded flesh. As he flattered and oozed charm with her, I had little doubt that his objective was to fuck her as well as myself before the get-together ended. To hurry the proceedings along, I accused him of deserting me, obviously he found Jenny more attractive.

'You see how New York has affected your dear sister,' Violette said coquettishly to Jenny. 'It's a very wicked city. There she sits, a happily married woman, making light of her – friendship, shall we say – with another man. And we can take Miguel nowhere, of course, because of his disgraceful behaviour. I hope you're not offended—?'

Jenny, on her fourth or fifth glass of champagne, said in a wicked giggle that she did not mind at all. 'Not if he intends to finish what he's started, getting me all hot and bothered. Much more and I won't be responsible—'

To give credence to the plan we had hatched, I thought it necessary to pretend to issue a warning. 'It's the drink talking, Jenny,' I said as if worried. 'These people mean business. Don't start something you may regret—'

'I'm enjoying myself for once,' Jenny declared in protest, on cue. 'I'll bet you've done things in New York you haven't been sorry for, with Harry away. Let it all happen, I say. I'm in the mood for fun.' As if in defiance of me, she took Miguel's hand and placed it over one of her big breasts. 'Don't be a spoilsport—'

'Exactly,' Violette piped up delightedly. 'Perhaps your sister is a little jealous of you, stealing her lover. Dare I say that she and Miguel have been quite intimate while her husband is absent—?'

Jenny hiccupped and giggled, her face to Martinez as his hand sidled into her dress, cupping a full breast. 'Naughty you,' she teased. 'You fucked my sister—'

'More than once, I recall,' he said, smiling. 'She has such an eager juicy cunt when being screwed by a big stiff prick like mine. I should very much like to complete the double by fucking her sister.'

'Ooh, plain talk, I like it,' Jenny burbled. 'In front of all our guests? Wouldn't that be naughty? Fun, though, I expect – what would they think?'

'That you are one of us, a highly sexed lady like your sister, not afraid to submit to her basic instincts,' Marcel Lefarge spoke up, eager-faced. 'To get us all in the right mood, I suggest we all disrobe. I'd like to compare you nude with Diana, to see how your charms match.'

'Yes, let's undress,' Gloria Stazak agreed. 'I think her tits are even bigger than her sister's. I'm going to strip and show them mine, the biggest of all—'

And the fattest and most pendulous, I could have said, as we all took our clothes off. The maid came back from the kitchen naked, carrying a refilled ice-bucket with cooled champagne, looking at my nude body and smiling. Gloria eyed me like a starving wolf too, her bare tits hanging like marrows over her rounded while belly, a great muff of hair between her fat thighs surrounding the thick-lipped cunt she obviously intended to have me suck and tongue during the proceedings. I felt Marcel Lefarge's hand press palm inward over my bottom cheeks, the middle finger insinuating into the tight crease, scratching the serrated ring of my anus and bringing a little gasp from my lips.

'I think,' I suggested, 'for what is obviously about to take place we should use the main bedroom. There's a king-sized bed which is much more comfortable than the settee or floor. I might have known this would happen—'

'And you love every wicked moment of it, Diana,' Violette said, putting her arms about my neck and pressing me to her naked body as her husband entered my arse-hole with a questing fingertip, making me quiver. Our breasts met, nipples sharp against rounded flesh, her mound and bush rubbing against mine. 'I have the most delicious desire to dildo you, *cherie*, right after Marcel has enjoyed your bottomhole, which treat I will allow my husband to have, naughty man. And Gloria will want your mouth again, of course. Miguel wishes to fuck you after he has had your dear sister and Lysette will want her turn too. Poor Diana, you are in for a busy time—'

And so I was for, in the bedroom, with naked bodies entangled on the bed, hands roving, mouths seeking, pricks and cunts thrusting, it was impossible to resist. Face down, with Marcel Lefarge up my bum and shunting his cock into me, directly in front of me Jenny was being strenuously fucked by Martinez who crouched over her while Lysette's lips went in turns from my sister's mouth to her nipples. Behind the kneeling maid, Gloria was fingering the girl's rear-pointed cunt and anus. Then Marcel was groaning and shooting deep into my back entrance and I was unceremoniously rolled over onto my back, my arse twitching and leaking spunk. Immediately Violette was between my thighs, nudging at my cunt with a large dildo strapped about her.

'My turn, Diana,' she hissed into my face, pushing herself into me. Eight inches of the dummy prick entered me and I drew in my breath as she moved against me in a fucking motion. Her belly pressed to mine had the soft sensuous feel of a woman and her breasts flattened against my own excitingly. Truly the mind is as much a sexual organ as a cunt or prick, for the very idea of the Frenchwoman fucking me so expertly brought me heightened arousal. She sensed it from the curling of my arms and legs about her soft body as I met her thrust for thrust, my cunt tilting to receive the plastic prick that felt so good.

'Yes, do, fuck it all up me, Violette,' I groaned as she worked her slim hips to piston the heavenly object deep within my receptive cunt. 'Don't stop – don't—' I heaved up and down, shuddering in a succession of climaxes as strong as any I had known. 'Bitch, bitch, dirty bitch!' she was screaming as she bucked and floundered over me, coming in helpless diminishing jerks on the other end of the double dildo up her cunt. We lay together gathering breath, still joined, bodies clinging and damp with sweat after a delirious bout. Around us the others were sitting up, their activities halted, entranced by the sight of two females having sex in the most uninhibited manner.

Before I could regain my breath and recover somewhat from a succession of shattering orgasms, both Gloria and Lysette were at me. The pair of debauched females sucked at my mouth and nipples in turn in a fury of lust. And, so help me, I was returning their kisses, my tongue in Gloria's soft warm mouth, clasping her ample

Sin and Mrs Saxon

flesh to me, then exchanging her lips for Lysette's – our hands roving and seeking, squeezing breasts, fingering moistened cunts. We were out of our senses, a trio of women wild with ecstasy. Now the big dildo had been withdrawn from my cunt, I welcomed Lysette's soothing mouth laving it. Meanwhile Gloria was settling her broad buttocks over my features, muttering her pleasure as I lapped and licked up at the pink flesh on offer. Then the telephone beside the bed rang out sharply, returning me to my senses and reminding me of the reason why we were there.

'Ignore it,' Gloria said tensely as I pulled my face from her thighs and sat up. 'Let it ring, Diana. Carry on with what you are doing—' Lysette too, interrupted in her mouthing my cunt, looked up in frustration, and nodded her agreement. Behind her, crouching in position, Martinez was in mid-stroke as he fucked the maid who had been tonguing me, annoyance on his dark face at the sudden halt of our *ménage*. Beside me Jenny was on her back, knees raised, with Violette Lefarge poised over her, the dildo now penetrating my sister while Marcel watched. The ringing of the phone persisted. 'Leave it!' Violette ordered curtly. 'Let it ring off, Diana! Let whoever it is call back—'

'It's probably my husband,' I said, getting off the bed, 'and I must talk to him. I'll use the phone in the lounge. I'm sure there's enough of you to continue the fun while I'm away.' I went through, still naked and with my nipples hard and cunt throbbing, and carried the phone as far away from the bedroom as possible, up to the main door of the apartment. Peter Dulay's voice came excitedly over the receiver.

'Got them, got them, almost right away,' he exulted in

Sin and Mrs Saxon

his delight. 'All the pics plus the negatives in a manilla envelope tucked away in a cubbyhole in old Marcel's roll-top writing bureau—'

'Oh, wonderful,' I rejoiced with him. 'Clever you!'

'It was the first place I looked,' he added, 'and it wasn't even locked. How are you doing over there? Has it been hectic?' Without waiting for an answer, he said, 'Is your sister with you? Ziggy needs you two out of the way to get the goods on them—'

'I'll get her,' I said. 'Hold the line, Pete.' Back in the bedroom plenty was still going on. I disengaged Jenny from Marcel Lefarge's tool and said that her husband was on the line from Scotland to speak to her. Still naked, we went back to the telephone by the door. Giggling at our deceit, we stood together with the instrument held between us as if sharing the call. Long minutes passed, in which time we hoped Ziggy was taking explicit photographs of those we had left in the bedroom. Then, to our concern, Martinez joined us, his big prick swinging flaccidly over his balls as he approached.

Jenny placed a hand over the phone's mouthpiece, giggling as Martinez came up. 'It's Macpherson, my husband,' she said wickedly. 'If only he knew what we'd been up to today—' She pursed her lips and pecked a little kiss at Martinez. 'We've been so rude and naughty. Standing here naked and taking his call, I feel a perfect ass—'

'So do I,' Martinez said in an amused whisper, 'two perfect asses, in fact,' his cupped palms giving a squeeze to both of our bottoms. 'Tell him goodbye and come back and join us, for Christ's sake. I intend to fuck the pair of you—'

I made a signal to him to be quiet, seeing him lift one of Jenny's breasts and run his tongue around her nipple.

Sin and Mrs Saxon

'This is Diana now,' I said, taking the phone from her and pretending I was speaking to her husband. 'Yes, Jenny is having a fine time, enjoying every minute.' She certainly was, having her tits groped and nipples sucked while she rubbed a big stiff cock. Martinez then led her back towards the bedroom and Jenny gave me a wave. Alone, I saw Ziggy Kaplan furtively appearing from the passageway that led to the other door of the bathroom. He held up a clutch of square photograph prints of the instant type.

'Fucking, sucking, you name it,' he said happily. 'I got the whole crowd of 'em at it after you left. Even Madame Lefarge shafting her old man with her dildo as he screwed his maid. Jeez, it was better than the porn flicks I direct. Want to see them, Diana?'

'No,' I said. 'It's better you take them through to Peter. He's found the photos of me, so he can make the switch. It's all gone to plan, hasn't it, Ziggy?'

'What you lot were up to!' he whistled through his teeth in admiration as he slipped through the door. 'It's given me ideas for my next movie. I'd like you and your sister to be in it—'

'No chance,' I laughed. 'We're going respectable after this. Peter's waiting for you – get going!'

He was back in moments, Peter beside him handing me a sheaf of photographs and negatives. 'Yours to burn or keep as souvenirs, Di,' Peter said proudly. 'Ziggy's pictures are in their place, so they're out of your neighbours' clutches. We're off to the bathroom to see how you handle them now you're off the hook.'

'That will be a pleasure,' I said. Back in the bedroom I poured myself a glass of champagne, watched by the group reclining on my bed.

'Gloria wants you to finish licking her out,' said Violette. 'We want to see that, just like last time, with Miggy fucking you as well. Don't keep us waiting, Diana.'

'You can all go fuck yourselves,' I said sweetly. 'The game's over, *chérie*, no more fun at my expense for you lot. Get to hell out of my apartment right now—'

Violette regarded me with narrowed eyes. 'Aren't you forgetting one little thing?' she said spitefully. 'The scandalous evidence of your infidelity? Photographs you wish never existed—'

'I don't believe you have them,' I said boldly. 'I've only your word for it.'

'Lycette,' the Frenchwoman ordered her maid. 'Get them!'

Silence fell upon what had been an animated group as the girl left the room, no doubt popping across the hallway naked, to return moments later triumphantly bearing the envelope that used to contain them. 'I'm sure your husband would be delighted to see what you have been doing while he is away,' Violette smirked, lifting the flap. A split second later her face fell. '*Mon Dieu*,' she gasped. 'What—?'

'Surprised?' I asked. 'We've got more, on film as well. So you can all get out of my sight for good and don't think I'm finished with you yet, you bastards.'

They made a sorry procession trooping out of my apartment, Violette and Gloria glaring hate, Marcel bemused, Martinez regarding us sorrowfully as if denied future pleasures. As they left, Peter and Ziggy joined us, dancing little jigs of triumph, clasping my naked sister and I in pure joy.

'We must drink a toast,' I declared, filling our glasses,

'with their bubbly! What else can we do to thank you boys for coming to my aid so gallantly—?'

Jenny giggled and the two men exchanged hopeful glances. 'I expect we'll come up with something,' Peter grinned. 'In fact it's just about up already, seeing you two standing there in the nude. As for Ziggy, is that a spare roll of film I see in his jeans or is he just glad to see you girls *au naturel*?'

I lolled back on the bed, eyes closed, feeling Peter nuzzling my breasts and then drawing his face down between my thighs as he parted them with his hands. Looking up, I saw Jenny helping Ziggy out of the green velvet jacket, undressing him urgently. It had, I decided, been a very good day, with the Lefarges foiled nicely and now more pleasures to come. I reached down to hold Peter's head, remembering with pleasure that on the morrow my wayward sister and I would wing off to a paradise island where who knows what adventures awaited us?

Chapter Eighteen
ENGLAND

Escorting the suspected spy, Walensky, certainly took me to the liveliest and most expensive night spots in wartime London. Given *carte blanche* to keep an eye on him, I slept in his flat most nights, suffering the cruel sexual indignities of a perverted mind. A favourite habit of his, if I somehow displeased him, was to bind me face down by my wrists and ankles to his bed and cane my bottom before using it for another purpose. At night I wore evening dress more than my uniform as I accompanied him around town, careful not even to look innocently at other men as it ensured more degradation and punishment later. Occasionally he was so dead drunk on our return – times that I welcomed – that I undressed him and he slept in a stupor, allowing me to search his rooms. Reporting back to Gerald Moffat invariably led to a session of heated sex on his bed. We could not get enough of each other.

I told Moffat all I discovered about Walensky and his activities: that the flat was stocked with black-market goods and details of all the people he contacted and the visitors he received, including the fat Mario. When drink flowed for his male guests, to show his complete dominance of me I was made to serve them naked. This practice began when a man made remarks about my breasts, their size and shape revealed by a clinging silk gown, saying he would love to see them. Walensky ordered me to bare them and, when his guests clamoured for more, I was told to strip. Aroused by this, enjoying my humiliation, he made it a regular feature of the entertainment. Seemingly he did not mind others fondling my exposed bottom, cunt and breasts while I served them as long as their host was acknowledged as lord and master of such an attractive slave girl.

To further prove my complete subservience, if he considered I was not entering wholeheartedly into the spirit of these boozy evenings, at his order I would lie meekly across his knee for a good bottom-smacking. Sitting so, my bum reddened and warmed, he would part my cheeks and invite the others to inspect me – my puckered arsehole and hanging cunt. My ears burned at the lewd remarks and suggestions made by the onlookers. Once, when still parting my buttock cleavage, he invited them to feel my exposed parts. Several men fingered me deeply in both orifices, at times two together. Of course I squirmed under the treatment and gave out with soft moans and sighs despite my resolve.

'She loves it, the little bitch is on heat,' I heard a voice crow salaciously. 'Much more and she'll come—' It did not please the man whose knees I was across. To show he was the only one allowed to have me, I was pushed to the floor and mounted, his prick iron hard, and for once I came to orgasm as he thrust angrily at me. My helpless heaves up to him while in the throes made the watchers cheer as I came off. Well, it can happen, even with someone you bitterly detest, if you are aroused enough and the cock up your cunt touches the spot and triggers off the mounting excitement that brings on that unstoppable climax.

Proud of his prowess that evening, he fucked me on other nights, giving erotic exhibitions to his guests. I can only suppose some deep predilection for humiliation, increased by being forced to perform before an audience making the foulest remarks, was what invariably gave me multiple comes. There were other indignities. One evening, with the guests well in their cups and urging their host for something especially lewd as I lay across his knee naked and well spanked, they were treated to a demonstration entirely new to me despite all my past experiences.

The inebriated Walensky dumped me unceremoniously on the carpet from his knee, held his right shoe to my face as I sat up on my knees, trying hard to conceal the hate I felt for him. At his curt order I removed both shoe and sock and took his foot in my hands as he lolled back in his armchair. 'Suck!' he said sharply. 'Go on, girl, lick my toes and suck them.' At my surprised look he repeated the command, so I grasped the foot and bent to obey. I licked them, took each toe in my mouth and sucked, pushing my tongue between each one, hearing his sighs of pleasure as I continued. 'The big one,' he said. 'Concentrate on my big toe, make it good and wet.' I covered his big toe with my lips, sucking and licking though it was so unlike the feel of a prick in my mouth, without the taste, warmth and pulsing throb I so enjoy.

When he withdrew it from me, glistening with my saliva, his foot went to my breasts, roving across both, pushing at them so that I had to steady myself, sitting up on my knees with my chest thrust out. He parted my tits,

Sin and Mrs Saxon

tried to nip my nipples, then used the flat of his foot to push me down on my back before him. Again he employed the foot to part my legs, putting the sole to my crotch, wiggling his toes on my cunt lips, working the calloused ball of his heel into the undercurve of my mound. 'Raise your cunt,' he said, 'tilt it forward.' When I complied, he worked his moistened big toe into my slit, determinedly entering it to its full depth on the forward thrust, ostensibly fucking me with it.

The gloating eyes of men looking down upon me, the crude comments, the hard big toe, rub-rubbing my clitoris tormentingly, had me stretching up to it as I lost all control. I clutched harder at the foot, pulling it into me, lifting my bottom, jerking against it in abandon, eager to get relief with the churning in my lower belly and cunt demanding satisfaction. My throaty aaaaghs and ohhhhs, my heaving flanks, all signs of my surrender, were received with whoops of elation by my audience. What more could men ask for? They loved watching. One of the opposite sex floundering naked before them with breasts jumping and hips heaving as she was brought off by a toe burrowing into her cunt. When Walensky withdrew his foot following several fierce climaxes, I lay with my arms across my face, degraded in the extreme by my perfidious sexuality. Above me I heard exclamations of congratulation being showered on the one who had so expertly toe-fucked me.

That Walensky revelled in the praise was made obvious by his eagerness to repeat the exercise on other occasions, varying the procedure at times by having me face down on the floor, a cushion under my thighs raising my bottom so he could use his big toe to penetrate my rear portal. These indignities I endured with the thought that I was helping in his final downfall. I was assured my work was proving of use, Walensky's contacts had been named by me and were being kept under surveillance. I had searched the flat thoroughly between times, finding nothing incriminating, often while Walensky slept after having me in a variety of perverse ways. If things got too dangerous or physical, my officer lover informed me, I was to hurl a chair or other object through a window, where a man stationed below would rush to my aid. It was an exciting time in more ways than one, living with a violent man whose temper exploded at the least thing and who was dangerously possessive.

One morning, on my back with an aroused Walensky fucking me in bed, I noticed one of the large ceiling tiles was slightly out of place, an edge resting half-an-inch on its neighbour. Even while moving against the body above me, as his long thin prick thrust into my cunt, it struck me that there could be an accessible loft up there and the last person to visit it had not properly replaced the trapdoor. That afternoon, when Walensky was at his office, I asked him for the key to his flat to clean the place. He gave it to me without thought of any ploy on my part. Alone in the flat I placed a chair on the bed and stood on it, wobbling precariously as I reached up. I found that the tile lifted and could be pushed aside easily. My fingers groped around the edges of the entrance hole and found a switch. I flicked it and above me a light came on, illuminating the loft.

Grasping the edge of one side of the square hole over my head, breathing heavily with excitement, I pulled myself up, squirming forward on my stomach until I was able to stand upright. There was a desk, a wardrobe, a chair and an old-fashioned tailor's dummy which looked as if it had been left by a previous occupant. The desk drawers revealed another pistol, writing pads with words and symbols in a foreign language and wads of English banknotes. In the wardrobe was a thick winter coat and a scarf, naval issue and new. Lastly, and trembling with high excitement and fear at my daring, I inspected the tailor's dummy. Shaking it, I heard a rattle from inside and discovered the top part of the female shape lifted off to the waist.

It was all there, what I had sought: a crude-looking radio transmitter and receiver, with valves and dials, a morse code sending key, earphones and a coiled roll of aerial wire, all of which fitted neatly into the waist of the tailor's dummy. As I replaced the bust section, elated by my success, sounds came from the front door of the flat. A key turned and the lock clicked, then Walensky loudly called my name. In a turmoil, heart pounding wildly, I lay on my stomach out of the attic entrance and reached down to the back of the chair on the bed. I hoisted it up, then switched off the light and replaced the ceiling tile, hardly daring to breathe in the dark.

I plainly heard his footsteps below me in the bedroom. One thing I silently gave thanks for was that I'd had the forethought to park the naval staff car away from his door in a side street. Scraping sounds floated up to me and I realised in my desperation that he was sliding the bed from under the loft entrance. Nowadays it would be said that my adrenaline was pumping; then it was the less sophisticated theory of danger sharpening the senses, what was known as the survival instinct. That he was coming up to his secret transmitting space was certain. I thought of the automatic pistol in his desk and dismissed the idea as I had no experience of weapons; I didn't know whether it was even loaded. A better means of defence was right at my hand, the chair I had hauled up to hide the fact I had clambered up into his den.

The loft cover was pushed aside, revealing Walensky as he stood on the folding step-ladder I had seen in the broom closet of the kitchen. The chair was raised high as he glanced up and saw me poised over him. There was a look of shock and horror on his ratty face. 'You!' he screamed. 'You—' It was all he had time to say.

'Yes, me!' I hurled back at him, smashing the chair down and the edge of the back of the seat struck his forehead. He didn't even groan, falling back lifelessly across the bed beside the foot of the stepladder, the bed on which he had often used and abused my body. When I climbed down to look at him at first I thought he was dead, but he rolled his head and gave a moan in his unconscious state. Going to the drawer where he kept the ropes he used to bind me, it was my pleasure to tie him securely by his wrists and feet to the bedposts. Then I went to the telephone and dialled the number given to me by Colonel Moffat.

'I think you'd better come over to Commander Walensky's flat,' I said, proud of myself. 'Don't worry, I'm not in any danger now.' Replacing the phone, I giggled with relief and went to the bathroom to splash water on my face. I took a wet flannel through to the bedroom to see if Walensky had come to after his mighty crack on the brow.

He was conscious, his forehead raised in an angry bump, eyes black and glaring hate at my approach. 'Bitch,' he cursed. 'Little cow. You set me up.' He strained at the bonds holding him. '*Gott in Himmel*, do you know what they will do to me—?'

Sin and Mrs Saxon

'I know what you did to me,' I told him, placing the wet flannel on his swollen brow. 'Now it's your turn.' I had left the front door open and Gerald Moffat came hurrying in. 'I had to clonk him,' I explained cheerfully, as he looked with amazement at Walensky's face and the cords tying him. 'He caught me up in his loft. It's all there, radio and code books—' Then I was swept into his arms.

'Clever girl!' he said. 'Thank God you didn't come to harm. From the look of it, Walensky was the one that needed protection—'

'I'm afraid I've blown his cover,' I said. 'You can hardly use him now as you intended, can you?'

'No problem,' I was assured. 'He'll still have his uses. Are you fit to drive back to the Admiralty, Diana? I have men coming to go over this place and I think we need a doctor for your prisoner. I'll see you later.'

That evening I was ushered into an admiral's domain, the gruff old man regarding me with a smile as Gerald Moffat introduced me. 'Such initiative as you showed, Leading Wren Mackenzie, deserves a medal, but we don't give them for operations that must remain secret. Instead I'm recommending you for a commission. How do you like the idea of becoming an officer?'

I liked the idea very much, me, Diana Mackenzie of humble origins. 'After a spell of leave, sir,' Gerald Moffat put in. I didn't know that he was intending to include himself but next morning we were driving north together to his Scottish home. That evening we arrived at the ancient home of the Moffats of Abercrombie, a castle of weathered stone. A butler and footman, also of ancient vintage, carried in our suitcases and welcomed their laird. They seemed to regard my presence as no

Sin and Mrs Saxon

great surprise. 'Dinner will be served at eight,' Gerald said, coming into the bedroom I'd been allotted, large four-poster bed and all, which adjoined his own. In his hands he held up two evening dresses on hangers, ones I had kept in Walensky's flat. 'I took the chance to liberate these for you, Diana, so you may dress for dinner. The servants would look down on a guest who didn't keep up appearances, even in wartime. Besides, I want to see you in your finery.'

Later in bed that night, after a long slow fuck that was his speciality and guaranteed to give me multiple orgasms of the gut-wrenching kind, he cuddled his naked body up to mine. He locked me in his arms, a hand at my tits and the other at my sopping cunt. 'I suppose,' I teased him, 'you'll be writing a full account of all our sexual activities this coming week to your wife. I do hope it will be something worth the telling.'

'You'll be able to tell her yourself,' he said, kissing my breasts. 'Once you've gained your commission, I've wangled it that you go out to Ceylon. I got the admiral to promise me that as a reward for your services, plus the fact that I know my wife is dying to meet you after the reports I've sent—'

'Sod, you crafty sod,' I laughed. 'You want her to have me! The husband and wife comparing notes on having me in bed. Who says I go in for that sort of thing?'

'My dear,' he rejoined, 'you're a very sexual creature, and my wife is an attractive woman and *very* persuasive.'

I found this out for myself after I had completed my officer's course and arrived at the naval base at Tricomalee, Ceylon. Not without some trepidation, I reported to the senior Wren officer, immediately noting a silver-framed picture of her husband, Gerald Moffat, on the desk of her office. She was tall, svelte and extremely attractive in her white tropical uniform, her sharp-pointed breasts swelling the front of her starched blouse. 'You know my husband,' she said, welcoming me. 'What a coincidence, isn't it? Gerald has written very complimentary things about the services you performed for him. I expect similar service of the kind from you here, Third Officer Mackenzie. Your duty will consist of helping me run this office here. *All* duties,' she added sweetly.

I discovered on unpacking my gear that we shared a double-bedded quarter. There were two narrow iron-framed beds in the room, one of which was never used as on that first night she crossed over to mine. 'Tell me how you liked my husband to fuck you,' she said at one. 'No use beating about the bush, Diana, I want you and he's said what a randy little piece you proved to be with him. Have you had sex with another woman before? I think you'll find it rather nice for a change. You're very attractive, I'm sure other women have approached you—'

She knelt by my bed, nodding her head when I admitted I'd known other women that way and her hand slid under the sheet to run her fingers in my pubic hair. 'What a lovely bulge you have down there,' she said, flicking the folds of my cunt lips. 'That's where Gerald loved to stick his big prick, wasn't it? Do you like it licked, my dear?'

'Yes,' I murmured, pulling back the sheet and parting my legs for her.

That became the pattern for the two years that I served in Ceylon, enjoying golden beaches and swimming, and passing the tropic nights making love to the

Sin and Mrs Saxon

avaricious Mrs Moffat who was every whit as eager to enjoy my body as her husband had been. Then I was returned to Britain and served out the rest of the war at various naval bases until I was released from service. Then Harry Saxon returned to make an honest woman out of me. Not before time, you might well say!

Chapter Nineteen
AMERICA

Santigue Island lived up to its reputation as a tropical paradise set in sun-speckled blue sea, the private province of the ultra-rich. The carefree holiday atmosphere of our jaunt began with farewell drinks at Milo Circassion's mansion and continued on the chauffeur-driven ride to the airport and on his private jet. Soon we became light-headed, so much so that the irrepressible Jenny flirted outrageously with the pilot, a suave type who needed little encouragement to return her suggestive remarks. She returned from the cockpit to inform me he had felt her leg and ogled down her dress at her tits. 'Pity he's got to fly this thing,' she said, giggling.

As we flew south over the sea, sipping champagne cocktails, Roger the pilot strolled aft to join us, the sole passengers. 'I'll serve these ladies, go and take a break in my seat,' he told the steward. 'We're on automatic pilot for a while,' he informed us. 'May I join you ladies?'

'No so much of the ladies,' Jenny laughed at him. 'I daresay you've done this trip before for your boss Milo. We're here for services rendered, you must know—'

'You said it,' he nodded, enjoying her candour. 'Why not be honest about it? I'm in his pay too, screwed around at the old bastard's beck and call. I must say you two are the best of his collection that I've flown to the island.' He made himself comfortable in a seat opposite us, glass in hand. 'What the hell can a blind old guy who can't get it up do with you girls?'

Jenny and I exchanged amused glances. 'That's for us to know,' I said. 'You're a very forward person. Is it nice to speak to us in that manner?'

'I'm enjoying it,' Jenny said wickedly. 'Do go on—'

'If you insist,' Roger grinned. 'I like it myself, plain talk between like kinds. Very cock-arousing I find it. Did you two ladies get your little quims felt by the old lecher? I'll bet he went a bundle on feeling up your big tits. Fess up, girls—'

'He's not nice to know,' Jenny laughed. 'He'd like to feel our quims himself and fondle our tits. Shall we let him, Di? I feel like a good fuck. There, I've said it!'

Below us the ocean disappeared in cloud cover. I never did much enjoy flying and was glad to have my mind otherwise occupied. 'This is getting beyond it, really,' I said, chuckling myself at the turn of events. 'You two do what you want. I presume the plane flies itself quite safely while you're otherwise engaged?'

'Flies better without me,' the pilot quipped. 'Jeez, but I'd love to see you two undraped. What do you say?'

'Strip, Jenny,' I said. 'His tongue's hanging out. You started it, don't keep the man waiting—'

She stood up between the seats, undressing happily, and soon stood naked before his eager eyes: a veritable feast of voluptuous snowy-white breasts waiting to be gorged upon, rounded thighs with the bulge and thick forest of reddish hair between broad fleshy buttocks. I wanted to see my sister being fucked and, as Roger rose to throw off his jacket and unbuckle his belt, I urged them on. 'Yes, yes,' I said, my excitement growing. 'Fuck her, Roger. Fuck the arse off my sister. Take her and screw her rigid—'

Roger was peeling off his underpants hastily, the sole remaining garment still to be discarded. His prick bobbed up free, long and exceedingly thick, poker stiff. 'Lower the seat,' he said urgently and I pulled the handle till the seat where Jenny had been sitting went back in a fully reclined position. Roger kissed Jenny's mouth with open wet lips, devouring her, while she clung to him, forcing her cunt against his rampant member. In indecent haste, desperate to use each other, they fell back beside me on the seat. At once Roger nuzzled her breasts, sucked hard on the erect nipples, then slid down to lap noisily at her cunt.

'Later,' I heard her moan. 'Do that later. Fuck me now – shove that big hard cock up my cunt – please, please! Give it to me—' As he came up between her widely parted thighs I plainly saw his prick homing in, the bulbous knob pushing the folds of her lips inward as it slid up inch after inch. As they fucked like wantons beside me, grunting in their lust and Jenny's arse cocked high for the deepest shafting, one of my hands slipped down to pull up my dress and rub hard at the gusset of my panties. Roger's hand stole across to squeeze my breasts and pinch my nipples. He fucked Jenny into such a delirious state that she was almost dismounting him in her throes, garbling out oaths and cries. One might call it a dead heat as we came off together, bodies jerking in climax. Finally we sagged in a heap, drained of movement.

We touched down on an airstrip at a neighbouring

island and were taken by Landrover to a jetty where a sleek motor launch awaited. Our pilot had come along for the ride, pointing out a low green islet some miles away across sparkling ocean. 'There it is, girls,' Roger said, 'Santigue, probably the most exclusive piece of real estate in the Caribbean. You two should have a ball—'

'Why don't you join us?' Jenny said, much taken by the virile and handsome flyer. 'We could continue what we started on the plane. Besides,' she added wickedly. 'You haven't tried my sister. Wouldn't you like to have had us both—?'

'Hired hands like me are not allowed there,' he said sadly, 'except for the permanent servant staff. Much as the thought of laying you both intrigues me, Mrs Gideon-Blane would send me packing on sight, the haughty bitch. Don't let her overbearing presence phase you girls while you're there, not that I think you'd let her. You're Milo Circassion's special guests, so let her know that right off.'

'Who is she?' I asked, thinking it better to be forewarned. 'You make her sound like some kind of dragon woman—'

'Your estimate is a little generous but otherwise correct,' Roger laughed. 'She's what you Brits would call an impoverished gentlewoman, of a good family, widowed and stoney broke, so she has to earn a living. You could say she's got enough breeding to run Santigue without embarrassing Milo's important guests like European royalty, heads of state, financiers and the people the boss entertains there for his own needs. Basically Rhoda Gideon-Blane is a paid hostess, a hired hand like me, but so snooty you wouldn't think so—'

'She'll go a bundle on us two then,' Jenny giggled, still

tipsy and in high spirits from a good fuck. 'I enjoy taking her kind down a peg or two. See you on the return flight, Roger. I presume you'll be our pilot again?'

'I'll make sure I am,' he called as our launch pulled away. Santigue was approached along a coastline of crescent bays of white sandy beaches with leaning palms almost to the water's edge. On landing, following the boys who carried our luggage, we saw a scattering of neat bungalows surrounding a larger building, all designed to blend in with the lush tropical landscape. Gorgeous flowers abounded, tended by locals in straw hats and shorts, all youthful men with strong graceful bodies. Jenny was impressed.

'I wouldn't say no to one of those,' she said earnestly. 'I've never tried a black one, but I don't intend to die wondering. I'll bet you have, Di. All those years you spent in East Africa—'

Whatever I might have answered was suppressed as we walked up a paved path to the main building and a woman emerged onto the patio. In her late thirties, she cut a handsome figure in a tailored white linen suit. She was slender but shapely, with blonde hair cut short in a fashionable bob and wearing large horn-rimmed spectacles. We were offered a limp handshake as she announced in an ultra-refined voice that she was Mrs Gideon-Blane, our hostess for the week we would be spending on Santigue. 'I was warned of your impending arrival,' she added coolly, 'and have had a bungalow made ready. I presume you have an acquaintance with Mr Circassion?'

She turned, leaving us as if an unsavoury duty had been accomplished, our luggage bearers obviously forewarned of the bungalow allotted to us. Inside it was

Sin and Mrs Saxon

luxurious in the extreme, with a comely black maid waiting to show us around the rooms and inform us she would attend to our every need. 'You have the island to yourselves, for there are no other guests until next week. Amos will cook for you so you can eat here, unless madam has invited you to join her for meals—'

That seemed hardly likely. For the next two days Jenny and I lazed and swam, ate and drank of the best, and sunned ourselves. We were good company for each other and enjoyed reminding ourselves of our childhood days. We rarely got sight of Mrs Gideon-Blane and had no need to seek her out with Ninah, the pretty girl servant attending to us. We made friends with her and discovered that she came from St. Kitts and was working in Santigue to save money to start a boutique in Jamaica, which was her ambition. She was invited to sit and chat with us and enjoyed talking about her life. Ninah in turn accepted us as women hardly likely to report anything she revealed about previous guests to the snobbish Gideon-Blane. It appeared that the sexual activities of the rich and famous in the complete privacy of the island included swapping partners. Frequently the maid servants and local male staff were involved. We'd noticed that they seemed to have been picked for their handsome physiques and potential virility.

'It is expected of us, of course,' Ninah said shyly, lowering her eyes, as if making a reluctant admission. 'I do what my guests require and every time I remind myself that the generous tip they give me when they leave goes to help me start my boutique.' She gave us both a little shrug as if to say 'do not think the worse of me'. 'Even the ladies – they want me – or they want me to be with their husbands while they watch.'

It was evident to me that the sweet Ninah, with her wide eyes and full-lipped mouth, was testing us for a reaction, one that might possibly be to her gain. Glancing at Jenny I saw from her interest that the girl's intention had not escaped her. The past days, though exceedingly pleasant for us, had been devoid of one essential element – exciting sex. Sun warmed while swimming naked, full of excess energy from the indolent holiday life, my sister was eager for relief other than by her own hand. She held Ninah's slender arms, kissed her cheek, then her mouth. The girl clung to her, returning the embrace. 'Madam would like me to undress?' she said. 'I know what European ladies like—'

Watching her unbutton the white overall and strip to her smooth brown skin, I guessed she had often done this before with white women, catering to their holiday whims. Ninah naked was indeed a tempting sight. The tits high on her chest were perfectly matched pear-shaped protuberances with thick purple nipples that begged to be sucked. Between her rounded thighs her cunt seemed lipless, just plump folds inturning to the split and the mound shaved clean to emphasise the effect. Watching us, she squeezed one breast in a hand, raising it to lick the nipple, her other hand stroking her cunt. Jenny was already undressed herself and pulled Ninah down onto the bed, kissing her mouth hungrily, going on down to her breasts. They swung around, heads between each other's thighs, Ninah covering my sister. She pulled her thighs around her face and both worked their tongues.

The excitement of watching them and the heavy scent of their sex, had its effect on me. The swell of the black girl's bottom cheeks made me reach down to fondle

Sin and Mrs Saxon

them and she immediately squirmed her buttocks against my roving hand. I parted her cheeks, saw Jenny's face below as she lapped and licked. With my finger in her tight bottom-hole, Ninah gurgled and shuddered. Jenny was coming off too, thighs clamped around the maid's head, crying out her helplessness. When they rolled apart, Ninah lay straddled on the bed, legs over the edge and widely parted.

'Go on, Di,' Jenny urged me. 'Don't you want to? Look at the minx lying there like that. She wants you to suck her now.' Ninah nodded, parting her cunt with two fingers, revealing the startling red interior, glistening with Jenny's saliva. I left my chair, kneeling, my eyes on her sex, the crevice drawing me to it. I tongued and sucked on the stiff clitoris, then Ninah groaned and went into spasms against my face. My thighs grinding together, I came with her, hearing Jenny's ribald laugh as she saw my gyrations.

It was the first of several calls upon Ninah that week. Jenny and I were unable to resist the girl, having her in turn or together. The day before we were due to leave, sitting beside the swimming pool with tall drinks, Rhoda Gideon-Blane approached us for the first time, apologising for not being much in evidence during our stay. 'There are so many important guests to cater for next week,' she went on, 'that I've been fully occupied seeing to the arrangements. You will dine with me tonight, I hope. Mr Circassion says he'll telephone while you're with me. He's tried several times to contact Mrs Saxon, but you've been on the beach or otherwise engaged—'

I wondered what she meant by 'otherwise engaged' and if Ninah had informed her of our goings-on. That evening Jenny and I were received in her bungalow and treated like royalty. There were flowers and candles on a beautifully set table, we were served a meal of delicious local fish followed by pheasant and attended to by a handsome male servant our hostess addressed as Ciro. Wine flowed and loosened Rhoda's tongue. 'It's a pity you won't be here next week,' she said. 'There are such interesting people arriving. Lord Semple for one and in his party will be the Countess of Brechin—'

'I know her,' Jenny threw in cheerfully. 'We met at the Royal Highland Show and I got pissed on champagne in the hospitality tent with her. Then the Queen singled us out to chat to about our cattle. That was quite a day—'

'You know the countess and have talked with our Queen?' Rhoda said doubtfully. 'I'll tell the countess you were here then, if she remembers you—'

'Give her my regards,' Jenny said, enjoying Rhoda's patent disbelief. 'Diana here will be meeting the Queen before long too, seeing as how her husband is to be knighted. Lady Saxon, it doesn't bear thinking about. My little sister—'

Rhoda looked at us both with a newfound respect, I thought, so I raised my glass to her graciously. We were all quite friendly following that exchange and merry on the excellent wine served by Ciro. When the telephone rang, Rhoda handed it to me and Milo Circassion asked how we were enjoying our stay on his island. 'Couldn't have been better,' I told him, unable to prevent a loud hiccup which made him chuckle as I answered. 'One last thing,' he added. 'I've got the Lefarges by the balls if you wish me to break them. I own them, all they've got. If I call in my loans to them, they're paupers. Do you wish me to, Diana? It's up to you—'

'I don't want that,' I said. 'Just keep them on the hook

Sin and Mrs Saxon

until I get back. I could have some fun with them—'

Back at the table, Rhoda, drinking steadily with Jenny, stared hard at me. 'Milo thinks a great deal of you,' she said in admiration. 'You are a lovely woman, Mrs Saxon. Would it be revealing a confidence if I said I know that the girl Ninah has been – close – to you and your sister this week?'

Jenny gave an inebriated giggle. 'She means we've been having it off with the maid,' she laughed. 'In the absence of male company, what else was there? It was very good—'

I rose to excuse myself, requiring the toilet. On my return Jenny and Rhoda had pulled their chairs close, heads together. I felt a plot had been hatched. My sister looked at me wickedly. 'Rhoda here fancies you herself, Di. She told me she wants to make love to you—'

The suddenness of it made me tremble. 'Don't joke,' I said. Rhoda watched me dewy-eyed, either with drink or passion.

'It is true,' she said solemnly. 'Even though I was married once I've always been that way inclined. I do so want to kiss you—' I stood stock still as she approached and kissed my mouth lightly then quite passionately, her tongue fluttering over mine. Then her hands went down, moulding my tits, squeezing them gently and fondly. Despite my surprise my heart pounded, I wanted her to see me naked, to show her my ripeness and offer it to her. I returned her kisses, yielding to her embrace.

'Let us go through to my bedroom,' she whispered, her voice low and hoarse with excitement. 'You want this as much as I do, I know.' She teased my erect nipples with her fingers, my legs weakening at her touch.

Sin and Mrs Saxon

'Will your sister join us? Would she prefer male company?'

'Bring on whoever you have in mind,' said Jenny eagerly. 'I could do with a real cock up me.' The answer to her plea was the sudden appearance of the tall and strapping Ciro, emerging from behind the door as if on cue. Jenny gave a shout of pure glee. 'Him!'

'Ciro has serviced many of our women guests most happily in the past,' Rhoda said, pulling me in the direction of her bedroom. 'I'm sure your sister will find him virile in the extreme.'

By her bedside we drew off our clothes, Jenny and Ciro doing the same. Despite Rhoda's kisses on my mouth and her hands fondling my tits and cunt, I still could not resist glancing at our companions. I was envious of Jenny. Ciro was indeed well-made, an admirable specimen. His cock was huge in her hand, immensely thick and considerable in its length. I yearned to cup his big heavy balls in my hand. As I was lowered to the bed, Jenny was laid beside me, giggling wickedly.

'Here we go again,' she laughed, drawing Ciro over her divided thighs. 'Take a feel of this,' she offered, holding up Ciro's rampant prick. 'It's hot and hard and you know where it's going. Lord, am I going to enjoy this!'

Even as Rhoda's open mouth nuzzled at my breasts I reached across, lifting the heavy rounds of Ciro's balls with my fingers before curling them around the thick stalk. I wanted him badly and Rhoda knew it, slapping my hand to release my clasp.

'Don't!' she ordered. 'You can have that later. I want you now to myself.' Her mouth came hard against mine again, tongue probing, her agitation great. I was touched

Sin and Mrs Saxon

and stroked expertly, roused to a fever as she caressed my tits, cunt and bottom-hole. She nipped my clitoris, flicked and rubbed it until I was lifting my cunt to her. 'How moist you are there, Diana,' she said breathlessly. 'Drenched, my dear. Oh yes, I shall kiss it, lick it all out for you. Ohhhh—'

Then her head was between my thighs and the sound of her lapping at my cunt, her moans and sighs, had me working with her, pulling her hair, feeling the rising surge within that foretold my climax. Beside me, our bare shoulders touching, Jenny was crowing out her unbridled joy as Ciro manfully fucked her.

The bed creaked with our exertions. I loved watching the pair beside me as Rhoda plied her tongue to my crack. Ciro's broad buttocks rose and fell as he pistoned his great prick up my sister, who grappled him with crossed legs and hands that hauled him to her. An obvious stayer, Ciro had her crying out she was coming before his flanks increased pace and his load was deposited up her cleft. I lay beside her, sated by my own several strong orgasms, Rhoda smiling down at me benignly, pleased with her effect on me.

The night was young, as they say. After more wine and congenial talk about the fucking, intoxicated with drink and lust and ourselves, the foursome continued. 'Isn't it a splendid prick?' Jenny enthused, Ciro's cock in her hand. 'You must try it, Diana.' I nodded, holding his balls, enjoying their roundness and weight, while Rhoda sat up behind me with her hand in the crease of my arse. I couldn't wait to try Ciro, and he knew it, standing up proudly. 'Let's get it really hard for you,' Jenny said, lowering her head to cover his knob with her lips. Again, I liked watching it, stirring me to new heights of lust. Jenny's mouth sucked greedily on his stalk and it was Ciro who withdrew from her, indicating to me by turning the big prick in my direction that he wanted to fuck me.

'On your knees for him, Diana,' Rhoda instructed. 'Kneel on the edge of the bed with your rear offered. He likes it that way and penetration can be so much deeper.' As long as I was to receive his length I did not care and I turned to position myself. I groaned, feeling the girth and heat of him going in, his large balls nestling in my bottom cleft. As his strokes increased, I heard both Jenny and Rhoda encouraging him. His weight bore me down until I was flat to the bed, legs outstretched. The poking was hard, fast and deep, my passage was stretched as his knob ground in a twisting motion that had me coming over and over until at last I sensed his own urgent need. His flanks buffeted me as his load jetted out in a succession of thrusts and spurts.

The following morning when we departed by the launch, Rhoda kissed us both a fond farewell, adding the hope that we would return to the island. We found that we shared the aircraft with other passengers on the return flight, much to our friendly pilot Roger's obvious annoyance. To our surprise, at New York the Lefarge's limousine awaited us and a very contrite Violette greeted us. Her chauffeur held open the door as we got in the car beside her. Right away she pleaded for me to get Milo Circassion not to ruin her husband and herself. 'He says it's up to you, Diana. Do be kind,' she grovelled. 'What we made you do was very wrong, but no great harm was done. I'll do anything to make up for it—'

'Anything?' I queried, with a wicked thought in mind. 'I'd quite like to see your chauffeur fuck you, with your husband present, of course. He can take photographs of that as a keepsake. I don't suppose Clarence would object, do you?'

'Must it be Clarence?' she said miserably, and I knew why. Their driver was big and black. I had never known the Lefarges to treat him as other than the most servile of humans. I knew he hated them. It gave him and myself the greatest pleasure when later in the Lefarges' apartment he screwed her lustily on her bed, with Violette's husband taking his pictures at my bidding. To add insult to injury, he watched his wife climax strongly whether she wanted to or not while Clarence shafted her front and back. As an added touch, I made her kneel and suck him to hardness again for a second bout, warning her as she protested that in no way was she to fire her chauffeur later or a call to Milo Circassion was a certainty. Jenny and I left them at it, returning to my apartment in high spirits.

Once inside, the first thing I noticed was my husband Harry's suitcase unopened in the lounge. I guessed he had returned, tired by the long flight from Somalia, and gone to bed. I signalled to Jenny for silence and we tip-toed through to the bedroom, finding the curtains drawn and Harry fast asleep, his clothes draped over a chair. 'So I get to see that elusive husband of yours at last,' my sister whispered to me, studying my slumbering spouse. 'He's got the handsome look of his father. Seeing him reminds me how often his old man used to fuck me—'

'Me too,' I agreed quietly, amused by a wicked idea forming in my mind. 'Undress and pop in beside him, Jenny. Let's see if he'll know the difference between us when he's still sleepy. You know what I mean—'

'Are you sure he wouldn't mind when he finds out it's

Sin and Mrs Saxon

not you?' Jenny said, undecided but wanting to.

'You know men,' I argued, still in our conspiratal whispers. 'Harry's no different, it would be a treat for him. Go on, I want to see it—' I began to undress beside her. 'Don't worry, I intend to join you later on the other side of him. We'll give him a homecoming he won't forget, two lookalike sisters with him in the middle!'

'If you insist,' Jenny said gleefully, shedding her clothes and drawing the covers from Harry. He slept naked, sprawled as if in exhausted sleep, the big prick I loved and that had serviced me so well in our marriage lolling limply in a curve sideways from his balls.

'Like father like son,' Jenny said in admiration, her tits drooping forward as she bent over my husband. 'I shall give that a few gentle sucks to see how he reacts. For what he's about to receive, let's hope he'll be thankful—' I watched her take the flaccid dick gently between finger and thumb, lifting it to her lips. Her tongue circled the crown of the knob, then she covered it and sucked slowly and quietly for a moment. 'It's coming to life,' she informed me, turning her head before resuming. 'What a good thick girth he has and the length to go with it. I can feel the throb and the bollocks are tightening too. It's lovely in my mouth—'

Harry stirred in his sleep, gave a low moan and parted his legs, his prick stiffening as Jenny sucked harder on the shaft. 'Oh, Diana,' he muttered. 'Oh, yes. It's been too long—' In his half-awake state he drew Jenny down beside him and rolled over to get between her thighs, thrusting his hips. She in turn directed his prick to her cunt and clasped her legs about his back. Penetrating, only knowing, I was sure, that he was snugly embedded up a very receptive cunt channel, his arse worked

Sin and Mrs Saxon

furiously as if he desperately needed a fuck. I presumed that he had not had one during his time away from me. Seeing them buck to each other so eagerly, bellies slapping and flanks heaving, made me touch myself up, masturbating as they coupled urgently.

After Harry came, with a loud 'Aaagh!' of ecstasy, he sat up with Jenny still beneath him. His eyes focused in the dim light, returning to full awareness. 'What? What the devil?' he exclaimed. 'Who are you? You're not my wife! You look like her but you're not Diana—'

I switched on the bedside lamp and joyfully jumped on the bed to press my nakedness to his body and kiss him fervently. 'Welcome home, darling!' I said happily. 'You've just met my sister Jennifer. We played a little trick on you. She does resemble me, doesn't she?'

'You minx,' Harry laughed, embracing me and returning my kiss. 'I really thought it was you.' He turned to regard Jenny beside us in all her lush nakedness, extending a formal hand. 'A bit late for introductions after what we did,' he admitted wryly, 'but the pleasure was all mine. God, Di, your sister's tits are so like yours, I didn't think there were two pairs made the same.'

'Now you know,' I told him, 'and it's my turn next. The pair of us are here for the night. Feed him your tits, Jenny, while I work on him below. It's been a long time without for me too,' I lied cheerfully.

'For all of us, it seems,' Harry said, lying back in state as we worked our wiles upon him. 'I could get to like this. Actually I've returned to fly back to England with you, Di. The date of the investiture has been fixed. This time next week we go to the Palace in our finery and I get knighted. Then you'll be Lady Saxon—'

'Some lady, hearing that with a prick in her mouth,'

Jenny giggled. 'I can remember when she had to wear my hand-me-down dresses—'

And so could I, looking back on a life filled with the utmost sexual pleasures I'd enjoyed just being myself. What next, I wondered? Men, and women, still looked at me with desire, and I'd always found it impossible to resist their advances. My happy misadventures have been recorded in this story and the earlier admissions in my book *Sex and Mrs Saxon*. Would there be more? I smiled at the thought, sucking at Harry the while. *Lust and Lady Saxon* perhaps. Could be . . .

A selection of Erotica from Headline

FONDLE ALL OVER	Nadia Adamant	£4.99 ☐
LUST ON THE LOOSE	Noel Amos	£4.99 ☐
GROUPIES	Johnny Angelo	£4.99 ☐
PASSION IN PARADISE	Anonymous	£4.99 ☐
THE ULTIMATE EROS COLLECTION	Anonymous	£6.99 ☐
EXPOSED	Felice Ash	£4.99 ☐
SIN AND MRS SAXON	Lesley Asquith	£4.99 ☐
HIGH JINKS HALL	Erica Boleyn	£4.99 ☐
TWO WEEKS IN MAY	Maria Caprio	£4.99 ☐
THE PHALLUS OF OSIRIS	Valentina Cilescu	£4.99 ☐
NUDE RISING	Faye Rossignol	£4.99 ☐
AMOUR AMOUR	Marie-Claire Villefranche	£4.99 ☐

All Headline books are available at your local bookshop or newsagent, or can be ordered direct from the publisher. Just tick the titles you want and fill in the form below. Prices and availability subject to change without notice.

Headline Book Publishing PLC, Cash Sales Department, Bookpoint, 39 Milton Park, Abingdon, OXON, OX14 4TD, UK. If you have a credit card you may order by telephone – 0235 831700.

Please enclose a cheque or postal order made payable to Bookpoint Ltd to the value of the cover price and allow the following for postage and packing:
UK & BFPO: £1.00 for the first book, 50p for the second book and 30p for each additional book ordered up to a maximum charge of £3.00.
OVERSEAS & EIRE: £2.00 for the first book, £1.00 for the second book and 50p for each additional book.

Name ....

Address ....

....

....

If you would prefer to pay by credit card, please complete:
Please debit my Visa/Access/Diner's Card/American Express (delete as applicable) card no:

Signature .... Expiry Date ....